praise for

"Deliciously creepy, bittersweet everything I want in a ghost story—but it's Olive's voice that will stay with me: yearning, biting, angry, despairing, loving, curious, and real, she'll stay with any reader who's been scared to lose what they love."

—Maxine Kaplan, author of *The Accidental Bad Girl* and *Wench*

"Darkly charming in its explorations of grief, love, and what happens after death, and filled with a diverse cast readers are sure to love, *Here Lies Olive* is the queer cozy horror novel we've all been waiting for."

—Sarah Glenn Marsh, author of *The Girls Are Never Gone*

"Anderson's debut novel is beautifully narrated, with lyrical prose that lets you fully immerse yourself in Olive's world. Olive is a relatable character in her quest to grapple with life's unexpected twists and discover what comes next after death. At its core, *Here Lies Olive* is a fantastically eerie, atmospheric novel with a fun, engaging plot and great queer representation."

—A. J. Sass, award-winning author of *Ellen Outside the Lines*, *Ana on the Edge*, and *Camp QUILTBAG*

"*Here Lies Olive* is a terrifyingly stunning debut about living life after death. With haunting prose that will keep you up at night, Anderson crafts a thoughtful story of platonic and romantic love, struggling with one's mental health, and accepting the darkness to get to the light. Chilling and atmospheric, this horror will grip you till its final pages."

—Robin Alvarez, author of *When Oceans Rise*

"With shades of *Wednesday* and Madeleine Roux's *Asylum*, this wonderfully spooky and mysterious read should be on every Halloween lover's bookshelf!"

—Kat Ellis, author of *Harrow Lake*

"*Here Lies Olive* asks us to face our own mortality with courage and a good pair of Converse. White Haven is the retro-goth town of your dreams . . . and nightmares."

—Lindsay S. Zrull, award-winning author of *Goth Girl, Queen of the Universe*

"A haunting tale that dares to ask hard questions about life, death, and what truly matters. Darkly creative and richly imagined, *Here Lies Olive* will captivate readers through the final chilling twist."

—Linda Kao, author of *A Crooked Mark*

"*Here Lies Olive* is a unique exploration of the afterlife expertly woven into a haunting ghost story that will have you screaming for more! A perfect fall read."

—Rachel Menard, award-winning author of *Game of Strength and Storm* and *Clash of Fate and Fury*

"Set in a charming small town that peddles in all things macabre, *Here Lies Olive* is a delightful exhumation of a grisly topic. After nearly dying herself, Olive is determined to answer her questions about death, chasing one ghostly lead after another. Anderson offers an undeniable main character with a relatable quest. *Here Lies Olive* is a compelling read, infused with warmth and humor to balance its grim themes."

—Kyrie McCauley, author of *If These Wings Could Fly* and *All the Dead Lie Down*

KATE
ANDERSON

Mendota Heights, Minnesota

First Edition
First Printing, 2023

Book design by Karli Kruse
Cover design by Karli Kruse
Cover illustration by Raluca Burcă

Flux, an imprint of North Star Editions, Inc.

Library of Congress Cataloging-in-Publication Data
Names: Anderson, Kate, 1985- author.
Title: Here lies Olive / Kate Anderson.
Description: First edition. | Mendota Heights, Minnesota : Flux, 2023. |
  Audience: Grades 10–12.
Identifiers: LCCN 2023021163 (print) | LCCN 2023021164 (ebook) | ISBN
  9781635830910 (paperback) | ISBN 9781635830927 (ebook)
Subjects: CYAC: Future life--Fiction. | Ghosts--Fiction. |
  Lesbians--Fiction. | LCGFT: Paranormal fiction. | Novels.
Classification: LCC PZ7.1.A5255 He 2023 (print) | LCC PZ7.1.A5255 (ebook)
  | DDC [Fic]--dc23
LC record available at https://lccn.loc.gov/2023021163
LC ebook record available at https://lccn.loc.gov/2023021164

Flux
North Star Editions, Inc.
2297 Waters Drive
Mendota Heights, MN 55120
www.fluxnow.com

Printed in Canada

To Jason: your wife wrote a book and all you got was this lousy dedication.

CHAPTER 1
DEAD INSIDE
COUNTS TOO

A pack of skeletons jog down the middle of the street, all dangling plastic bones and glow-in-the-dark tutus. The runners in the Skele-10K clatter past me as I walk toward White Haven, New Mexico's annual Festival of Death.

Today is the kind of fall day where I shiver in the shade and sweat in the sun, with a sky so blue that it makes me blink. Dry cottonwood leaves rasp across the road, and the air is thin and crisp; it smells like rotting apples and falling leaves and smoldering wood, a combination of dying things that I inexplicably want to capture in a scented candle. Like all North American basic white girls, I have a sudden urge to put on a chunky scarf and ankle boots and carry a punny mug with me everywhere I go (Zero Fox 🦊 Given).

The town square looks like it's straight out of a Tim Burton film: skull-shaped streetlights draped in black bunting, cast-iron cauldrons on each corner overflowing with black velvet petunias and creeping, veined ivy. A long line twists around a hearse parked next to the cemetery wall. *Food to Die For* is scrawled on the sign in dripping red letters. This apparent health code violation doesn't stop tourists from waiting an hour for loaded Gravedigger Tots and Death by Chocolate Cake.

"There you are!" Dad calls. He's setting out Styrofoam blocks and dull butter knives at our family's booth: Morana Memorials Carve Your Own Tombstones. At the end of the weekend, the best one wins a tiny headstone that he shapes out of scrap marble and engraves with the winner's name. "I've been here for an hour already. Grab me more knives, okay?"

I tap the badge pinned over my heart. It's a hard, plastic cartoony tombstone with HERE LIES OLIVE engraved on it.

"I would, but I take my civic duty very seriously," I say, even though my track record would beg to differ. "I have to help at the Junior Reapers information booth."

Mom and Dad were thrilled when I joined the city's youth council. Let's just say community involvement has never really been my thing.

But Junior Reapers has its perks.

"Oh, of course!" A faint smile tugs at Dad's lips. "Go, go! Enjoy your day!" He waves me off, turning to a bossy-looking woman who's eyeing her watch like she's running out of time. At the festival or in her life, I don't know, but she looks like the kind of woman who doesn't make a distinction.

"Lolly!" Dad calls after me. "Do you have your EpiPen?"

It's been two years, two months, and nineteen days since I bit into a crab rangoon and almost died. Now Dad never fails to remind me to take my EpiPen everywhere, even though a shellfish allergy isn't like a bee allergy. It's not like a shrimp can swoop out of the sky and ram itself down my throat. I can just, you know, *not* eat any shellfish. Still, I pat my skull-shaped purse to make sure the EpiPen is in its zippered pouch, then roll my eyes at him. "*Yes.* And stop calling me Lolly!"

I push through the crowd, but the campy festival feels darker as I think back to those moments when my throat closed and my heart stopped beating.

My family isn't religious, but I still expected to see a light at the end of a tunnel or a lot of fluffy white clouds, the kind that pile up in the sky on summer afternoons like whipped cream. One of those trite interpretations that the media uses to give shape to the vague concept of Heaven.

Instead, I floated in a dark sea of nothing. It could have gone on forever in every direction, like the never-ending cold of space—or it could have been a thin membrane that fit around me so neatly that I couldn't even feel it. I closed my eyes and opened them again, but there was no difference. Just an endless void that I hung suspended in, alone with my racing thoughts: *Is this it? Is this death? There's nothing here.* Then, with dawning horror: *There's Nothing here.*

No white clouds. No angels wearing flowing silver gowns with tinsel in their hair. Nothing. Nothing. Nothing. The word beat in my chest like the ghost of my heartbeat. I was dead, and instead of going to Heaven, I was alone in the Nothing.

Then the paramedics restarted my heart, the tight fists of my lungs opened, and I swallowed a chestful of air that scraped like gravel going down.

But I still saw the Nothing every time I closed my eyes until my whole world went dark.

It's kind of hard to care about next Friday's biology test when you've just escaped eternal midnight. And texting my friends dropped to the very bottom of my to-do list. Why bother, when I was just going to end up as Nothing?

Someone bumps against my shoulder, snapping me out of my current existential crisis. The crowd spills around me as I stare at the Junior Reapers booth looming just ahead. What was I thinking when I signed up for this? I should be spending the day at the hearse races, snacking on sugar skulls, and sampling all the entries in the funeral potatoes cook-off. Last year the winner used French's Fried Onions as a topping instead of the traditional cornflakes. A bold move, but one that paid off with a $50 gift card to Sue's Custom Urns. What if someone tries something equally risky this year and I miss out?

"Olive! Hurry up!" A voice like bells spills out of the tent. Not the silvery sound from a church bell; this voice is more like the gong that warns of an impending invasion.

Maren effing Seymour. She's one hundred percent the complete opposite of me. Straight A's, president of Junior Reapers, captain of the debate team, and manager of the robotics club . . . Maren is one of those kids who always have their hand in the air and their nose in everyone else's business.

Spoiler alert: She also has very little patience for my apathy. And I'll live to regret it if I stand her up for our shift in the information booth.

I take a resigned breath and duck under a strand of tissue paper ghosts trailing from the edge of the canopy. Maren is leaning over a paper map, tracing a route to the nearest bathroom for a harried mother (up the marble staircase in city hall and past the statue of Maasawu, the Hopi god of the dead). Long red hair flows down her back like rivers of blood.

As soon as the mom and her hopping child hurry into the crowd, Maren turns on me with her arms crossed. The flutters in my chest grow into a gale as her green eyes meet mine. "You're—"

"Late, I know." I force myself to sound bored, and even hold up one hand to examine my chipped black nail polish until she turns that dynamic gaze on someone else and I can finally suck in some air. It's hard to remember to breathe when Maren has you fixed in her stare like a rattlesnake. "Sorry. You've been a Junior Reaper since you were twelve. I figured you'd be okay."

"Nice," she snaps. "So because I'm responsible, you don't have to be?"

"Okay, okay." I raise my hands in surrender. "I officially repent of my irresponsibility. There. Better?"

We spend the next few hours answering questions,

pointing out the most popular booths on the map, and collecting stray sunglasses for the lost and found. The cemetery tour schedule fills up before lunch, and then we have a wave of questions about the best places to eat in town.

I slump into a folding chair and put my feet up on the table as soon as there's a lull in the crowd. "If I have to answer one more inane question about the difference between the sanitarium and Seymour House, I'm going to—"

Maren prods my feet off the table, scowling at me. "Honestly, Olive," she mutters. "Junior Reapers are supposed to be the face of White Haven. You could at least try to make a good impression."

I let my feet thud to the ground. I'm wearing black high-top Converse with my black Poe-ka dot dress: a rockabilly cut with tiny Edgar Allan Poe faces dotted across the full skirt. Very demure. With the sneakers and my signature purple-black lipstick, I'm the very antithesis of Maren, who's staggering around in actual kitten heels. If it were me, I would kick them off and go barefoot, but everything Maren does has to be perfect.

No wonder we've never gotten along. A walking disaster like me doesn't fit into her world of sweater sets and pearls.

"You know what I don't get?" I say, mostly to myself because Maren is back to straightening a stack of pamphlets about the history of White Haven for the thousandth time. "The number of people who have asked me what the Festival of Death is. White Haven is in the middle of nowhere. If they're not coming specifically for the festival, why are they here? Imagine wandering into White Haven and having no idea what to expect."

"Imagine *moving* to White Haven and having no idea what to expect," a girl chirps from the front of the booth. She's wearing a T-shirt printed with a retro pinup girl in a witch's hat, and a seashell-pink ribbon looped around her neck. Her hair is blonde and shiny, curled in loose waves around her pale, heart-shaped face, and her eyes are such a deep blue that they're almost violet. She glances around at the kids weaving through the crowd with black poison candy apples, the families posing for pictures with a life-size skeleton wearing a bow tie. "I have to admit, this is not what I thought New Mexico would be like."

And without her saying anything else, I know exactly what she was imagining. Everyone thinks New Mexico is all dried chiles, aliens, and turquoise jewelry. Spanish missions and pueblo and cacti. Georgia O'Keeffe and Walter White. Sand and stone and sky above.

But White Haven has a distinctly retro feel. You know how people think of the 1950s as kind of idyllic, even though it really wasn't if you were anything other than a rich white man? That's pretty much how White Haven is: 1950s aesthetic, but make it goth. In the world of dark tourism, White Haven has a reputation of being a morbid Stars Hollow. The happy little town that embraces death, where kids ride their bikes to an elementary school housed in an old mortuary and neighbors wave on their way to work at the morgue.

Around here, when people say they have skeletons in their closets, they're apt to be actual skeletons.

Maren wheels away from the brochures and jumps in before I can say anything.

"Maren Seymour," she says, leaning across the counter so she and the blonde girl are nearly nose to nose. The girl takes a step back at Maren's aggressive energy. "And this is Olive." Maren gestures at me like an afterthought, then straightens her lacy black wrist-length gloves.

"I'm Vanessa Fitz," the girl says. One hand drifts to her pink ribbon, wrapping the trailing end around her pinkie like it's a promise. "I just moved here from New Orleans."

That's right; I saw her at school last week, sitting by

herself at the edge of the cafeteria, watching everyone with a guarded expression like she wasn't sure any of us were worth her time.

I get that.

"Um, so this is kind of embarrassing." Vanessa rolls her eyes with self-deprecating charm. "But I got all turned around in the catacombs maze, and I can't remember how to get home. Could either of you tell me how to get back to Blood Orange Street?"

"I'll show you," I volunteer. Maren raises an eyebrow at my willingness to do more than the bare minimum required, so I wave the ghost tour schedule under her nose. "I have a tour in ten minutes, anyway. The Ghouls Just Wanna Have Fun ghost-hunting club from Las Vegas." I snort. "Sounds like a bunch of understimulated suburban moms who get together to drink wine and try to convince themselves that their husbands' night farts are really ghosts trying to communicate with them."

Vanessa bites her lip and giggles as she follows me into the crowd. "It was nice to meet you, Maren," she calls over her shoulder. We sidestep a kid with an ice-cream cone from the bright orange I-Scream truck.

Davis Wills nods at me. I give an awkward thumbs-up as Vanessa and I walk past his dad's real estate booth. Davis and I haven't talked in . . . a while, but it feels weird to see him and not say anything.

The cemetery gate is blocked by a group of middle-aged women wearing badges shaped like ghosts. One is saying loudly to anyone who will listen, "I feel right at home in the cemetery now that I'm so old!" Her braying laugh sets my teeth on edge.

"Looks like your description was spot-on," Vanessa murmurs, pressing her lips into a tight line to keep from laughing.

"What did I tell you?" I sigh and point at the path that

winds through the wrought iron gate and into the cemetery. "Go straight through the cemetery to the gate on the other side. Blood Orange Street is one block east."

"Thanks, Olive," she says. "See you at school on Monday."

I wait until she's halfway across the cemetery before turning to the Ghouls and introducing myself as their tour guide. "I hope you're ready to delve into the darkest, most disturbing history of a very dark and disturbed town," I rasp in a low voice.

Lie. The cemetery is filled with the graves of B-list movie stars from early Hollywood and other minor celebrities who came to White Haven to die of tuberculosis in the sanitarium, which was more like a world-class resort than a hospital. None of their deaths were gruesome, suspicious, or otherwise disturbing.

But I'm good at setting the mood, and the Ghouls squeal with delight and link arms as we pass through the gate.

Believe it or not, I actually like this part of being a Junior Reaper. Remember those perks I mentioned? Junior Reapers may be cheesy and filled with earnest overachievers who are way too concerned with their GPAs, but it *has* come in handy for ghost-hunting. How else would I have gotten access to the basement furnace at the sanitarium where they burned consumption victims' personal belongings, or had a chance to light the candles at the White Haven Home for Foundling Wraiths and Spirit Children?

The only problem is I haven't actually found a ghost yet. But it's only a matter of time. Living in the dark tourism capital of America, I'm bound to run into one sooner or later.

I spend the next hour steering the Ghouls through a maze of elaborate mausoleums and crumbling stone angels, resolutely avoiding any paths that would take us past Mrs.

Hernandez's grave. My heart sinks a little lower every time I catch sight of her headstone, still pure white and new. I haven't been able to bring myself to visit, even though it's been nine months; I wasn't even at her funeral. When it came down to it, I just could not step through the cemetery gates. Nothing Mom or Dad said could unlock my frozen feet, so they finally went in without me and I watched the whole procession from the street.

I didn't want to see her—my person, my grandmother by something stronger than blood—being lowered into the ground. It was bad enough being there when she died. We had been laughing about how silly I looked in a too-small hat Mrs. H was knitting for her granddaughter, the bright colors garish against my black lipstick and dress, when all of a sudden, she stopped laughing. She looked past me, and her eyes went all distant and faraway like she could see something I couldn't.

"Oh, Lolly, oh Lolly—" she said over and over. She shook her head, but her eyes stayed still, fixed on this spot over my shoulder.

"What is it? What do you see?" I grabbed her hand. "What's wrong, Mrs. H?" My heart felt like it was hardening, like it had been dipped in embalming fluid. I flailed for the call button at the side of her bed; alarms started shrieking in the hall.

Mrs. H held on too tight for me to run for a nurse, but she didn't say anything else. I didn't need her to. I knew what was happening. The Nothing was coming for her, just like it had come for me, just like it's coming for everyone. There was no escape, but I tried to hold her back anyway.

"Don't go. I love you," I whispered. "Stay with me."

Her hand was going slack as nurses rushed into the room. Just before her eyes went flat and blank, they changed—lit up with recognition, like there was someone in the empty doorway behind me.

"Mom," she breathed out. Her chest didn't rise again. Her hand slipped out of mine, and her eyes were dull and cloudy, like marbles. She was dead.

Her last word. It was just her brain firing its last synapses, like the sparks that escape a collapsing fire. That's what I told myself in the confusion as the nurses rushed into the room and saw the DNR tag on her wrist.

I knew what happened after we died; I'd been there.

But I couldn't stop thinking about the way her mouth lifted at the corners, or how she looked past me at someone only she could see. I guess I'm not as jaded as I thought, because . . .

What if I was wrong?

Maybe the Nothing I drifted in during my allergic reaction isn't the end after all.

Maybe there's something on the other side, a place where Mrs. H's mother was waiting for her—a place where Mrs. H is waiting for me.

And who better to ask about the afterlife than a ghost?

CHAPTER 2
to a Better Place

I'm sitting at the kitchen table with a bowl of chocolate pudding on Monday morning when Mom bounces down the stairs.

She positively radiates energy. She's carrying a hamper full of laundry—folded. And I don't mean clean laundry. I mean my mother folds her dirty laundry.

"Olive! What are you doing at home?" she scolds. "Why aren't you at school?"

"It's a late-start day." Which is technically true. I'm going to school late today; therefore, today is a late-start day for me.

"I thought you were going to start taking school seriously this year."

"Don't know where you got that idea." I concentrate on my pudding so I don't have to see the exasperation on her face. I don't think Mom has ever gotten over the fact that I'm more likely to use my textbooks as doorstops than to read them. School just seems so pointless to me.

Back in ninth grade, not long after my Close Encounter of the Anaphylactic Shock Kind with the crab rangoon, I was assigned a paper analyzing a poem of my choice. I was going through a nerd-rock phase, so I chose "Undone (the Sweater Song)" by Weezer and wrote a paper about feeling vulnerable and exposed while the world fell apart around me. Ms. Dunson was not pleased. She scrawled "Rivers Cuomo is not a poet!" under my grade: C–. My mom talked her into letting me write a new paper, but I never did. Ms. Dunson said the assignment was to help her get a glimpse into our minds, but she really just wanted everyone to fall in line with what was comfortable and acceptable.

My world isn't comfortable and acceptable anymore, but no one wants to see that. So why bother?

Mom opens the washing machine, unfolds her laundry, and examines every piece for stains before adding it to the machine. "If you don't want to go to school, why don't you do something worthwhile? Come with me to Evening Bell. I'm doing manicures this morning before work."

I feel like I've just been whipped in the face by a stray tree branch. It's like when Dad calls me Lolly. He and Mrs. Hernandez were pretty much the only ones who still used my childhood nickname, and every time he says it, it brings back that last day with Mrs. H: the slushy snow melting on the floor of her room, the click of her knitting needles, the ropy veins under the thin skin of her hands clutching mine as she died.

I haven't been back to the retirement home since, and I don't think I can bear to see how the paper snowflakes taped to the doors have been replaced with die-cut black cats and pumpkins, because that means it's been nine months since Mrs. H died, three seasons that she's missed, and Earth has almost completed one full orbit of the sun without her here to see it.

I pretend to consider before shaking my head. "I'll pass."

Mom tilts her head to the side and sighs. "Oh, sweetie," she says, cupping my cheek with one hand. "I miss her, too. But just because someone you love died doesn't mean you give up on everyone else. Mrs. Hernandez wouldn't want that."

She's right. I visited Mrs. H every day after school until she got suspicious about why I had so much free time. *Get involved*, she told me. *Don't waste your life.* So I joined Junior Reapers, but she died before I even got my badge, and now

I kind of regret everything.

"You need to come with me to Mrs. Hernandez's grave sometime so you can say goodbye. That's the only way you're going to get closure," Mom says. She drops a kiss on my head. "But first go to school." Grabbing a set of keys, she disappears through the back door.

I'm not done with my pudding, but it loses its appeal when I remember the way Mrs. H always let me finish hers at Evening Bell.

We got to know her when Mom first started volunteering a few months after takeout night almost turned into a visit to the morgue. She thought it would be good for us to "give back to the community" and "bond as a family after our shared trauma." But Dad fought about politics with the old dudes too much, and I never knew what to say to anyone. Mom's parents both died before I was born, and Dad doesn't talk to his, so I've always been a bit nervous around old people. They have that smell, you know?

Plus, I didn't like the reminders everywhere of how fragile life is. Maybe Mom thought it would make me feel better, to be around all those decrepit walking skeletons clinging to life with both hands, but all I saw were the tubes and monitors and trays of pills keeping them alive. It would be *so easy* for them to slip away. Cut this wire, flush this medication, and they'd be gone, just like I would have been if the paramedics had taken a wrong turn.

Then Mrs. H rolled up to me in her wheelchair one day and said, "What's a gal like you doing in a place like this?"

It turned out she was new, too, and just as awkward as me. I was surprised by how funny she was, and how she didn't shy away from talking about death like everyone else did. She just snorted and said she wondered what was taking so long. When I told her I was afraid, she said she was, too, instead of rushing to reassure me that I was safe and everything was okay, like Mom did anytime I tried to talk to her about the Nothing.

It's like Mom and Dad are afraid to admit the truth: that for a few terrifying moments, I was dead. As in, my heart stopped. My lungs deflated. But they act like as long as they don't say the words, it isn't true. Death cannot exist for me, because the paramedics came! Now you have an EpiPen! We'll be more careful in the future! There was no harm done!

As long as we don't talk about it, they can pretend it never happened.

But I don't have that privilege because I fell into the Nothing, and I think a part of me never left.

I get to school in time for third period. The bell rings just as I slide into my seat behind Maren.

"Cutting it close, aren't you?" she mutters under her breath, tapping a pencil on her desk.

"I considered not coming at all," I shoot back, my eyes tracing the smooth curve of her neck as she turns back to the front of the classroom. The freckles that dot her skin are the same color as the desert sand at golden hour, when the sun is just dipping below the Sangre de Cristo mountains.

"Settle down," Mr. Hudson calls over whispers and the rustle of notebooks. The door squeaks open again, and he scowls at the latecomer.

"Sorry, Mr. Hudson," Vanessa breathes from the doorway, sidling into the classroom without looking at anyone. Mr. Hudson just flaps one hand irritably at the empty seat next to Davis. Vanessa sinks into it, flashing me the barest hint of a smile before letting the blank mask drop back over her face.

My eyes drift out of focus as soon as Mr. Hudson begins his lecture on *The Crucible* and Cancel Culture:

Twenty-First Century Witch Hunts. He drones on and on, and it doesn't take long until I'm completely zoned out. I don't come to until there's a hollow smack as a book hits the tile floor.

"Oops," Vanessa squeaks, flustered. Her copy of *The Crucible* is lying between her desk and Davis's. She leans forward, brushing the trailing ends of the pink ribbon tied around her neck out of the way, but Davis grabs the book before she can.

"Here." He slides it back onto her desk, smiling just enough so that the dimple in his left cheek shows. Vanessa just drops her gaze, her cheeks a soft pink, and spends the rest of class fiddling with her ribbon.

I'm sitting in my usual deserted corner of the cafeteria when they come in together five minutes after the end of the period. Davis bends down to say something to Vanessa, then motions toward the table in the middle of the room where he usually sits. It's filled with the main characters in every teen movie ever made: jocks, cheerleaders, a nerd who's beautiful but doesn't know it. Davis exists at the edge of their group, but I don't think he even talks to any of them outside of school.

Vanessa shakes her head, biting her lip, and surveys the room. Her gaze falls on me while I'm still watching. I blush at being caught staring, but she just taps Davis on the shoulder and makes her way across the room to me. They're only a few feet away when Davis realizes where she's headed and his entire body goes stiff.

"Hi, Olive," Vanessa says, sitting down at my table like it's the most normal thing in the world. "So you survived the middle-aged ghost hunters?"

"Just barely," I say.

"We met at the festival," Vanessa explains to Davis. "Olive was leading tours in the cemetery."

Davis sits down next to Vanessa, angling his body away

from me. He cut his black hair sometime over the past two years. Instead of brushing his shoulder blades, it's trimmed short at his ears and swept back over his forehead. "So I wasn't imagining things," he says without looking at me. "You really are a Junior Reaper."

"I joined this year." I don't blame him for being surprised. Davis and I have been next-door neighbors since we were babies, so if anyone witnessed my complete withdrawal from all social interaction after my Almost-Withdrawal from Life, it was him. For fourteen years, Davis was my best friend—the person I called in the middle of the night when I thought I heard a ghost in the attic (turned out to be raccoons) and the only one I confided in when I cheated on a math test in sixth grade (he didn't rat me out).

But I didn't tell him about the Nothing.

It was the first thing I didn't share with him. The first thing I *couldn't* share with him. I had been alone in the Nothing, and so I had to carry it alone. There was no light at the end of the tunnel. There was no one waiting for me.

I knew that if Davis got me on my own, I would crack and spill my guts, so I started avoiding him: ignoring his texts, staying in my room when he came over for dinner. I was *scared*, dammit.

And out of that fear grew apathy, and the apathy turned to detachment, and now the only thing left between me and Davis is a ghost of our friendship.

"Where's the friend you were working with? Maren Seymour, right?" Vanessa glances around the cafeteria, but Maren is nowhere to be seen. She spends her lunch period in the teacher work room, where she has special privileges with the copy machine.

Davis snorts into his soda. "Olive and Maren, working together? God, that must have been fun. Couple of besties, those two."

He's not wrong—Maren and I spent most of elementary school at each other's throats. She was an even bigger know-it-all back then, and I've always been a contrary kind of person. Naturally I had to argue with anything that Maren stated as fact, no matter how insignificant. She can't let anyone else be right.

Anyway. I glare at Davis and change the subject. "So New Orleans—what was that like? Big houses and that creepy moss that hangs from trees?"

Vanessa shrugs. "It was kind of like White Haven—the part where I lived, at least. Lots of ghosts and vampires and cemetery tours. You should see a New Orleans funeral. There's a jazz parade from the funeral home to the cemetery and everyone dances in the street. My father was actually writing a book about death rituals around the world, but . . ." She twirls her spoon through her yogurt and puts it in her mouth. "He got some firsthand experience before it was finished."

I grin, then put together what she just said. "Wait, what? He died? God, I'm so sorry." The smile slides off my face like oil on water.

Vanessa's eyebrows rise into sharp crescents at the stricken look on my face. "It's okay. He wasn't my real father. More like an adoptive father figure. I barely knew my real father."

Still. If I'm this traumatized by the death of Mrs. H, who I knew for less than two years, it must have been hard for Vanessa to lose her surrogate father.

I settle back in my seat. Everyone deals with death in their own way. And I of all people have no right to judge how Vanessa handles it.

Shudders creep up my spine as a cool breeze wafts over the back of my neck. Davis clears his throat, raising his eyebrows and looking at something over my left shoulder. I turn and come face-to-face with Maren Seymour's phone.

"Gah," I splutter, batting the screen away. "What are

you doing?"

"Congratulations, Olive," Maren says in a clipped voice. "The Ghouls emailed Ms. Hunter to tell her what a great tour guide you were at the Festival of Death. They said that you're the best one they've ever had." Her face twists into a smile that looks like it takes a lot of effort.

"Really?" I grab the phone and scan the email that Ms. Hunter forwarded to her. "Huh. Maybe *I'll* be president of Junior Reapers next year."

Maren snatches the phone back. "Yeah, right," she mutters, rolling her eyes as the bell rings and everyone gathers their things to go back to class.

Davis stifles a laugh as Maren storms away. "Did you join Junior Reapers just to get under her skin?"

I almost grin at him before catching myself. It's been a while since I've been around him, and even though we didn't really talk at lunch, I can already feel my heart cracking at the thought of having him in my life again. It's that fake-casual way he mentioned me being a Junior Reaper, like he still pays attention to me even after two years of radio silence. Like I'm always on his radar. And as much as I've pushed him away, I miss him. I don't think I realized how much until now.

But I can't make the same mistake with Davis that I did with Mrs. H. I thought it would be okay to let her in a little bit because she was so old and sick and I knew she was going to die. I thought it wouldn't be a big deal because her death was inevitable. But then it actually happened, and I was there in the room, and watching her disappear into the Nothing was almost as bad as being trapped there myself.

As much as I miss Davis—his friendship, his steady presence, his laugh—there's no way I can let him in again.

But the next day at lunch, right when I've scooped a spoonful of peanut butter out of the jar I keep in my locker, there they are again: Davis and Vanessa, headed straight for my table.

And the next day.

And every day for the rest of the week.

I don't know why. I definitely don't do anything to encourage them. Vanessa keeps trying to draw me into their conversation, but whenever I answer her, Davis goes silent, and vice versa. It's less like the three of us are sitting together and more like she's carrying on two completely separate conversations.

By the end of the week, I have a better sense of why Vanessa is content to sit with me on the sidelines instead of letting Davis introduce her to the popular crowd. They tried a couple times, waving to Davis and calling him over, but Vanessa walked right past them, her face guarded and cool. At first I thought she just has resting bitch face, but then I realized that the blank mask she always wears? That's really her trying to hide how insecure she is. I figured it out when I noticed how often she tugs at the ribbon around her neck: when she's called on in class, or when someone whispers something as she and Davis walk by. Her hand always goes straight to the ribbon in a nervous habit. And what I took for disinterest in our classmates is really just anxiety at being thrown into a new school where everyone has known each other since kindergarten.

I've never been the new kid, but it probably sucks to try to break into a group that has been friends for years, having to laugh at inside jokes that you don't get or pretend to know who they're talking about. She doesn't have to worry about that with me, because I don't have any friends. I must feel safe and unthreatening.

Friday is nacho day in the cafeteria, and as long as I've known Davis, he's never passed up an excuse to eat his body weight in melted cheese. He gets in line as soon as they walk into the lunchroom, leaving Vanessa to find my table on her own. A couple girls that are friends with Davis corner her before she makes it across the room, fake smiles plastered across their faces. They gesture toward his normal table in the middle of the room, their voices pitched high enough that I can hear them imploring her to join them.

"Come sit with us! We miss Davis!" one of them squeals while the other tugs at Vanessa's hand. Vanessa's mouth drops open in alarm, and her free hand twitches toward her ribbon.

I press my lips together in a grimace. I know what it feels like to be dragged, kicking and screaming, out of your comfort zone. It's exactly how I feel whenever Mom schemes a new way to pull me out of my apathy, whether it's volunteering at Evening Bell or asking a teacher for extra credit.

"Vanessa!" I shout, waving my hands over my head. I don't realize what I'm doing until her name is already out of my mouth. "Over here. I saved you a seat!"

She stares at me with the same hard, closed look she has on her face whenever anyone tries to talk to her in class. For half a second, I think I've completely misread this whole situation—maybe Vanessa was just sitting with me until something better came along, maybe I just made a fool out of myself in front of half the school—but then she untangles herself from Davis's friends. Sudden, startled relief flares in my chest. I bite down on my tongue, reminding myself that Vanessa and I aren't friends. I was just saving her from the kind of aggressive awesomeness that would eat her alive.

"Thank you," she breathes. The tense set of her shoulders relaxes as she sits down. "That group is a little intense for me." She straightens her ribbon and glances back at the two girls, who are scowling with their heads bent together in gossip. "They *really* want Davis to sit with them again."

I pop an Oreo in my mouth. "Of course they do. Almost all the girls in our grade have crushes on Davis. I'm probably the only one who doesn't."

I mean, objectively I can see his appeal. He's as cool as James Dean in *Rebel Without a Cause*. Smoldering and mysterious. Brooding. But this is a good time to make something totally, one hundred percent clear: I've never been into Davis. Not like that.

Vanessa lifts one delicate eyebrow. "So why don't you?"

I snort. "Let's just say that I remember when Davis thought tampons were for nosebleeds. It's kind of hard to feel romantic about a guy when you have a mental image of him with a tampon stuffed up his nostril after getting hit in the face with a Frisbee."

Actually, to be perfectly honest, it's hard for me to feel romantic at all, and it's not just Davis. I've never had that knotted feeling in my stomach about a boy, the one that makes my eyelids flutter and my heart skip a beat.

Davis drops a tray loaded with tortilla chips and congealed neon-orange cheese on the table. He pecks Vanessa's cheek as he sits down.

"Ew." I side-eye the nachos. "Those look radioactive."

For the first time all week, Davis makes eye contact with me just to make sure I see him stuff an entire chip in his mouth in one bite.

"What are you doing tonight, Olive?" Vanessa asks. "We're going to Davis's mom's diner. He says that's what everyone does on the weekend."

Davis presses his mouth into a thin line and drums his fingers on the table. The diner was a sore spot between him and his mom back when she first opened it, and he doesn't seem much more enthusiastic about it now.

"Pretty much." I say this like I know, like I actually do stuff with other people, like I won't be sitting alone in my room lighting candles and muttering made-up spells to summon the dead. "Either that, or to the drive-in movie theater, or up to Seymour House to hook up or scare each other."

Vanessa's eyebrows shoot up. She leans across the table. "What's that?"

I hesitate, crinkling my nose. Seymour House is White Haven's dark side. "It's an old house in the woods behind the cemetery. It started out as Seymour House Asylum for the Poor, then became a mental hospital, the really messed-up kind from before mental health care reform, like real *American Horror Story: Asylum* shit."

"There are all kinds of creepy stories about Seymour House." Davis lowers his voice to a husky drawl. "Doors that slam by themselves and lights that flash on and off, even though there hasn't been electricity there for years. An urban legend about a hitchhiker trying to escape from the house. He always disappears as soon as the car leaves the grounds." He scoffs to show how ridiculous this is, but it gives me an idea.

After all, there's a kernel of truth in every urban legend.

"Let's go there after the diner," I manage to choke out. "See if the stories are true."

"Oh, were you planning on coming with us tonight?" Davis says, narrowing his eyes at me. His eyes are dark as onyx, but they're anything but one-dimensional. There's sparks of irritation at their centers. I don't blame him. I've spent two years ignoring him, and now here I am, everywhere he looks.

"Well—yeah," I say. "That's what people do on the weekend, right? Hang out with their friends? Unless you didn't want me to come," I add, glancing at Vanessa.

"Of course we want you to come! This'll be so fun." Vanessa shivers, the kind of shudder that rolls through your shoulders in a mixture of pleasure and dread. "An asylum. That sounds so creepy."

"Then it's a plan." I fight back a little guilt at taking

advantage of Vanessa's obvious need for a friend at her new school. But I'll do whatever it takes to find out if there's any possibility that Mrs. H is still out there somewhere. Mostly I'm just surprised that I haven't thought to do this before. Seymour House should have been the first place I tried, instead of gathering wildflowers and laying them on the pyre at the Phoenix Project, or burning old love letters at the Museum of Macabre.

Seymour House is the kind of place where kids go and come home with their hair gone stark white, where the police see flashing lights and hear screaming, even when no one is there.

In other words, the perfect place for me to find a ghost and ask what's on the other side.

CHAPTER 3
BUCKET LIST

A cracked white candle. A book of matches. A pinch of salt wrapped in a square of foil. A heart-shaped planchette I found with an ancient Ouija board in the attic. A stubby piece of chalk, forgotten in a corner of the garage from my last childhood game of hopscotch.

This is how I will summon a ghost.

I'm no witch—I wouldn't even call myself a ghost hunter—but Mrs. H believed in all that: palm readings, crystals, horoscopes, and smudging. She was kind of a spiritualist. I mean, it's not that unusual in New Mexico. People here are all about art and mysticism and stuff. Even in White Haven, which was influenced way more by New England than the rest of the state. I know of at least three spiritual wellness stores where you can buy salt lamps, incense, and amber jewelry. And when my mom turned forty, she went to a spa for a sound bath. She literally paid $200 to lie on a mat in a geodesic dome while some hippie played the rim of a singing bowl.

So between the internet and White Haven's mystical district, I've put together a ritual meant to draw spirits out of the darkness and back into our world. Just long enough for me to look them in the eye and ask the question that took root in my chest after Mrs. H died:

Where do you go after you die?

I'm still thinking about Mrs. H as I get ready for the night, shuffling through a dusky rainbow of lipstick in my desk drawer—Vamptastic Plum, Medusa, True Blood, Cherry Vixen—before settling on Black Honey. It's deep purple black, the same color as the juice that bursts from overripe blackberries. Leaning closer to the mirror, I blot my lips on a tissue and study my reflection. The dark lipstick casts shadows on my round face and almost makes it look like I have cheekbones.

"That's right," Mrs. H said with a hard glint in her eye when I showed her this shade. "Get lost in the darkness before you lose yourself in it."

She never tried to get me to swap my dark lipstick for bubble-gum pink, like Mom does.

Like most of the adults in White Haven, Mom's career centers on death. She's a mortuary cosmetologist, which means she's the one who takes withered Aunt Edna after she dies and tries to make it look like she's sleeping. No shade on Mom—I'm sure she's great at her job—but she's not fooling anyone. Old Aunt Edna doesn't look like she's going to wake up and stretch and ask how long she was out; she looks *dead*. No amount of concealer, blush, and lipstick can change that.

Plus, isn't it weird that Mom spends so much time volunteering and getting to know the residents at Evening Bell, only to end up doing their makeup when they die? Doesn't it startle her to fold back the sheet and see Mrs. Kane with her cheeks sunken in and her teeth in a jar of cloudy water? Or Mr. Gonzalez without his toupee, veins crossing his scalp like a street map? Does she remember their laughs as she dabs concealer over the age spots on their necks or think about stories they told as she smears blush into the grooves of their paper-thin skin?

Does she wipe away tears as she bends over the photo someone dug up, comparing the smile or the laugh or the scowl on the paper to the empty husk on the table? Or is it all so routine to her, so normal, that she hums and thinks about where to go out to dinner after work?

I can't decide which is worse: living in a constant state of mourning or being so empty inside that grief has no place anymore.

I tuck a strand of hair behind my ear. It's strawberry blonde, like Mom's, but hers is always sleek and shiny, while mine looks like the frizzy hair on a decade-old Barbie doll.

Our similar coloring is where the resemblance ends. Mom wears sunshine yellow and ruffled dresses printed with a hundred hot-air balloons; I dress all in black. She's upbeat and bright; I'm sarcastic. And it's no secret that I ended up completely macabre with none of her whimsy.

I'm turning to go when the heavy silver locket pooled in my jewelry dish catches my eye. I hesitate, then grab the necklace and drop it around my neck as I tumble down the stairs.

This locket is the only thing I have that belonged to Mrs. H, and technically it's stolen.

After she died, the nurses let me sit with her while they called her family. I slipped the locket over her head and put it in my pocket, where I could hold it and pretend it was her hand in mine whenever I felt like I was falling. I wasn't going to keep it—I was planning to give it to her sons when they came to White Haven for the funeral. But then I panicked at the cemetery and skipped the graveside service, so I never got a chance to pass it on.

I've left it in the jewelry dish on my desk for nine months, worried that if I wear it anywhere, someone will accuse me of grave robbing.

But who's going to recognize it? Mrs. H's sons live out of state and all her friends are dead.

It fits perfectly in the hollow of my chest, a dull gleam of moonstone and silver against black lace. It feels nice to have a part of Mrs. H with me. The locket is like a talisman of her love, one piece of her that isn't drifting in a fathomless void.

Outside, there's a chill in the air that wasn't there yesterday. Mom is bent over a bin of Halloween decorations in the front yard, her arms clasped around a plastic rib cage as she heaves out a skeleton. "Oh, oops, he lost his tibia. Could you grab that please, Olive?"

This is Hank. He's been our skeleton as long as I can remember. Every house on Front Street has one, and we all arrange and rearrange them in little scenes throughout the fall. Skeletons doing yoga, skeletons roasting marshmallows over fires made of fake logs and orange string lights, skeletons wearing old band shirts and holding microphones.

Mom rummages in the bin as I reattach Hank's lower leg. There's already a wreath made of glow-in-the-dark eyeballs on the front door, and three headstones, one for each family member, arranged in the flower bed. *RIP RON. BELOVED BETH. HERE LIES OLIVE.*

I've never told her how much I hate seeing my name on a headstone, even if the headstone in question is just made out of plywood sponge-painted gray. It feels pretty morbid, considering the fact that they almost had to pick out a real one for me. But Mom lives for Halloween. She decks out the whole house in decorations, and even sticks tiny costumes on all our family pictures: fake mustaches, googly eyes, paper witch hats and brooms.

My grandparents on her side of the family died in a car accident around Halloween, before I was born. That might make some people dread this time of year, but Mom always says that it was fitting. To her, Halloween is a time to celebrate the dead and remember their lives.

Still, something tells me Mom wouldn't approve of my plan to summon a ghost and ask about the afterlife—that definitely doesn't fit her definition of getting closure—which is why I'm not going to tell her what Davis, Vanessa, and I are doing tonight.

The door of the house next to ours slams shut, and Davis comes jogging down the front steps, a set of keys dangling from his hand. He pulls up short on his side of the property line, marked by a row of bright orange mums potted in plastic cauldrons.

"Hi, Mrs. Morana," he says. The setting sun washes over him, bringing out the warm undertones in his russet skin and highlighting a dark smudge of stubble along his jaw.

Mom pushes herself to her feet. "Davis! It's so good to see you."

He grins. "Good to see you, too." Davis used to barge through the kitchen door without knocking on Saturday mornings and steal the pancakes right off my plate. Mom always took his side, scolding me for not offering any to our guest. "The front yard cemetery looks great."

Mom brushes the dirt off her hands and surveys her handiwork. Along with the headstones, there are ceramic statues of children praying and an angel with spreading wings, all lit with bruise-purple shadows cast from a string of blacklights in the grass. "Hmm, I think it needs something else. Maybe a gargoyle."

"I think I saw one at the thrift store. Maybe it's still there." He turns to me, shuffling his feet and not quite meeting my eyes. "Uh—ready to go?"

My mom absolutely lights up like a pinball machine. Her smile is so big that it could reach all the way around her head and lop off the top two-thirds of her face. "Oh, Olive, you didn't tell me you were going out. What are you kids up to tonight?"

"Nothing!" The word bursts out louder than I mean it to. Sweat beads on my palms, and I'm convinced the shape of the planchette is showing through my purse.

Mom gives me an odd look, but Davis just rolls his eyes and answers her. "We're just going to my mom's diner with another friend from school."

Oh. Right. The diner. I was so focused on what I'm

planning to do after that I forgot about that part.

"Well, have fun," Mom says. "It's been too long since you've spent time together."

"Tell me about it," Davis mutters. I wince. Mom doesn't notice the frostiness between us, but I would be annoyed, too, if he ignored me for two years and now suddenly insisted on hanging out, no explanation.

I climb into the back seat of Davis's car, sliding to the middle so I can lean forward and talk to him.

"You don't have to sit in back," he protests.

I shake my head. "Vanessa can have shotgun." I'm trying to be considerate, but he just scowls as he backs out of the driveway.

"I feel like I'm driving a hearse," Davis mutters. His eyes meet mine in the rearview mirror, then dart away. The expression in them is soft and bruised like a wound just beginning to heal.

"That would make me dead." It's supposed to be a joke, but it falls flat.

Maybe because our friendship is dead.

I fiddle with a loose thread on the cuff of my sleeve and try to think of something to say. We used to talk about everything, but now Davis is a stranger. It's like we're getting to know each other all over again. I put my elbows on the console between the two front seats. "So what have you been up to?"

"You mean what have I been up to for the two years since you stopped talking to me?"

Ouch.

"I didn't 'stop talking to you,'" I say, bracketing the words in air quotes. "I just . . . stopped talking to you. And to everyone."

"I know," Davis says. He seems to regret bringing it up at all. "It's nothing. Forget about it. I've been working for my dad a lot lately. He's busy getting ready for the groundbreaking of his new development."

Davis's dad is the pushiest real estate agent in White Haven, but a few years ago he decided to branch into developing, too, and he sank all his money into a land-development firm called Wills and Son. Davis is supposed to be the "son" in that entity, but last time we talked about it, he wanted nothing to do with the family business. I would have expected him to move on to something else by now, but he sounds like he's resigned to the future his father has planned for him.

Vanessa lives on the other side of town, on a street lined with big Victorian-style homes. The old bed-and-breakfast that she moved into is a hulking shadow at the very end.

Davis pulls up to the curb and peers into the darkness that surrounds the house. It feels like it's watching us.

"Uh," he mutters. "I'll just go knock—"

Before he can finish, what looks like every light in the house turns on, illuminating a xeriscaped yard full of native plants in shades of silver and purple: black mondo grass, creeping plum sedum, green-gray sage, and lavender bushes. Vanessa sweeps off the porch in a long, fitted black coat that flares at the waist. She weaves her way through the dark flowers and lets herself out of a gate with roses worked into the wrought iron.

"Hey," she says, sliding into the front seat. "I'm starving. Does your mom make good fries?"

Only the best in White Haven. Davis's mom, Poppy, bought one of those old silver railroad car diners at an auction after she and his dad got divorced three years ago, and moved it out to the very edge of town, where White Haven borders the Navajo Nation. She and Mr. Wills both grew up on the reservation, and most of Davis's family still lives there. Poppy's Dinér—which is a play on Diné, the word Navajo people use to refer to themselves—serves the most amazing Navajo southwest fusion food. The green chile cheese fries may be responsible for the most euphoric experience of my life.

Every booth overflows with kids from school and from the reservation, spilling into the narrow aisle between tables and crowding around the jukebox. Poppy lights up when she sees us, wiping her hands on her apron and bringing us a basket of fry bread drowned in honey and powdered sugar before I can order one.

"Well, hello there! I didn't know you were coming tonight." Poppy tries to catch her son's eye, but he avoids her gaze, scanning the menu like he doesn't know it by heart, so she turns to me instead. "Olive, it's been too long since you've been here. I was starting to think you didn't like my cooking anymore."

"Never," I insist. To prove it, I try to stuff a whole piece of fry bread in my mouth at once and end up inhaling a cloud of powdered sugar. While I'm coughing and sputtering, Poppy nods at Vanessa, who is tucked under Davis's arm.

"Davis, aren't you going to introduce me to your new friend?"

"This is Vanessa," he says. "Vanessa, this is my mother." They disappear behind the menu. Poppy hovers for a moment before offering me a tight smile, half shrugging like his dismissal doesn't sting.

We order burgers served on nanniskadii—a fluffy, savory flatbread that's a million times better than regular hamburger buns—fries, and cactus pear lemonade. Davis fishes the lime out of his drink and hands it to me before I can ask if he's going to eat it. As I pop it in my mouth and slurp the juice down the back of my throat, loving the tang, he reaches over and snags a fry dripping with green chili sauce and creamy cotija cheese from the basket in front of me. It's so natural, passing our food back and forth without waiting for the other to ask or offer, that for a second I feel like the past two years never happened. It's like a glimmer of our old friendship, a sign that maybe we're not too far gone.

But then I remember how Mrs. H always let me have the dessert from her dinner tray, and how the peanut butter cookie crumbled to dust in my mouth on the night she died, how it rained down my throat like dirt burying me alive. And suddenly the tart lime from Davis's lemonade is so bitter that I feel like I'm going to choke. I spit it into my napkin and swallow to try and clear my mouth, but it's too late. Everything is sour.

"Oh—Maren!" Vanessa calls. My stomach teeters at the edge of a precipice as Maren pauses beside our table, a takeout bag in hand.

She tugs at a strand of her long red hair. "Hi. How was school for you this week?"

"Intellectually stimulating," I quip, but Davis is the only one who laughs. He's always gotten my sense of humor, even when no one else does. Hearing him laugh is like a sunburn, all heat, sting, and regret rolled into one.

"It was really nice. Everyone has been so friendly," Vanessa says, smiling. "Do you have plans tonight?"

I give my head a minuscule shake, trying to warn Vanessa not to say anything. Maren is touchy about her family's involvement in Seymour House.

But Vanessa either doesn't notice or pretends not to. "Olive is going to show me the asylum. Want to come?"

Maren flushes and glares at me. "Whatever." She doesn't look back as she stomps out the door.

Great. All I need is for Maren effing Seymour to have another reason to be mad at me. Not only am I unreliable and irresponsible, but now she's going to think that I'm spreading rumors about her family.

"Don't bring up Seymour House in front of Maren. She

hates talking about it," I hiss at Vanessa. "Didn't you see me shaking my head?"

Vanessa claps one hand to her mouth. "Oh! I thought you were having a neck spasm. I hope she doesn't think I was trying to make her feel bad or anything." She tugs at her ribbon, her blue eyes round.

"Ugh, don't worry, she'll be mad at me, not you. It was my idea anyway. Speaking of . . ." I glance at my phone. "Are we still going?"

"Sure." Davis downs the rest of his lemonade in one swallow. "Let's get out of here."

Poppy calls out to us while we're stuck behind a group at the cash register arguing over splitting the bill or just Venmoing each other later. "Davis, yázhí—where do you think you're going without saying goodbye to your mother?"

Davis stiffens and slips his hand into Vanessa's, fitting their fingers together. "I know how busy you get."

Poppy kneads a lump of fry bread dough behind the counter. Flour rises with each thrust of her hands, settling over her dark hair like cobwebs. She doesn't miss a beat as she tries to laugh off Davis's snub. "Do you want to stay and help me close up? We could watch a movie after we do the dishes."

"No. Your apartment is way too small for two people. Besides, we have plans."

This time Poppy's face ripples with hurt. She lives in a tiny apartment attached to the back of the diner, and when she first moved in, she told Davis it wasn't big enough for both of them and left him with his dad. Davis barely saw her that first year that the diner was open unless he was here mopping floors. And Mr. Wills made sure that Davis was too busy working at his land-development firm to ever help his mom. It was like he was caught in some weird custody battle between his parents, but instead of fighting over who he got to live with, they fought over who he had to work for.

The diner is filled with laughter and music from the jukebox in the corner, but the atmosphere between Davis and his mom is as tense and silent as the air just before a lightning strike. In the desert, summer is monsoon season and you can see storms coming from miles away. The rain moves like a sheet across the steppes, lightning forking in a sky that seems to go on forever. But the real dangers during a desert thunderstorm are flash floods: torrents of water roaring through washes that are dry for three hundred and sixty days a year, destroying anything in their path. That's what it feels like now, like Davis or his mom or both are going to wash away anything that's left of their relationship if someone doesn't do something.

"I just love your diner," Vanessa says, running her fingers along the tattered ends of her pink ribbon. "I've never had Navajo food before."

I exhale in relief. Vanessa must have felt the tension, too.

Poppy clears her throat and forms the dough into a ball. "Thank you. Sharing my culture's food is my passion."

Vanessa gestures at a set of silver-and-turquoise bracelets on a rack on the counter. "And these are so beautiful. Does someone local make them?"

"Davis's aunt on his father's side. She lives not far from here, just over the border in the Navajo Nation." Poppy tries to smile at Davis, but he's busy scrolling through his phone. "Maybe your boyfriend will buy them for you."

Davis presses his lips into a straight line as he hands Vanessa the bracelets, still refusing to look at his mother. Vanessa slides them onto her wrist, twisting the ribbon that binds the bracelets together in her hand. Davis hovers by the counter for a moment longer, then turns toward the door. His eyes look flat and dead. I glance at Poppy as I follow, my stomach tight.

"You know, you can stay if your mom needs your help," Vanessa says as we cross the parking lot.

He shakes his head. "She made it clear she didn't need me years ago. It's not my fault that she suddenly decided she wants to try."

I really start to regret polishing off all of my green chile cheese fries plus a good portion of Davis's, because I basically did the same thing. I was a complete nonentity in his life for two years, and now here I am, out of the blue, totally using him to deal with my own existential dread.

"Do you spend a lot of time with your relatives in the Navajo Nation?" Vanessa asks as Davis heads out of town and into the hills where Seymour House crouches like a slumbering beast.

He jerks his shoulders in a shrug. "We used to go to dances and powwows more often when I was a kid. But then my dad got obsessed with work and it's like he forgot about everything that was important to him."

The muted orange glow of a streetlight fills the car as Davis pulls off the main road, idling in the shadow of a billboard that proclaims *DESERT HEIGHTS: COMING SOON FROM WILLS AND SON!* The billboard has a retro-style illustration of a man in a hat and a woman with a vapid expression staring at a McMansion surrounded by cacti and yucca. After they bulldoze the woods surrounding Seymour House, Desert Heights will be the kind of high-cost, low-quality housing development with white fences and fake candles in the streetlights and gazebos that no one ever sits in.

"Like this fucking suburban nightmare." Davis nods up at the billboard. "This whole area used to be Navajo land before the Seymours took it. He should have ceded it back to the Navajo Nation after buying it from the Seymours, but all he cares about is money."

"So the asylum is around here?" Vanessa leans forward, peering into the dark trees.

"At the end of that road." I point at a pair of rutted tracks that snake into the woods. *Scary Road*, the kids in town call it (we're very poetic here in White Haven). I've spent my fair share of time exploring these woods, but I've never broken into the moldering old mansion at the end of them. Seymour House has always given me the creeps. It's not like the cemetery or the funeral pyre, where people are laid to rest by those who love them. Seymour House was a place full of forgotten people who lived in misery and died horrible deaths. My tongue curls just thinking about it.

Davis scrolls through his phone before putting it back on the console and pulling onto the narrow track. The opening notes of "Thriller" fill the car as the trees close over us. He turns the music up loud, smirking at me in the rearview mirror.

"Stop it," I groan. "This isn't fair." I was terrified of "Thriller"—terrified!—when I was a kid. Vincent Price still haunts my nightmares.

At the end of the song, Davis turns out the headlights and laughs maniacally along with Vincent. The hairs on the back of my neck stand up and my heart races, but I can't help laughing, too. It's fun to hang out with Davis again, even if I feel like Vincent Price and I are double-dating with him and Vanessa.

When he turns the headlights back on, Seymour House looms over us. It's an old, sprawling clapboard Victorian, the elaborate trim along the porch roof sagging and missing in places. The wrought iron fence is a nod to the one around the cemetery in town.

Shivers rush over my skin as we get out of the car. This is where Maren's ancestors made their fortune, on the backs of the poor and unwanted. I feel dirty even standing on the grounds.

I expected Vanessa to be the type to whimper in mock fear and take advantage of the atmosphere by getting handsy with Davis, but she's the first one through the gap between the gate and the fence.

"What are we waiting for?" She laughs. "Come and find me!" She beckons to Davis before disappearing into the gloom that surrounds the house.

Davis looks at me, moonlight tracing the planes of his cheek and flashing off his eyes. "You don't have to come in. I can leave the keys out here, and you can listen to the radio."

I wish I could agree, tell him I'll stay in the car, but out of all the places I've looked for a ghost, Seymour House is the place most likely to have one. Hundreds of people died here over the seventy years it was open.

This is my chance to put aside my fears of what comes after death once and for all.

This is my chance to see if Mrs. H is still out there somewhere.

"Why not?" I say. Bits of rust flutter onto my hair as I lumber through the gap. Davis shrugs and follows, slouching toward the house with his hands in his pockets and his collar flipped up. That's the Davis I remember, still cool at a haunted mental hospital.

A heavy wooden door stands at the top of the bowed steps. It looks like it's going to swing open any second, and Maren's great-grandfather is going to usher me into the house where I'll die like so many others. I take a deep breath and creep into the shadows, following the wraparound porch to a pair of French doors with shattered glass.

Davis shines his phone flashlight through the doors. The dust is thick on the floor, and there are footprints everywhere, way more than just Vanessa's.

"Vanessa?" I croak into the dark. I think I can hear her

somewhere in the shadows. Scratch that: I know I can hear *something*, and I really, really hope it's her.

I shoulder my way through the broken doors and into the house, Davis ducking behind me. The air is stale, and it smells like dust and mouse shit and dead leaves and something else that I don't want to think about. We're in a small room with bookshelves lining the walls—some kind of office?—and there are moldy books and torn paper all along the floor on one side. The room opens onto a large, formal entryway with a sweeping staircase and a soaring ceiling.

I take a few hesitant steps deeper into the house, waiting for my eyes to adjust to the dark. The floor, gritty and squeaky under dirt and trash, is set in an elaborate parquet pattern. Moonlight shines through a cracked stained-glass window, casting foggy colored shadows on the floor. It's like looking at a distorted rainbow. There's a rusty screech from somewhere in the shadows and a burst of wild laughter—Vanessa exploring the second floor.

"Davis!" she calls. Her voice draws him like a moth to a flame and he drifts away, leaving me alone in the entryway. The dim light that filters through the windows is broken only by the pinprick of Davis's flashlight bobbing up the stairs. My nerves are a bundle of live wires. The darkness is a heavy, oppressive kind that is more than just the absence of light. It clings to my skin like spiderwebs.

This darkness feels expectant.

I take a deep breath and finger the locket that hangs over my heart, reminding myself what I came here to do. It would be hard to explain to Davis and Vanessa if I started lighting candles and chanting incantations, so instead of following him, I wait until he and Vanessa disappear down the dark hall on the second floor, then turn to survey the entryway. I have to find a place where a spirit might linger.

A sideboard filled with broken china stands along one wall. Possessions are always a good place to start. Despite the well-known adage that you can't take it with you, people tend to be overly attached to their things, and all the ghost-hunting websites say that spirits are more likely to stay near their worldly goods.

The glass panes in the cabinet doors are smashed. I'm reaching for a tarnished silver spoon when something jerks me back.

Heart racing, I catch a gasp in my throat and spin around. I half expect a figure cloaked in black to be hovering over me, hands curled into claws and darkness flooding out of the place where its eyes should be. The Nothing blooms before me, as dark and terrible as I feared, but then I blink and realize that my sleeve is just caught on a jagged piece of trim.

Keep it together, kid, I chide myself, letting out a shaky laugh.

I work the fabric loose from the rough wood and a hidden door in the wall falls forward under my hand, opening into a cramped passage with a low ceiling and plain paneled walls: a servant's corridor.

I glance back at the ruins of the once-grand entry hall. Paint peels from the walls in great swathes, and underneath it the wood is dank and rotten.

Just like this place. The sooner I can get out of here, the better, and that means performing this ritual undisturbed.

I duck through the doorway and down the hidden hall. It ends in a narrow staircase that climbs into darkness, with a yawning doorway next to it. The air is close and heavy, draping over me like a shroud. Something inside me twists tighter and tighter. The empty doorway beckons to me, coaxing me forward with promises of nightmares and visions alike. My heart thuds so hard that I think Mrs. H's locket is going to leap off my chest as I swim through the tension and fall through the doorway.

Inside is a long room with a tiled floor and a drain in

the middle. Ransacked cabinets line the walls, and empty pill bottles litter the floor. Piles of moldy canvas fill the corners. A rusty gurney with dangling, rotting leather straps stands in the middle of the room. My throat closes when I notice the crank on one end.

Straitjackets. Shock therapy. My mouth twists. This room was used for what passed as treatment in that horror age of mental health care.

Out of all the places I've searched over the past nine months—a funeral pyre under the blue dome of the New Mexico sky, the bell-lined path that winds through the children's section of the cemetery—this is the only time I've felt tension draw me forward and coil in my chest like a rattlesnake, ready to strike. Like there's something lurking in the shadows, waiting for me to stumble so it can snatch me up.

The only light is the dim shine of the moon filtering through cracks in the boards that cover the windows. Streams of silver cross the floor like veins of blood.

I try to breathe out all my hesitations in a long exhale. Am I ready for this? I wasn't so nervous the other times I tried this, and I'm getting second thoughts. If the ritual works . . . is that what I really want? What if I don't like the answer I get?

Mrs. H's locket seems to pulse with my heartbeat. I close my eyes and touch it, imagining it's her hand in mine. I need to know. I can't let fear of the Nothing hold me back.

I drop to my knees in the center of the room. With shaking hands, I pull my ghost-hunting supplies out of my purse and lay them out in a line like surgical tools.

The linoleum floor is sticky and gritty against my palms as I crawl in a rough circle, sketching a pentacle with the chalk, then sit back on my heels to survey my work. It's uneven—one of the points is more of a misshapen blob—but I think it's close enough.

I grit my teeth at the squealing sound the foil packet makes when I tear it open, then empty the salt into my hand. It's like holding a handful of stars. Following the rough lines of my pentacle, I outline the five-pointed star with salt.

It takes me three tries to light the match. The flame flares blue orange in the dark. I hold the candle over the center of the pentacle, letting the wax drip like blood, then stand it upright so that the flame casts looming shadows on the wall.

Closing my eyes, I focus on the steady beating of my heart until it seems to fill the room. Blood pounds in my temples like the rush of speeding death. I ease out a long slow breath and open my eyes. The room flickers around me in the light of the candle. Shadows move at the edge of my vision, just out of sight, just out of reach.

Waiting for me to speak.

Waiting for me to ask.

This is what I've been looking for—not just since Mrs. H died, but since I almost died two years ago. I didn't realize it at the time, but everything has led to this moment.

Mrs. H's locket swings forward as I kneel over the dancing flame. The light of the candle catches it and holds it in an ever-changing grasp, illuminating the cloudy moonstone, the tarnished fingerprints along the edges where Mrs. H's hands fit, the fine links of the chain that ties me to her.

The locket flashes silver as I sprinkle the rest of the salt into the flame.

"To bind the spirit," I murmur. The candle flares brighter and brighter until the room is as light as a summer day. Delirium swoops in my belly, a hot, liquid feeling that sends goose bumps racing over my arms. A chorus of savage screeching fills the room, like the wind whipping through the trees on an October night.

I catch a flicker of movement out of the corner of my eye, but when I spin to look, there's nothing there. Swallowing hard, I reach one hand into the empty air.

"Hello?" My voice is low and rough. "I need to know—"

A crash resounds from the front room, followed by a bellow of fear.

Then Davis begins to curse.

CHAPTER 4
BEYOND THE GRAVE

The shadows whirling on the wall freeze and the candle flame shrinks to a spark as I surge to my feet. I race toward the door, pulse hammering in my temples. Panicked thoughts spin through my mind. This is it. I finally did it—I managed to summon a ghost and got someone killed in the process. My sleeve catches on another rough piece of broken trim around the doorway, but this time I jerk it, the fabric ripping with a snarl as I dart back down the servant's corridor.

I burst into the entryway to find Davis shouting "Shit!" at the ceiling and shaking out his hand. Vanessa cowers against the banister, both hands clapped over her mouth.

"What happened?" I ask.

Davis lets out another roar and points into a corner, where a shadowy figure lurches toward us. The edges of my vision swim as my heart pounds to keep up with the fear pulsing through my veins. Then a sliver of the figure drops to the floor with the tinkle of breaking glass, and everything becomes clear.

The tension I felt crouching over the candle leaks away. Of course my back-alley ritual pieced together from tips I found on paranormal investigation websites didn't work. It never has before. What would make tonight any different? There's no spirit in Seymour House.

Giggles spill out of my mouth as another piece of the mirror splinters; I've always been a nervous laugher. I shine the flashlight on my phone into the corner. Our reflections are a network of cracks in an ornately framed floor-to-ceiling mirror. Davis's punch landed right at his eye level. I'll give him this: he does have good aim.

"I thought I saw someone," Davis insists. He picks splinters of glass from his knuckles, blood trickling over his fingers and dripping to the floor.

"Your own face was so terrifying that you punched yourself," I wheeze.

"I think we've had our fun, haven't we?" Vanessa says. I shiver as the moonlight catches her pale face in an eerie illusion: for half a heartbeat, it looks like her severed head is floating above her body. But then I realize that the dark line across her throat is just the black velvet ribbon that bound the silver bracelets together at the diner. She must have swapped her normal cotton-candy pink for it. The bracelets jangle at her wrists like handcuffs as she tugs at the ribbon. "Let's get out of here."

Davis just grunts in response. My fit of giggles dies away as we duck back through the broken French doors, and with it goes the unease I felt at the candle flame flickering brighter and brighter.

I feel the same kind of disappointed relief that comes after Maren passes me over for a committee in Junior Reapers. It would be nice to be chosen, but do I really want all that responsibility and shit?

Ignorance is bliss.

Maybe I should just focus on what Mrs. H said right as she died. She didn't talk about the Nothing; she didn't say anything about feeling empty or alone. Her eyes lit up, and she said, "Mom." I mean, what else could that mean? She saw a previously departed loved one waiting to greet her on the other side.

I should hold on to that glimmer of hope, let it pick at the crack in my heart until it's big enough to let some light back in. Maybe I could make myself forget the Nothing altogether without finding a ghost to answer my questions about the afterlife.

Outside, the gate rattles in a swelling wind. Bare trees scratch at the black velvet sky. The thin light of a fingernail moon glints off one of Seymour House's broken windows, like an unseeing eye that follows us as we pile back into the car. Davis reaches for a dirty shirt balled up next to me on the back seat and wraps his bleeding hand in it before driving into the overgrown woods that lurk around Scary Road. Branches scrape against the windows, setting my teeth on edge. It's the same squealing song I heard in Seymour House—there must be a tree standing close enough to the house for the branches to rub on the boarded-up windows in this wind.

Just as I'm starting to relax, a shadow steps from the trees and holds up its hands. Too scared to even scream, I just gasp as Davis slams on the brakes.

"What the hell," he murmurs. The shadow solidifies into a boy about our age, tall with blond hair that brushes the collar of his shirt. He's pale with skin like moonlight.

I let out a squeak. All of the urban legends I've heard about Scary Road rush back to me: bloodthirsty fiends who stalk innocent teenagers, shadowy figures who beg for a ride before vanishing into thin air.

My heart sputters like the flame of the candle when I sprinkled the salt. *Nothing happened*, I scold myself, but I can't stop the unease that spreads through my body like a virus. The only reason we're here is because I wanted to look for a ghost, but now I'm feeling a little regret at suggesting we come. Okay, a lot of regret. Lighting the candle and sprinkling the salt felt a lot more like a game when there wasn't a pale figure standing on the side of the road on the way home.

"Davis, don't—" I whimper as he reaches for the button to lower the window. "He—he could be dangerous."

"He's our age," Vanessa says. "He was probably just

driving around and his car broke down."

"It's fine, Olive." Ignoring my protests, Davis rolls down the window. "Hey, you okay?"

The boy is at Davis's window before I can think of how to save my former best friend from being murdered by a creep in the woods.

"Thank you for stopping," he says. "Could I have a ride to White Haven?"

"Get in," Davis says. "Olive, scoot over."

"This is a bad idea," I insist, but the boy is already opening the door and sliding in. I shiver as a wash of cold desert air rolls across the seat. He must be freezing. Instead of a jacket, he's wearing a baggy plaid shirt buttoned up to his neck and a pair of threadbare corduroy pants. The shirt is thick and looks like it's made of wool, but there are holes in the elbows where the fabric has worn out.

Davis puts the car into gear. "I'm Davis."

"Jay—Jay Henderson," the boy says. He runs his hand over the split leather seats, yellow foam poking out. "Swanky car."

Swanky? Davis's car is older than he is, and even when it was new, I don't think Toyota Corollas were considered swanky.

"Are you new in town, Jay?" I don't bother to keep the edge of accusation out of my voice. "I haven't seen you around before."

"Actually, Olive—"

"Wait—how do you know my name?"

"Davis said it when he asked you to make room for me."

Oh. Vanessa sighs, and I catch a glimpse of her in the rearview mirror. She gives me a look that clearly says *bless your heart*, which I know is southern for *you're ridiculous*.

"Anyway, I've been in White Haven a long time, but I've been ill, so I haven't had a chance to meet many people," Jay explains.

"Convenient," I mutter. Davis and Vanessa seem to accept Jay's story without question: he was walking in the woods and got turned around; the sun went down before he realized how far he had wandered.

The red lights of the dashboard glint off my locket like drops of blood. Jay leans forward, examining the heavy silver filigree. His eyes are the pale blue gray of granite.

"Where did you get that locket?" he asks.

The blood in my veins curdles as I remember lifting it over Mrs. H's head. I jerk away as far as I can go.

"It was my friend's. She died a few months ago." Davis frowns at me in the rearview mirror, probably wondering which of my friends died recently. "Why?"

"It looks like one I've seen before," Jay says. His voice is even, but there's a hard edge to it, like a bone about to crack.

The orange glow of a streetlight fills the car as we reach the clearing where Scary Road meets the main road.

"Gotta make a quick stop," Davis announces. He parks in the shadow of the billboard, only mildly inconvenienced by the makeshift bandage still knotted around his hand. "It's not vandalism if it's all gonna be mine someday," he adds, shrugging as he pulls a carton of eggs from under his seat

"I don't think that's how that works," I mutter, but Vanessa's giggles drown me out.

"Something tells me you're not planning on making an omelet," she says.

"Call it an expression of repressed needs," Davis explains. "The eggs are my feelings, and the billboard is my douchebag dad." His voice is smooth and cool, but his jaw is as tight as rigor mortis. He's trying to play this off like vandalizing the billboard is just a childish prank, but it goes deeper than that.

Davis and his dad have clashed on everything since he

was old enough to talk. Davis has always felt connected to his Navajo heritage, even wearing his hair long until last year, but his dad is a different story.

"You have to understand how he was raised," Poppy tried explaining to me once after Mr. Wills refused to go to a powwow that Davis was dancing in. "His parents both grew up in boarding schools where they weren't allowed to speak their language or live their culture. Those schools caused a lot of shame and trauma. It was ingrained in them that the only way to be successful was to leave their heritage behind and try to make it in 'white society.'" Her mouth twisted when she said those words. "They moved back to the Navajo Nation when Davis's dad was a little boy, but the damage was done. He's a product of what happens when you forcibly remove someone's culture and heritage. The effects can last for generations."

Poppy kept Davis and his dad from each other's throats for a long time, but after the divorce, she was busy opening the diner, and things got pretty bad. Sometimes I could hear Davis and his dad shouting at each other from my bedroom. Then Davis would storm over to our house, and Mom would make him pancakes and put him to bed on the couch. She never badmouthed Mr. Wills, but it was clear she was on Davis's side.

Earlier tonight he told me himself that he's been working for his dad, but it doesn't seem like he's had a change of heart. Again, I wonder why he finally gave in to the pressure.

Then I realize what changed: me.

Two years ago, Davis had me and my parents to back him up and support him. To throw him a lifeline when he was drowning in the chasm between him and his dad. Then I got lost in the Nothing and came back a different person, unable to help anyone but myself. I'm sure my mom would have stuck by Davis's side, but it must have gotten hard for him to come to our house when I disappeared into my room as soon as he walked through the door.

So he stopped coming, and no one noticed that he was going under.

My heart squeezes so tight that it hurts as we get out of the car. I should have been there for him. I should have seen that he needed me—needed anyone.

Broken glass glitters like stars in the dirt around the billboard. Davis and Vanessa whoop and run into the clearing with the eggs, leaving me and Jay to stand still as ghosts next to the car.

My chest pinches as I watch Vanessa wind up and hurl an egg. It's a mix of emotions: resentment at the thought of her knowing Davis the way I did, regret that I wasn't there for him when I should have been. Jealousy that he has someone like her and I never will. She's definitely on board with wrecking the billboard; maybe she'll be able to support him in more meaningful ways, too . . . help him work through his problems with his father, let go of some of his anger.

"Come on, Olive." Davis drags me forward and hands me an egg. Foul yellow goo already streaks the billboard. "Throw an egg. It'll make you feel better."

But his offer only makes me feel *worse*, because even after two years of me not realizing he was drowning, he can still sense when I'm upset. I just shake my head and shuffle my feet, waiting for him to finish nailing the man on the billboard with eggs.

Finally, Davis holds up both middle fingers to the billboard, then tucks the empty egg carton under his arm. Apparently he draws the line at littering.

"Where's Jay?" Vanessa asks. "Did he get back in the car?" She peers inside, but it's empty. We circle the clearing, but there's no sign of him.

"There's something weird about that guy," I declare.

"Did you notice how cold it was when he got in the car?"

Davis rolls his eyes. "It's fall in the high desert. Of course it was cold when he opened the door." He shrugs and climbs into the car. "Come on. He must have gotten tired of waiting and started walking along the main road to hitch another ride."

There's still a pocket of cold air in the back seat, but Davis is right. It's freezing outside, and the engine has been off long enough for the heat to fade. But I can't stop a shiver from creeping across my skin when I remember the way Jay just appeared in the woods. Then there's the funny way he talked, using words like swanky . . .

I've been in White Haven a long time, he said. *But I've been ill.*

Ill, like someone who died of consumption at Seymour House a hundred years ago.

"Uh, no, he vanished into thin air because he's a freaking ghost!" I blurt. My eyes feel as big as saucers, and my breath is fast and shallow.

As soon as the words are out of my mouth, every pop culture image I've ever seen of ghosts flips through my head: a luminous woman with long, dark hair floating in the hall; a kid draped in a white bedsheet; Shaggy and Scooby-Doo clutching each other and crying "A g-g-g-ghost!"

I sound ridiculous.

There's a beat of silence before Vanessa dissolves into giggles, brushing tears off her cheeks. Davis puts the car into gear.

"You let your imagination run wild," Davis manages to say between snorts of laughter. "Grow up, Lolly."

CHAPTER 5
ASHES TO ASHES, DUST TO DUST

Okay, so Davis isn't entirely wrong. I've always had an intense imagination. When I was seven or eight, I convinced him that Mrs. McKinley down the street was a witch. In my defense, she *did* have about a dozen black cats and she favored long, flowing dresses, but it turns out she was just a lonely old lady and not a mistress of evil.

And when Jessica Bowen started missing school once a month in fifth grade, I told everyone her absences lined up with the full moon, so obviously she was a werewolf. I got in huge trouble when her mother called mine and told her the real reason Jessica was missing school was because of debilitating cramps.

The point is, I have a track record of reading into things.

I don't realize my locket is missing until Davis pulls into his driveway. I catch a glimpse of myself in the rearview mirror when the dome light ticks on, and the place where the locket hung is so empty that I can't believe I didn't notice it earlier.

"Oh no," I moan. "My locket's gone." My hands flutter over my chest like I've been stabbed.

"I'm sure it's here somewhere," Vanessa says, twisting in her seat to look through the cupholders. I stuff my hands in the crevices of the back seat, coming up with a few candy wrappers. Even Davis sweeps his hand through the crumbs on the floor, but eventually we have to accept that the locket is gone.

"It probably just fell off at the Desert Heights sign,"

Vanessa says consolingly. "We can go back and look for it tomorrow."

Davis makes a noise of derision in his throat but doesn't argue. I barely hear Vanessa saying goodbye before she follows him into his house. A sick feeling gnaws in my stomach as I cross his yard to my own door. I should have left the locket in my jewelry dish.

No—I should have left the locket around Mrs. H's neck. I should have let her be buried with it. I didn't think about taking that away from her, that comfort she must have felt every time she held her locket and remembered her mother. And now she's lying in her coffin under six feet of dirt, alone and in the dark. The spot over her chest must feel so empty as the flesh decays and falls into the hollow of her ribs. I stole her locket from her, and I stole any peace it might have brought her in the Nothing.

I crawl into bed without changing into my pajamas. All I want to do is sleep like the dead. But even the feeling settling in my bones like the muddy silt left behind after a flash flood reminds me of Mrs. H, because she's the one who taught me the word to describe it when we were doing the Sunday crossword together: Weltschmerz. It means the feeling of being weary of the world. There's not really an English equivalent, but I understood it as soon as she started explaining. It's like:

The assault-rifle-wielding, Second Amendment zealots that followed the March for Our Lives rally I went to in Albuquerque after three back-to-back school shootings;

Another unarmed Black man killed in the street because an officer in riot gear didn't recognize his humanity;

The acrid taste of smoke that coats my tongue every summer while the West burns.

I roll onto my side and clamp my arms around an extra pillow. Sometimes it feels like the entire world is bustling around, passing hammers and nails and planks back and forth. They say they're building something together, but I'm the only one who can see that it's a casket.

That's why finding a ghost is so important to me. If I can prove to myself that there's something on the other side, something after this life, then maybe I'll stop picturing myself lying in a bed of dirt with the weight of the world piled on top of me.

Not gonna work, a voice chides in my mind. It sounds suspiciously like my mother's. I punch the pillow into a more comfortable shape to drown it out, and fail. *You're just avoiding the real pain, and it's not going to go away until you face it.*

Who doesn't want to avoid pain, though?

I'm up by seven the next morning, which is unheard of for me. I've never been much of a morning person. Shocker, I know. But I spent most of the night lying awake with my gut twisted into knots, and by the time the sun comes up, I'm buzzing with nervous energy that won't be eased until I have the locket back. I pull on a pair of jeans and wrestle my way into a sweatshirt, my mind racing up the road that climbs into the hills out of town, following its curves to the Desert Heights billboard and Scary Road.

When I get downstairs, Dad is standing at the stove wearing an apron with a glow-in-the-dark headstone. "Compliments to the Chef" is written in old-fashioned script under a skull and crossbones.

"Morning, Lolly," he says, flipping a pancake. "What are you up to so early?"

"Don't call me Lolly," I mutter, grabbing a handful of the chocolate chips he's adding to the pancake batter and popping a few in my mouth. They melt into a slick of milk chocolate. Too sweet; I'm definitely a semisweet kind of girl. "I, uh, have a Junior Reapers thing this morning. I'm supposed to clean up trash in the woods on Scary Road. I mean, by Seymour House." I make it up on the spot, knowing Dad won't question anything I say is for Junior Reapers.

Vanessa offered to go back with me to look for the locket. Well. Kind of. She implied that she would. And Davis didn't say anything, which I'm taking as silent agreement.

After two pancakes smothered in peanut butter and syrup, I head over to Davis's house. He blinks at me with bleary eyes when he opens the door to my knocking. "What are—" His mouth falls open in a jaw-cracking yawn. "What are you doing here?"

I shift my weight to one side, suddenly aware of how stupid my hands look dangling at my sides. "I know it's early, but can you take me back to Scary Road now? So I can look for my locket."

"Uhh—" Davis frowns at me, shifting so that his body fills the doorway. The floor creaks behind him, and I get the distinct feeling he's trying to keep me from seeing something. "Come on. Really? You've barely spoken to me in two years and now you show up at the crack of dawn on a Saturday morning and expect me to drop everything to take you somewhere?"

He's right. Last night almost felt like old times, up until I realized how wide I'd dug the gulf between us over the past few years. That divide is a reminder that Davis is the last person I should be going to for help. It's not fair to expect him to do anything for me. Besides, as much as I wish I could go back to the days when Davis knew everything about me, he can't understand the Nothing. That's a place I went on my own, and I've been alone ever since.

My heart sinks. "You're right. Forget I asked." I start to turn away, hoping he doesn't notice me blinking back frustrated tears.

"Olive!" The door creaks wider, and Vanessa appears under Davis's arm. Her hair hangs in damp tendrils around her face, and she's wearing one of Davis's old T-shirts. My cheeks burn as I realize that she spent the night.

"I'm sorry. I didn't mean to walk in on—" I flutter my hands toward them. Whatever this is.

"It's fine." Vanessa leans against the doorframe, crossing her arms tightly over her chest, her cheeks soft pink like the sky at sunrise. "Of course we'll take you. We don't mind at all. I can tell this is really important to you. Right, Davis?"

He looks like he wants to argue, but Vanessa tilts her head to the side so the sooty ends of the black velvet ribbon around her neck fall across her collarbones. "Come on. It's a beautiful day. A nice morning for a drive," she adds in a breathy whisper.

Davis pinches the bridge of his nose before turning back to me. "Fine. We'll take you. But you're buying coffee."

Ten minutes later, drinks from Coffin Coffee Co in hand, we're rolling through town and onto Highway 89, windows down and wind blowing through the car. My hair is wild, tangled and flying in my face so that I can't see. I grab it in one hand, pulling it into a low ponytail that brushes the top of my neck.

The sky is a brittle, cold blue, and dry leaves skitter across the road as we drive into the hills behind town. Autumn in New Mexico doesn't look like the pictures I've seen of New England: white-steepled churches set in groves of vivid trees like a stained-glass window, or fields of orange pumpkins surrounded by split-rail fences. Here, the cottonwood trees and scrub oaks mostly just fade to muddy yellow and dull brown, but the woods by Scary Road are dotted with pockets of pure gold aspens.

Smears of yellow still drip from the Desert Heights billboard. The man in the illustration has a smile like Mr. Wills's: big and too tight at the corners, more like a grimace than a grin. I shiver under his gaze.

Davis pulls into the shadow of the billboard and puts the car in park. "Go ahead. I want to drink my latte before it gets cold."

"I'll help you look, Olive," Vanessa offers. "Let me just—" She takes a careful sip of her drink, closing her eyes and sighing a little as her cheeks flush from the steam. "Oh, that's so good."

I have to restrain myself from rolling my eyes.

"I'm fine," I say. "Finish your drink." Blowing out a tense breath, I step out onto the fine New Mexico dirt. The trees that line the clearing rustle in the wind, bending toward one another, whispering secrets not meant for me. Dancing shadows follow me like lost children as I turn in a slow circle.

I crouch, sifting through the broken bottles and dead leaves that litter the ground. My heart stops as I spot something gleaming in the half-light, but it's just a piece of glass.

There's a prickle on the back of my neck, like a hand trailing through my hair or the slightest breath of air. My lungs contract as a tingle rushes across my skin. I turn slowly, trying to brush off the feeling that someone is watching me, but it clings like cobwebs. The Desert Heights billboard casts a shadow across the ground. There's nothing there, I tell myself, half-disappointed and half-relieved, but the thought isn't even fully formed before the shadow shifts, unfurling into a figure that flickers like the heat shimmer at the end of the road on a hot day.

"Looking for this?" Jay asks in a voice full of dirt.

CHAPTER 6
EXISTENTIAL DEAD

he moves like a phantom, dark and fleeting, launching himself at me before I can blink. I flail backward, stumbling over a broken beer bottle. My foot turns on a root and I go down hard.

Before I can stagger to my feet, Jay is on me, one hand twisted in the hood of my sweatshirt, the other shaking the locket in my face. His hands are cold, and he's strong enough to rattle the teeth in my jaw. "Where did you get this?" he spits. "Dirty thief!"

"What the hell!" Davis shouts. I hear Vanessa shriek and the car doors slam as they scramble out, but I can't see anything through the chaotic fury that is Jay.

"Get off of me—" I try to push him away just as Davis grabs his shirt collar, and the moment we all make contact, the world goes gray. It's not the endless expanse of the Nothing, empty and dark as a tomb; this is more like all of the color, all of the warmth and light, has been sucked out. Everything is flat and hollow, and plumes of dark smoke creep along the edges of my vision. Shadows shift over Jay's face, turning his brow into the high, polished dome of a skull, his gray eyes to unseeing sockets, his mouth to a jaw that sags.

I make a noise in my throat like a bone snapping and scramble backward on my butt. Jay grunts as he hits the ground, clutching the locket against his chest and glaring at me. Vanessa yanks me to my feet, then claps one hand over her mouth in shock.

"What was that?" Davis wheezes, stepping in front of

me and looking up at the sky. It's perfect, a cloudless blue. The sun is ringed by a corona of light. "It was like the sun turned black. How did you—"

"How did *you*"—Jay points at me, his face twisted in rage—"get my mother's locket? Did you break into her room at the boarding house?"

"I don't know what the fuck you're talking about," I sputter, rubbing my neck where Jay's hand brushed against my skin. It burns with cold. "That locket belonged to my friend."

It's the truth, but there's also truth in what he called me: dirty thief. His accusation rings in my ears as my mind fills with unsettling thoughts about Mrs. H lying alone in her casket without the locket to bring her comfort.

"You're a liar, and I can prove it," Jay hisses. He places his forefinger and thumb on either side of the locket and squeezes gently. There's a slight pop, and the locket springs open. I jolt back, my limbs stiff. I never knew the locket opened.

Jay holds it out for me to see.

On one side is a black-and-white photograph of a boy wearing a newsboy cap and a collared shirt: Jay. The other side has a tiny flower made of flaxen hair held in place by a delicate clip.

"Is that one of those creepy things made of someone's hair after they die?" Vanessa asks.

"A mourning brooch," I say. I've seen these before, in the Museum of Macabre. There's a whole exhibit on Victorian mourning tokens: human molars set in delicate silver rings, photographs of stiff corpses propped against high-backed velvet couches with their hands folded in their laps, and dozens of brooches and bouquets of intricate flowers made of tightly twisted hair. Life (and death) was different back then. When someone died, they didn't leave behind a whole life documented on social media, a

digital footprint to outlive them. They were just gone. Forever. So the people they left behind would take any little bit
of them that they could and save it as a memento.

"My mother clipped that lock of hair before I went
to the asylum for the poor," Jay says, snapping the locket
closed. "I haven't seen her in months. No one is allowed
to leave the asylum grounds without permission." His face
tightens in fear, and for a split second I see the smooth
white curve of a jawbone again. "Momma would never
willingly part with this locket. Did she send you to find
me? Did she give you the locket as a token of trust and bid
you come?"

"No, I—"

"Someone else, then. Mrs. Murphy from the boarding
house? Did she send you to tell me that my mother is un-
well?" Cold flames burn in Jay's eyes. A shadow shifts behind his irises. "Have you come to tell me that she died?"

Davis, Vanessa, and I exchange a bewildered look.
Then the truth hits me like a sudden wind howling out of
the hills: *Jay* is the one who's dead—but he doesn't know it.

My stomach cramps with cold, sick dread as tendrils of
smoke fill his eyes. I thought this moment would be trium-
phant, like the musical montage of a 2000s teen movie: fist
pump, freeze frame. But instead all I feel is panic.

This is some freaky *Sixth Sense* shit right here. When
I set out to find a ghost, I figured he would be self-aware.
I wasn't counting on having to break the news of his own
demise.

I draw in a shaky breath, then stumble over the words.
"I'm not here to tell you that your mother died. I'm here to
tell you that *you* did. A long time ago."

Shadows brew on Jay's face. His eyes are silver and
cold, icy flames, and the skin on his face stretches, clinging
to his cheekbones and brow and jaw, tighter and tighter
until he's just a skull with yawning holes where his eyes

were. Darkness flows out of those holes and blocks out the pale sunlight, the same darkness that enveloped me when I took that fateful bite of crab rangoon. A bone-chattering cold sweeps over us. My breath rasps in my throat. The fathomless dark surrounds us, and my heart stutters to a stop. I hid from it for two years, but now my time is up. Jay is here to drag me into the Nothing.

"No." Jay's voice cracks in the still air like a shot echoing off the hills. My fingers twist into tight fists. "No, you're lying. You're trying to trick me."

Jay flings his hands out as though he's brushing away a cobweb, and the wispy darkness fades away. He covers his trembling mouth with one hand, Mrs. H's locket dangling from his fingers. The moonstone at the center has the same luminescent sheen as Jay's skin in the half-light under the trees.

"Dude, I think she's right," Davis chokes out. "It's been years since anyone lived at Seymour House. And the way you just appeared, like you were part of the shadow—"

"I can't be dead," Jay says, pacing across the road and back. He moves like something you see out of the corner of your eye when you're alone. "I was sick, yes, but I was well enough to sneak out of the asylum. I tried to hitch a ride back into town to see my mother, to say goodbye to her in case consumption finally took me . . . I can't be dead. Feel—"

He reaches for me, and his fingers are bones, long and shining white. I squeeze my eyes closed, sure that if he touches me with those skeletal hands, my flesh will warp and melt away like his and I'll be nothing but a skeleton, a pile of bones left in the dirt.

But when he touches me, it's just to take my hand and draw it against his chest. My eyes fly open in surprise. His face is gaunt, hollow under the eyes. He holds my hand tight against his chest, long enough for me to feel a heartbeat if there was anything warm and living left to beat. But my hand might as well be against a stone that's been dredged up from the bottom of a river. His chest is hard and cold and dead.

"What do you feel?" he demands.

"Nothing," I whisper.

He lets go of me and rips open his shirt, revealing a hollow blue-white chest that looks wasted away. Davis grabs for me and Vanessa and tries to tug us back toward the car, but I'm frozen in place watching as Jay presses his hands to his skin, feeling desperately—futilely—for a heartbeat.

"I died," he whispers. His voice is soft, disbelieving. He sounds like a child who's just been told that his parents are splitting up. Broken. He holds out his hands, examining them as though looking for proof that I'm wrong. Delicate bones flicker in and out of sight in the space of time it takes me to blink. "In the asylum . . . without ever getting well. I died without saying goodbye to my mother." He presses one hand to his mouth, then looks up at me, his eyes the same slate gray as the sky before a storm. "But if I died, then why am I still here?"

He's here because I summoned him here. But why did it work this time, after all my months of searching? What did I do last night that finally drew a spirit back to the land of the living?

The answer comes to me as Jay fiddles with the fine chain of the locket.

Last night wasn't the first time I knelt in a place steeped in death to search for a ghost, but it *is* the first time I did it while wearing Mrs. H's locket. The hairs on my arms stand up as I remember the way it swung over the candle. The lock of Jay's hair that his mother had carefully clipped and twisted into a mourning brooch moving over the flame, the salt sparking in the light as I spoke the words *to bind the spirit.*

I shiver as I realize Jay and I are linked by this locket in a way I didn't anticipate. It had belonged to his mother at one point, but Mrs. H had it when she died. When I took it from around her neck, it set me on this path to find Jay—to ask him the question that's consumed me for the past nine months.

"You're here because I brought you here. Last night. That's why I suggested we go to Seymour House," I admit, turning to Davis and Vanessa. "I was looking for a ghost."

Davis tenses beside me. "So you were just using me as your chauffeur. Good to know."

"I didn't—" I flounder, shaken by the brittle quality of his voice. It sounds like a pane of glass about to shatter.

"Why would you do that?" Vanessa cries. "Why would you want to find a ghost?" She shivers a little as Jay turns his gaze on her. The hollows in his cheeks deepen as his jaw sags open in shock. He must not be used to being referred to as a ghost.

"Yeah, Olive," Davis says. "Why?" Hurt deepens his eyes to polished obsidian, and I know that he's not asking why I was looking for a ghost. He wants to know if I have a good reason for using him.

"I've been trying to summon a spirit for nine months," I say. "Ever since my friend died. The one who gave me that—" I reach for the locket, but Jay twitches his fingers and it disappears before I can take it. My hands itch to snatch it away, hold it tight against my chest until it pulses in time with my heart, but I can't risk pushing Jay away. What he can tell me is more important than the locket, so I grit my teeth and continue. "I have a question that only a ghost can answer. I want to know—I *need* to know what happens after we die." I swallow hard, suddenly afraid of what he'll say. "Where do we go after we—you know—move on?"

Davis's head jerks up at my question. Vanessa's fingers

flutter over the ends of her ribbon. Maybe they've never thought about it before—maybe they've never wondered what comes next.

What luxury.

"You want to know what happens after we die?" Jay asks mournfully.

"Yes."

"Like if there's some sort of afterlife or if we just fade away?"

"Yes." My skin prickles under a flood of emotions strong enough to sweep away all reason. Because if he tells me that there is Nothing, that's it. I'll know for sure that Mrs. H has gone somewhere where I can never talk to her again, she's rotting under six feet of dirt, and someday I'll be there, too, I'll be Nothing just like her, just like everyone else, and what's the *point* of everything if it all ends in Nothing?

Suddenly I wish I could take the words back, snatch them out of the air and stuff them down my throat. I wish I could turn the hands of the clock back twelve hours and never set foot in Seymour House. I wish I could just be damn *satisfied* by that look on Mrs. H's face right before she died. Why couldn't I have accepted that as my answer? Why couldn't I have taken her last, fluttering exhale— *Mom*—at face value, and imagined her and her mother hugging in long white robes and tinsel halos? What's wrong with me that I've spent the past nine months seeking out darkness, like I'm determined to find my way back into the Nothing, like I *want* my worst fear to come true?

It's too late for all that regret because I lit the candle and sprinkled the salt and bade a ghost come, and now the ghost in question is standing in front of me, glancing around the trees as though looking for an answer. My skin prickles under the heavy weight of Davis's eyes studying me as I brace myself for Jay's response.

"How am I supposed to know? I didn't even know I was dead."

I feel like all the air has been sucked from my lungs, like I'm drowning on dry land. Out of all the possibilities I imagined while searching for a ghost, this was the one that never crossed my mind: that the dead would be as oblivious as I am. How can Jay have no idea what happens after this life? He died, didn't he? It must have been at least a hundred years since he took his last breath. So where has he been all this time?

The thought barely crosses my mind before I remember what Davis told Vanessa about the urban legend that surrounds these woods: *The stories say that he waits for a ride, trying to escape the asylum, but he disappears as soon as the car leaves the grounds.*

"Shit." I press a hand to my face, deflating. "You don't know what happens when we move on because you never did—you've been stuck here ever since you died, trying to escape these woods."

"The vanishing hitchhiker," Vanessa says with a little gasp. Davis repeats my expletive.

"Hitchhiker?" Jay glances between us. "That's the last thing I remember doing. We weren't allowed to leave the asylum. Mr. Seymour forbade it. But I tried to hitch a ride into White Haven so I could see my mother again." He squints toward the woods, tilting his head like he's listening for something. "I remember headlights coming at me through the trees . . . I was all turned around, lost in the woods. I thought I had made it off the asylum grounds, that I was on the main road. So I put my hand up to ask for a ride." He raises his hand in a mimicry of his actions all those years ago. "The world turned red and gray, and then—" His hand falls, and he looks at me, fear swimming in his eyes. "I didn't make it, did I? I never made it out of these woods."

I shake my head. "I don't think so."

"Instead I died . . ." Jay ripples slightly in the wind as he falls into the memory. He seems to be losing form as more and more of his death comes back to him. "I think I remember a man—Mr. Seymour's son—and a girl from the house, holding me down in a hole in the dirt until everything went dark. But instead of staying in my grave and moving on, I struggled out and stayed in the trees . . . waited for another car to come along and take me back to my mother."

My stomach churns at the thought of Jay's spirit rising out of his grave and wandering these woods for decades, his desperation to escape binding him to this pale imitation of life. It's like he's been stuck in a rut, repeating the events that led to his death over and over for a hundred years.

"If what you're saying is true . . . if it really has been so long since I died, then that means Momma is dead, too, and the only way for me to ever see her again is to move on. So what's holding me back?" Jay presses his hands to his skull in frustration. The more he loses control of his emotions, the less form he has. When the wind blows, it pulls away enough of his muted color that the trees show through him. I shiver, thinking about all the things those trees have seen. Jay, wandering through their haunted labyrinth for years, trying to find a way out . . . Jay, being left in a shallow grave.

His grave. I catch a breath and hold it for three heartbeats. After he died, his spirit left his grave to continue his escape.

And I bet he hasn't been back since.

"Your grave," I say. "You left your grave after you died. You aren't at peace because you can't find your grave." My bones ache with certainty. That's got to be it. If we find Jay's grave, he'll be released from this half-life that he's been stuck in. He'll be able to move on—to the Nothing, or to whatever else there is after death—and then he'll be able to answer my question.

"I could help you," I say slowly. "I could help you find your grave . . . but I want you to do something for me, too. I want you to promise me that you'll come back and leave me a sign or something. Just to let me know if there's something on the other side." A light at the end of the tunnel. I keep my eyes fixed on Jay, wading into the pools of still water that are his eyes.

"Olive," Davis mutters. He's looking at me like I'm holding an angry rattlesnake. "Maybe you shouldn't mess around with this."

"Why not? This is what I've been looking for."

"But what if it doesn't work? You heard what he said— he wasn't buried with the rest of the patients in the city cemetery, and he doesn't have a headstone. What are the odds you'll be able to find his grave out there?" He sweeps his arms out at the sprawling, overgrown woods that separate Seymour House from the main road where we stand. It's got to be a hundred acres of scrub oak trees with clawing branches and half-fallen stone walls waiting to twist ankles. "Not to mention this." He jabs a finger at the Desert Heights billboard. "Did you forget about that? My dad is breaking ground in just over a month, and when he does, Jay's grave will be destroyed."

My heart drops like an anvil onto a roadrunner. Four weeks. In four weeks, these trees will snap like femurs under bulldozers and Jay's chance at resting in peace will be gone.

If the grave is destroyed, Jay will be trapped here forever.

Vanessa clears her throat, clutching at her ribbon. "Davis. What will happen to Wills and Son if human remains are discovered at the site of their premiere housing development?"

There's a beat of tense silence. I suck in a sharp breath and chance a look at Davis. He folds his arms, leaning against the hood of his car as a sly grin creeps across his face.

"Holy shit," he murmurs. "You're right. No one wants to live on the set of *Poltergeist*. And my dad sank everything he has into buying this land from the Seymours. If Desert Heights doesn't happen, he'll fold. There won't be any Wills and Son Development Group."

"This could be your chance to get out of working for your dad once and for all," Vanessa says.

Davis taps his chin with one finger. "Okay. I'm in."

"You're in?" Relief colors my voice. I would have helped Jay either way, but I'm glad Davis is agreeing to help, too. It'll be easier with more of us. Plus, there's something so reassuring about Davis. Having him around reminds me of the years we spent side by side—the years before I saw the Nothing every time I closed my eyes.

"I'm in."

I square my shoulders as a plan starts to form. "Then it's time that I put my Junior Reapers badge to work."

CHAPTER 7
NOT LONG FOR THIS WORLD

I'm dreaming about the ocean, a black, oily ocean with waves that sweep bones onto the shore instead of sea-shells. The water washes up over my feet. It's achingly cold, and as it recedes, I look down and see in the silvery light of the moon that my feet are bones.

"We're all bones," Jay says. He reaches out with one skeletal hand and takes the end of a black ribbon knotted around my neck and tugs, and the ribbon falls, and with it is my head, falling, falling—

I throw out my arms to catch myself, my legs tangled in the sheets so that I hit the floor in a heap. My heart pounds in time with the blaring of my alarm as I wait for the last vestiges of the dream to fade away.

We're all bones. Someone more emotionally well-adjusted would say that dream is my subconscious's way of reaching out, trying to communicate that what I'm really afraid of is my own mortality, or something like that. I choose to believe it stemmed from the bowl of Funny Bones Ultra-Sugar Crunch Crisp I had before bed last night. That red dye'll get you every time.

Yawning, I drag myself to my feet and turn off the alarm before pulling a pair of black jeans and a deep red polka-dot blouse out of the hamper. I sweep my hair out of my face and pin it back with my favorite hair clip: a glittering skeletal hand covered in black rhinestones. But when I see it in my hair, the dream comes swimming back to the surface. Shuddering, I grab a Victorian-style brooch with an alabaster silhouette instead.

Maren corners me as soon as I get to school, her arms filled with posters for the Sock Hop. She grabs my wrist and drags me to an alcove at the end of the hall.

I rub my wrist, the skin tingling where she gripped me. "Ouch. What the hell?"

"Stay out of Seymour House," she says without preamble. "I know everyone thinks it's so fun to go hook up and party there, but it's my family's house. Bad things happened there. And I would hate for Ms. Hunter to find out about you sneaking around there. The most important part of being a Junior Reaper is being a good representative of White Haven, and I doubt she would think trespassing reflects well on the town."

I laugh. "Wait—you're joking, right? You wouldn't really go tattle on me to our Junior Reaper advisor."

"I never joke. You don't know what it's like to have a family legacy like mine."

I consider Maren's slightly menacing tone. The Seymours have never been popular in White Haven, but that doesn't mean they aren't powerful. Money goes a long way toward control, and Maren's family has more of both than anyone else in White Haven. So I don't doubt that she has enough influence over Ms. Hunter to make life difficult for me if I keep digging into her bloody family history.

Maren must take my silence for acquiescence because she shoves half the posters at me and thrusts a roll of masking tape into my hands.

"We need to hang these posters for the Sock Hop around school. You take the south wing and I'll take the north wing." Her oxford pumps clack on the tile floor as she speed-walks away. "And Olive—" she calls over her shoulder. "Do it right, or I'll make you fix it tomorrow."

The Junior Reapers host the Sock Hop every Halloween. It's supposed to keep teenagers from smashing pumpkins and having weird Halloween sex. I haven't ever gone.

It takes forever to hang the posters because the tape keeps twisting and sticking to itself (and, I'll be honest, somehow I get a wad of it stuck in my hair). Then I drop everything when I'm halfway up the stairs, and the posters all float back down to the bottom.

I have a hard time concentrating on my classes for the rest of the day, and not for the usual reasons. Instead, I'm going over everything I already know about Maren, her family, and Seymour House.

White Haven was founded back in the late nineteenth century when tuberculosis, then known as consumption—the white plague—swept across the country. People thought an arid climate would cure it, so they flocked to the desert. This part of New Mexico was already set aside as a Navajo reservation, but in true arrogant American fashion, the Seymours drove the Navajo out of this valley and founded a world-class consumption sanitarium. White Haven became something of a mecca for consumption-suffering minor celebrities and rich easterners, who came here to live out the rest of their lives in luxury on stolen land.

But the upper class wasn't the only one to be decimated by the white plague. The lower classes were even more likely to have it due to their poor nutrition and general wretchedness of life. And they came out west seeking a cure, too.

It was Maren's great-grandfather William Seymour—a younger son who didn't inherit the fortune his father made with the sanitarium—who opened Seymour House Asylum for the Poor. At first it just gave impoverished people a place to die, but after a while, people in the surrounding area figured out that it was a handy place to stash unwanted or unbalanced relatives. William dropped "for the Poor" from the name, along with any pretense of caring for the indigent. Instead, Seymour House became the kind of place where anyone with a mental illness, intellectual disability, medical abnormality, or societal flaw could be locked up for the rest of their life.

The sanitarium closed in the 1940s, when antibiotics slowed the spread of tuberculosis, but Seymour House was open until the mental health care reforms of the 1970s. When it finally closed, Maren's branch of the family made a big show of donating to the Mental Health Association of New Mexico. I always thought that was kind of gross considering they made their money running a for-profit mental hospital in the first place.

When I get to city hall after school, there's a bored-looking receptionist and a few people in line at the information desk. Luckily, I've been to the records department several times to do very important Junior Reapers stuff—shred old documents, mostly—so I bypass the line and head straight upstairs, down a series of corridors that grow progressively narrower and dimmer as I twist deeper into the old building.

Behind a door marked RE OR DEPA TME T is a table with three ancient computers. The harsh fluorescent lights flicker overhead and a copy machine behind the row of computers whines.

No one's around.

I sit down at one of the computers and wiggle the mouse to wake it up. The screen takes a long time to brighten, but finally the cursor blinks in a search box under the words WHITE HAVEN PUBLIC RECORDS.

I feel an iota of guilt as I type *Seymour* into the search bar and watch the screen fill up with results. Maren and I have never been buddy-buddy, but believe it or not, I'm not out to get her. The only reason I'm digging into her family history is to help Jay.

Something tells me she wouldn't see it that way.

The Seymour family has been prominent in White Haven for over a century, so there's a lot to wade through:

birth announcements, marriage licenses, bills of sale, property titles, bank liens. I'm not looking for anything in particular, but I find plenty of information. Like:

Maren's father received a dishonorable discharge from the Army twenty years ago.

Her great-uncle was married four times, with each wife dying in a freak accident more gruesome than the one before.

Seymour House had half a dozen liens on it and almost went into foreclosure twice while it was a for-profit mental hospital.

None of these little tidbits tells me anything that will help Jay, but they do give me some insight into why Maren is the way she is. With a background like hers, it must be hard not to feel defined by her family history. She must think that if everything she does is perfect, she can redefine herself. She can be someone else.

William Seymour's obituary: February 3, 1916. It's not clear how he died, but he was young, only in his sixties. I scan the article quickly and then queue it up to print.

I'm so absorbed in Seymour family history that I don't hear the copy machine stop spitting pages onto the floor behind the computers.

"Can I help you?" a voice says right in my ear.

I jump enough to knock the keyboard to the floor.

"Sorry!" I squeak. I'm not sure if I'm apologizing about the keyboard or being in the Records Department in general. "I didn't see anyone when I came in."

"What do you need?" The woman has parched lips pressed into a thin line and a pair of reading glasses on a chain. Her hair is cut in a *can-I-speak-to-the-manager* style— you know, smooth and chin length around her face but teased and gelled into punk rock spikes in the back. I bet her name is Karen.

"Well . . ." I angle myself in the chair so that maybe

Karen can't see what I was searching for. "I need to find some burial records. Burial records of patients who died at Seymour House."

Karen purses her lips tighter; they're in danger of disappearing. "Anyone in particular?"

"His name is—was, I mean, he died a long time ago, of course, he's definitely not still alive—Jay Henderson. He died sometime in the early 1900s."

"No records from Seymour House from before 1930," Karen says, waving her hand in the air and turning back to the filing cabinets. "They were all lost in a fire in the Seymours' personal residence."

The fire that destroyed the home just a week after Edward Seymour, William's son, took out a million-dollar insurance policy on it. Yep, I learned that little tidbit, too. "Hmm. Okay. Well, I know that the grave is somewhere in the woods behind Seymour House."

Karen shakes her head enough that her tacky earrings rattle like her only two independent opinions in her empty head. "There are no graves on the Seymour property. The Seymour House burial grounds are on the far edge of the city cemetery."

"Right . . . I know about those graves, but I'm looking for the other ones."

"There are no other graves." Karen is losing patience with me, I can tell.

"There must be, though. There are only about fifty Seymour House graves in the cemetery." I counted them yesterday, picking my way through the overgrown section where the poorhouse victims are buried. I figured I better do my due diligence before I drag everyone out into the woods, but none of the graves in the cemetery could have been Jay's—too old, too new, the dates too far apart or too close together. "Seymour House was open for over fifty *years*. So where did they put the rest of them?"

"Maybe you're overestimating the number of people who died as residents of Seymour House and remained unclaimed," she says. "Now, would you like to see the burial records from Seymour House from 1930 on?"

"I guess," I say. She disappears into her labyrinth of filing cabinets and comes back with a form and a pen.

"Fill this out, and I will submit it . . ." She checks her watch. "Hmm, probably not till tomorrow. Then you'll receive the records in eight to ten weeks."

"Eight to ten weeks? I thought death certificates and burial records were public!"

Karen shrugs. "They are, but Seymour House is, and always has been, a private entity."

"I forgot to show you—" I fish in my pocket for my Junior Reapers badge, then flash it under her pointed nose. "I'm a Junior Reaper. So can't you expedite it or something?"

"No," she snaps, pushing my badge away. "Fill out the form."

I shove the paper back to her. "Never mind. I can't wait that long."

"I'm sorry I couldn't be more helpful," she says, not sorry at all.

Stupid, stupid, stupid. Using my Junior Reaper status didn't get me anywhere—and now I have to worry about Karen poking around and mentioning my visit to Ms. Hunter. I grab my backpack and am halfway through the door when she calls after me.

"Miss—"

I spin back around. Maybe she thought of a loophole or something.

But she's just holding the page I printed between her thumb and forefinger. "You forgot this."

The page she hands me is still warm from the printer. I read it slowly as I walk back to the top of the marble staircase. I'm about to stuff it in my backpack, when—

"Olive. What are you doing here?"

I'm not usually so jumpy. Maybe it's the fact that I am now on speaking terms with a ghost, or maybe all the late nights are making me lose my nerve. Whatever it is, I flinch and drop the paper, which drifts from side to side as it falls to the marble floor at the bottom of the stairs, landing right at Maren's feet.

I half trip, half run down the stairs. "I got it! It's nothing, don't worry about it!"

But it's too late: Maren stoops to pick it up. Her green eyes widen as she scans what it says. When she looks up at me, her face is like a porcelain doll with a crack in it.

Maren is tough as nails. I've seen her talk over teachers until they throw up their hands and let her take charge. She bullies Ms. Hunter into changing all of our Junior Reapers plans to suit her. She has a withering stare that could petrify a basilisk.

She doesn't get sad; she gets mad.

But that broken look on her face? It stings like salt in a paper cut.

She crumples the paper and stuffs it in her pocket, before turning on her heel and bursting out onto Main Street. My shoes squeal on the polished floor as I hurry after her, following her through the wrought iron gates of the cemetery. She disappears into a miniature city of mausoleums that inter White Haven's wealthiest citizens—tiny adobe pueblos and Spanish mission–style cathedrals set on narrow, twisting cobblestone streets with actual working streetlights and street signs.

I find her sitting on a stone bench, facing an elaborate white stucco mausoleum with *Seymour* carved over the doorway in imposing letters.

"It's not what you think, Maren." I'm afraid to sit next to her—her fingernails are shaped like talons—so instead I hover over her shoulder. "I'm not just being a nosy bitch."

Maren pulls the crumpled computer printout from her pocket and smooths it out. In a deadpan voice, she reads, "William Seymour, beloved father of hundreds of White Haven's poorest citizens, died peacefully in his sleep in his home at 185 North First Street."

She rips the paper in half, then in fourths and eighths, and lets the wind take it through the iron gate of the mausoleum. I can vaguely make out the stumps of old candles and the spines of books inside and I shiver, wondering if she ever goes inside to sit with her family's bones. I imagine her climbing onto the stone bed and lying with her red hair spread like a halo and her hands crossed over her chest like a Madonna, pressed against her heart to stifle the beats that would echo off the cold walls. Would she close her eyes and imagine herself lovely as a corpse in that house of the dead, a blooming marigold surrounded by the wilted remains of her family? Would she trace her name written in stone?

"Do you know *how* he died peacefully in his sleep?" Maren's sharp eyes glint at me, and I shake my head.

"Because his youngest daughter, Mary, who was only thirteen, waited until he'd passed out drunk and then put a pillow over his face." Maren stands up and clutches the iron bars of the Seymour crypt gate. "Mary told her mother that he had been selling her to men to pay his gambling debts. Her mother didn't believe her, of course, and Mary spent the rest of her miserable life locked up in Seymour House."

My skin crawls as I picture a girl in an old-fashioned dress locked inside Seymour House. She looks like Maren.

Maren turns to me, her face hard as the white stone that surrounds us. "I know what you're doing, Olive. You're not the only one who wants to take down Maren Seymour, the frigid bitch who makes everyone miserable. Well, go ahead." She holds her wrists out to me. "I'm tired of trying.

It won't take much to prove that in my veins runs the blood of monsters."

I've never seen her get personal like this. Maren is usually one hundred percent polished, one hundred percent distant. It seems exhausting, to be honest. She never relaxes or lets down her guard, and the amount of emotional energy that must take doesn't leave anything for her to use on friendships. Instead, she spends all her time volunteering, probably because she's trying to right past wrongs, trying to make up for crimes that aren't even hers. No wonder she's always stiff and impatient. Maybe it's not personal; maybe it's a defense mechanism, the only way she can focus on doing what she has to do to feel safe.

And I can't believe I'm thinking this about *Maren effing Seymour,* but we're not so different. We both shut people out to protect ourselves. And we're both pretty screwed up because of it.

"You're not a monster," I say. "You work so hard to make White Haven a better place—"

"It doesn't matter!" Maren throws up her hands. "It doesn't matter that I'm the president of Junior Reapers, and I spend every Friday night manning the teen crisis line, and I organized the Walk to End Bullying. It doesn't matter that I volunteer to be the designated driver at *every single party.*" She draws a long, tremulous breath. "Do you know how many parties I get invited to? None. Nothing I ever do will make up for my family's part in White Haven history. I'll always be a Seymour. I'll always be covered in their blood."

Covered in their blood. I shudder at the image—Maren's tangled red hair doesn't help. It must suck knowing that your legacy is one of pain and suffering. I don't blame her for being willing to do anything to shrug that off.

Anything . . .

An idea takes root in my mind.

"But what if . . ." I say slowly. "What if there *is* something you could do?"

CHAPTER 8
DONE FOR

Maren waits for me in the parking lot after school the next day, leaning against her 1965 convertible, cherry red, the kind of car that James Dean died in. She wears big round sunglasses and has a silk scarf twisted over her hair.

"You ready to tell me what's going on?" she demands, unlocking the doors.

"When we get there," I promise, sliding into the front seat. Her car smells like Bath & Body Works and sunshine. "Go to Scary Road, and then I'll explain everything."

Maren looks at me with narrowed eyes, but doesn't argue. Pulling out of the parking lot, she hits the button to open the roof and turns on the radio. Tinny rock music pours out of the speakers. She reaches for her phone, but I grab her hand before she can change the song.

"Wait—I know this. Saves the Day, right?" Jangly guitars and clanging cymbals, a steady, throbbing beat under a keening voice. "This is good."

"Guilty pleasure," Maren admits. "I love nineties pop-punk."

"Maren, Maren, Maren . . ." I wag my head back and forth in exaggerated disapproval. "If you're not careful, you're going to end up with a mohawk and your clothes safety pinned together."

Maren lets out a short bark of laughter. "I said I like the music, not the scene."

She glances at me sideways. Reaching for the volume, she cranks it up, and we fly up the road into the hills.

The road climbs into the mountains outside of town,

toward the Phoenix Project Pyre, toward Scary Road, toward Seymour House. Toward everything new. Big waves of light wash over the car, and I try to catch the wind in my hand. Maren's scarf untwists and soars away, and her long red-gold hair uncoils and streams behind us like a flag. And I kind of don't want this drive to end.

But then we round a bend, and the Desert Heights billboard towers over Scary Road.

Maren parks under the billboard. "We're here," she says. "Explain."

I gesture toward the tree line, where Davis and Vanessa are standing. "Let's get out."

She scowls, but follows me across the weedy clearing and into the woods. Davis raises an eyebrow when he sees who I'm with, but doesn't say anything.

"Um—" I shift my weight, trying to figure out how to broach the subject without sounding like one of those people who believe every conspiracy theory that circulates on Twitter. "So have you heard the stories about—"

"This doesn't have something to do with the vanishing hitchhiker, does it?" Maren interrupts. "Half the school thinks there's a ghost in these woods."

Vanessa bites her lip to hold back a smile.

"You don't believe the rumors?" I ask.

Maren snorts. "Come on, Olive. I thought you were smarter than that. Those stories are just an urban legend meant to scare kids out of picking up hitchhikers."

Davis, Vanessa, and I exchange a look. "But what if the stories are true?" I say.

"There's no such thing as ghosts," Maren insists.

A gust of wind whips through the woods, blowing a vortex of dry leaves from the trees. Maren stumbles backward, clutching at my wrist with a grasp that tingles like fire as a figure blooms out of the woods, dark around the edges like a storm cloud. It's indistinct and ethereal before solidifying into a boy whose corn silk hair blows around his face. His outline doesn't quite match up with his movements, making his whole body appear to be fluttering as he walks toward us. Waves of bone-chattering cold flow off him, raising the hairs on my arms. His eyes are shadow gray and so cold they burn.

I gesture at his shadowy figure. "Maren, this is Jay Henderson—the vanishing hitchhiker."

Maren's fingernails dig into my skin before she abruptly releases me. I don't think she's taken a single breath since Jay appeared, so I take an extra deep one to compensate and explain how the only reason I came to Seymour House in the first place was to look for a ghost, and how we met Jay, who's been trapped in these woods for a hundred years.

It doesn't hurt that the ghost in question is standing before us, rippling slightly in the wind like smoke from a candle.

"So the reason I was looking your family up is because I was trying to find information that will help us find Jay's grave," I finish. "And then when you said you would do anything to make up for being a Seymour, I thought you might be able to help." My stomach twists into taut ropes as I wait for Maren's response.

"You're a ghost," she finally says to Jay, her freckled skin chalky with unease.

He smiles wryly. "In the flesh."

"Then tell me what happened to you."

Vanessa points toward the sagging corner of roof that shows over the trees. "Isn't that obvious? He died at the asylum." Her mouth puckers like the words taste bad.

Maren shakes her head once. "That's not what I asked. I want to know what *happened* there."

Jay frowns. "I don't quite remember. Everything feels foggy, like my memories are obscured by mist."

"Maybe the fog will lift if we go inside," Vanessa

suggests.

"Go inside Seymour House." Maren says it like a challenge, arms folded tight across her chest. Her voice doesn't shake, but her face is leached of color.

"The asylum was where he spent his last days. Maybe going back will help him remember." Vanessa fingers the ends of her ribbon, eyes darting from Maren to me like she's hoping I'll back her up.

"It's not so bad in there," I lie. I don't blame Maren for being nervous. It's late afternoon, and Scary Road is draped in shadows.

Maren glares at me. Her eyes get the same steely glint that they do when someone contradicts her. "Then let's go."

Seymour House rises out of the trees as we walk down the dirt road, a blemish against the blue sky. I watch Maren out of the corner of my eye as we follow Jay across the yard. I didn't mean to drag her here, to her family's legacy that lurks over town.

Jay slips through the gate like a shadow. When we catch up to him, he's standing just inside the house, in the office with its mildewed books and torn pages. It's completely dark, but I can still see him, his skin casting a weird glow. Davis pulls out his phone and hits the flashlight. That's almost worse. Now our profiles jump on the walls and I can see the open doorway, where shadows hint at what lies beyond.

"Well?" Maren's voice hangs in the air like a mote of dust. "Do you remember anything?"

Jay closes his eyes. My chest feels as empty as the hollows under his eyes. I force myself to focus on the thin beam of light from Davis's phone, but every time I blink, the shadows in the corners of the room seem to spread, and I can't help but wonder if instead of lifting, the shadows that shroud Jay's memories are darkening. Maybe behind his closed eyelids, everything has gone black.

Maybe he's drowning in the Nothing right in front of us.

The air in the abandoned study is heavy and stagnant, full of a century's worth of regrets. I gulp the dank air, but my lungs refuse to fill, withering like poppies in the summer heat. For half a heartbeat, my veins pulse with choking panic, but before I suffocate, Jay begins to speak.

"I got sick in 1910. We lived in Ohio. My mother was a laundress, and my father was a bum. After he died in a bar fight, there was nothing keeping us there, so we sold everything we had for two tickets to New Mexico. The dry air was supposed to cure me."

He speaks so softly that we have to lean in to hear him. A strand of Maren's hair brushes against my arm as we listen to his story like it's a eulogy.

"When we arrived in White Haven, we were penniless. We didn't eat a single meal on the journey—several days. And when the train pulled into the station, it disgorged us and hundreds of other poor, sick easterners, and we were left on the streets. I was weak. My mother was afraid. She found a place to live, a house already crowded with three other families. But I wasn't welcome there. They said I should go to where their sick loved ones were: Seymour House Asylum for the Poor."

A sibilant hiss fills the room when Jay says the word *asylum*, wrapping around us, drawing us closer. I can't tell where it comes from: one of us, or Jay, or the very motes of dust in this godforsaken place. It twists between us like a cat twining among ankles, tension spilling everywhere it touches. Davis's jaw grinds; a tendon stands out in his neck. Maren clasps her arms tight across her chest, like she's trying to hold herself together. Vanessa's hands are at her neck, thin fingers twisted in her ribbon.

"It was supposed to be a place of refuge for people like me. Those of us who were sick but couldn't afford the exorbitant cost of the sanitarium and didn't have loved ones wealthy enough to support us. My mother was going to send for me when she had found work and saved enough. But meanwhile I would be cared for at the asylum."

Jay's voice had been expressionless, timeless in the dark, but now it is bitter. "We fought like animals for clothing, water, food. I had only been here for a week when I saw my first murder. He was in the bed right next to me in the dormitory upstairs. We were packed so close together that I felt his blood spatter on my face when another patient cut his throat and stole his wool blanket. In the morning, I tried to leave, but Mr. Seymour stopped me. No one was allowed to leave the asylum grounds without permission. He brought me in here, into his office, and took out a ledger."

An iron pit forms in my stomach as a leather-bound book appears in Jay's hands. This is more than just Jay's reminiscences—this is his memory. Maren gasps as the light from Davis's phone reveals the initials *WS* embossed on the cover, still sleek and smooth after all these years. Jay's mouth twists in scorn, and he opens the book. A light blooms from its pages, spreading like flames over the broken, scuffed plaster of the walls and leaving a richly patterned wallpaper in its wake. The dust on the floor vanishes, and the hardwood shines. The bookshelves fill with handsome books and flank a heavy wooden desk. Jay puts the ledger, still open, onto the desk, and raises his hand with a flourish. Sumptuous velvet drapes fall over the window. And Jay is whole and alive. He's still pale and thin, but there's a ruddy flush of blood in his cheeks and a spark in his eyes.

My head spins as I take in the room around me. The edges of the furniture are hazy and indistinct like Jay, like the book on the desk, like a dream—or a nightmare.

"He showed me my name written in the ledger: Jay

Francis Henderson, born October 31, 1895. There was a whole column of numbers by my name. 'That's for your food,' he told me. And room and board, and the clothes they put on my back, and the delousing that they forced me into when I first arrived on the doorstep, even the ink needed to write this entry in the ledger." He taps his long finger on the page as we creep closer. The desk is polished to a sheen, and I can see our reflections in it when I look down into the book.

And there it is, just like he says: his name, written on thick, creamy paper in an old-fashioned hand. A faint wail comes from the hall, still dark through the open doorway, though the office is now lit by some cold, invisible light. I snap back, startled. Davis curses, and Maren takes a step back as the floor outside the door creaks; there's a harsh cry, and a sharp squeal of pain. Vanessa tilts her head to the side, listening to the voices. Her almost violet eyes swim in her face, unblinking. I hear singing, a low, tired woman's voice; the clatter of pots and pans from the kitchen; the chime of a clock in the hall; the slam of the front door. And a cruel, cold voice promising to note the extra portion of bathwater in his ledger.

"No matter how much I worked, I never earned enough. The numbers in the ledger only went up. I waited for my mother to come for me, but the other boys laughed and told me not to bother. No one ever left the asylum, except in death."

There's a fetid scum on my tongue, like the smell that hangs in this room has invaded my mouth. I sneak a glance at Maren. She's wrapped her wrists in coppery snarls of her hair, and her eyes are red-rimmed and staring. I don't know how she's still standing in this house, her family's house, a house of nightmares. If it were me, I would have run howling out the door as soon as Jay began his story. But Maren is made of stronger stuff than me.

"Every time I coughed, I could feel that I didn't have much time left. My pillow was red from blood in the mornings, and sometimes it felt as though my lungs were in a vise. I knew if I waited much longer, I would lose what remaining strength I had and Mr. Seymour would put me in the terminal ward. No one ever left the terminal ward.

"I finally decided to run. I thought I could hitch a ride into town and find my mother before it was too late. But I got turned around in the woods, and when I saw headlights, I thought I had made it to the main road. I held up my hands and stepped out of the woods. But the car didn't stop.

"They ran me down like a dog in the street: Mr. Seymour's son and a girl from the house, joyriding in his father's car. "They tossed me in a hole in the woods and held me down until I choked on my own blood." Dark blood trickles out of Jay's nostrils, flowing over his chin like a river. He steps closer, his eyes burning like dark flames.

Jay raises his hands to us. They're shining with blood that runs down his fingers. Drops hit the wood floor like bombs. Next to me, Maren shifts backward, her eyes fixed on the puddle of blood rolling toward her like a red tide. I can feel shame shuddering from her pores like sweat: sour and frantic. It hangs around her in a haze, invading my lungs.

Something twists inside me, pivoting from disgusted to protective. I don't want the blood to reach Maren—she's only here because of me. I step in front of her, bracing myself for the sticky liquid to coat my sneakers, but as soon as it touches my shoes, it disappears—all of it. The desk, the books, the light, the blood. I blink, startled to be back in the damp office again, surrounded by mold and rat shit and death. The thrum of tension fades away, but the sharp metallic taste lingers in the air.

"What was that?" Vanessa says in a hoarse whisper.

"How did you do that—show us all that?"

Jay turns his hands over, examining them for any sign of blood. His eyes sink deeper into his head as his skull flashes behind his thin skin. "I don't know. It was like the past was alive again, like my memories were haunting me."

My stomach cramps. I always knew that Seymour House had a dark history, but what happened to Jay is worse than I could have imagined. It's no wonder that he wasn't able to move on after he died. This house, these woods, should be filled with other trapped souls.

Maren presses against the wall, strands of hair twisted in her hands. "I'm sorry," she says. "God, I'm sorry. For what my family did to you. I want to make it right. My grandfather may be dead, but I'm a Seymour, too, and I can give you permission to finally leave the grounds. Go wherever you want, Jay. I wish you had had that opportunity in life."

Jay nods, but I'm not satisfied with this offering. Leaving the grounds isn't enough. Jay needs to be able to move on, and for that we need to find his grave.

"What about your great-grandfather's ledger?" I ask Maren. "Do you know where it is?"

Her eyes narrow. "No. Why?"

"Mr. Seymour's son didn't bury Jay in the cemetery—I already checked—but maybe he made a note of it."

"The ledger," Jay says softly, and he curses under his breath. "You're right—Mr. Seymour was meticulous about that ledger. He wrote down everything. There's bound to be information about where I'm buried in it!"

"If we find the ledger, we won't have to search the woods," Maren says. She nudges a pile of papers with the shiny toe of her Mary Janes. "But what are the odds we'll find it in all this shit?"

I pick up a moldy tome between my thumb and forefinger, wrinkling my nose. "Here it is," I joke, but no one's paying attention to me.

Davis and Vanessa start with a pile of loose papers that look like something has been using them as a nest. Jay hovers by the doorway, eyes closed. I wonder if he can still hear the ghosts of the past. A moment later, he shakes his head and pulls the drawers from the desk, emptying the contents onto the floor.

Maren starts by the bookshelves, pulling off the rotted remains of her great-grandfather's books and thumbing through each one before discarding them in a pile on the floor. Her hair is a wild halo around her face, and her eyes are hollow. It must have been terrible for her, watching the shadow-show of Jay's memories. She's been running from her family legacy her whole life, and here I am, dragging her back into it. It would be like if someone told me the only way I could make up for summoning Jay out of his fugue state would be to take his place in the Nothing. Face my worst nightmare. Could I do it? *Would* I do it?

She shouldn't *have* to do it. I got us into this mess. The only thing Maren has to do with it is her name, and she can't help that. I'm about to tell her so, tell her to get out of here and just ask her mother about the ledger later, when she pulls her hair back and twists it into a complicated braid to keep it out of her face. She's sifting through an armful of detritus before I can say anything, and I know by the set of her mouth that she wouldn't listen even if I did tell her to leave.

Maren effing Seymour. She never ceases to surprise me. Like I said, Maren is made of stronger stuff than me.

After an hour of pawing through piles of rancid garbage, there's still no sign of the ledger. Empty beer bottles, yes. Lotion and tube socks and tissues (ew), yes. Piles of tin plates rusted in unsteady towers, yes. But a hundred-year-old leather book? No.

I think I might bathe in lye when I get home.

"This. Is. Disgusting," Vanessa gasps, dropping a scrap

of disintegrating carpet back into the corner and hiding the decades of mouse shit that it's been covering.

"That book is our best shot at finding the grave," Davis grunts as he heaves an armoire to the side; the square of wallpaper behind it is eerily bright and clean. "Not to mention proving how many people are really buried back there."

A creak sounds from the doorway that leads into the hall, and I spin around, heart skittering in my chest like a frightened animal. Something is propped against the doorway, some piece of furniture like a long, thin hand with reaching fingers.

There must be a . . . a . . . grandfather clock with a bundle of walking sticks leaning against it out in the hall, or a rolled-up rug with stringy tassels. Something like that.

But just as I'm remembering that I've *been* in that hall—I walked down it last time I came to Seymour House, and it was empty then—the hand moves.

CHAPTER 9
BITE THE DUST

The fingers twitch, drumming on the doorframe jerkily. I jump and drop the moldy cardboard box I'm holding. I'm vaguely aware of a plump spider skittering out and across the floor, leaving a milky white sac of eggs behind—but my focus is on the hand in the doorway. If Jay weren't standing just a few feet away, sifting through a century's worth of garbage and grime, I would think the pale hand slipping into the room was his.

"Maren," I croak. I can feel her behind me, but she doesn't answer. The air around me thickens, heavy and oppressive like a blanket of snow, or like I'm underwater.

The figure moves deeper into the room. Its edges are indistinct and hazy, smeared like a pencil drawing that's been scrubbed out by a dirty eraser. Panic grips my heart when I see that instead of a face, there's only a yawning hole.

My arms erupt in goose bumps as a cold breeze ripples off the faint form. The cold invades my throat, claws its way into my chest. I feel it like an ache in the back of my throat, and when I swallow, the air is so cold that it burns.

Davis and Vanessa are bent over a stack of rotting tomes, oblivious to the presence creeping behind them. Out of the corner of my eye, I see Jay look up. His face shifts, the flesh melting away and leaving behind nothing but hard bone. Dark tendrils of smoke stir behind his eyes until they're the same inky void that has blotted out the figure's face. The paper he's been examining slips from his twitching fingers.

The faceless figure creeps closer, sending chills sweeping over my body like a swarm of spiders fleeing a flood. I try to move, try to stumble backward, but my legs are stiff and numb and all I can do is shuffle to the side. I bump into Maren, and pins and needles flare through my hip where it touches hers.

"Maren," I say again. My voice is just a wheeze.

"What?" she says. She doesn't look up from the drawer she's rummaging through.

My fingers flutter toward her, reaching for the spark of warmth in her hand. If I can hold on to her, it will spread through me, too, and then the figure will be gone. Black spots dance across my vision as the cold seizes my heart, but just before the darkness closes in, I inch my pinkie into her hand. I twine my fingers into hers, ignoring the throbbing pain of blood pumping back through my aching limbs. When our hands are linked, the pressure in my chest eases up, and I gasp, warm, damp air filling my lungs. The relief is sudden and all-encompassing, but the dark figure still bears down on Jay, and when it beckons to him, Jay stumbles forward, his legs stiff and dragging.

No. The thought flickers through my mind, bright as the neon signs on old Route 66. If Jay goes with that thing, I'll never get my answer about what comes next, and that is not okay with me.

With my hand still tight on Maren's, I stretch forward until I can grab Jay's bone-thin finger. As soon as I do, his face slips back into place over his skull and his eyes snap to mine.

"What, Olive?" Maren says, trying to shake me off.

The figure retreats back into the hall, but I don't let go of Maren. Her hand in mine is the only thing keeping me here, like the string of a kite that stops it from flying away. I'm afraid if I let go, I'll float after that thing, drift in its wake until the current catches me and sweeps me into that never-ending hole.

Maren's eyes narrow the way they do when she catches me goofing off during a Junior Reapers meeting. I half expect her to snap at me to get back to work, but her expression softens as I draw a shuddering breath. A crease appears between her eyes, and her hand tightens on mine. I'm suddenly very aware of the feel of our palms pressed together. I pull my hand out of hers and cross my arms.

She presses her lips together in an exasperated expression that's much more familiar than the one that she was wearing. "What's wrong?" she asks.

"There was someone in the doorway," I say. Davis looks up at the brittle sound of my voice. "Someone without a—" My throat works soundlessly as I try to find the words to describe the gaping chasm.

"It was someone like me." Jay's gaze is fixed on the doorway. No one else saw the faceless figure. No one but Jay and me. Jay, who is long dead, and me, who should be. The others haven't been touched by death the way we have, so they don't see the horrors of it.

"What do you mean, someone like you?" Vanessa twists one hand around Davis's and the other through her ribbon as she peers toward the empty doorway. "Another ghost?"

"Someone who didn't move on after death." Jay's face darkens. "I could feel its mania, its fixation with this place, rolling off it like waves of cold. Pain and fear. Confusion. Despair. Anger. All those things snarled together in a knot, tying it to the asylum."

"It was so cold," I say. My pinkie twitches toward Maren, but I won't let myself reach for her again.

"That's not like you, Jay," Davis says. "Yeah, you're dead, but you're not like a revenant or some shit. You're not *haunting* us."

My skin crawls with phantom bugs as I consider this. Most of the time Jay doesn't seem that different from us, but the shadow that twitched in his eyes was the same emptiness that beckoned from the doorway. It's hidden behind the mournful gray for now, but I've seen it twist and try to break free, and I know what it means.

"Not yet," I mutter.

"Pardon?" Jay says.

I clear my throat. "I said you're not haunting us *yet*."

An uneasy silence fills the room as everyone turns to stare at Jay.

"What do you mean?" Davis asks.

I sigh, then turn to Maren. "Do you remember what the curator at the Museum of Macabre said when he came to speak at our Junior Reapers meeting?"

I've never heard Maren whisper before, but she speaks so softly that her voice is like fading smoke. "He said the world is full of ghosts."

"The world is full of ghosts," I repeat, nodding. The words are just as poetic now as when I first heard them. "Spirits held back by their unresolved issues in life. He told us that as long as those spirits are ignorant to what happened to them, they're harmless. They're stuck reliving the trauma they experienced during life, trying to process it so they're able to move on. In other words, they only haunt themselves."

"How's that different from me?" Jay asks.

"It's not," I say. "But there are other kinds of spirits, too. Revenants and poltergeists. Residual ghosts. And that thing in the doorway—" I fight back a shudder, shoulders spasming, as I remember the void where its face should have been and the way it made me feel like I was falling . . . like I would never stop falling. "I think it was a shade."

The mythology of shades goes back to ancient Greece, where they thought that the dead lived in a world of shadows. In modern folklore, shades are believed to be an emotional imprint left after someone dies. I've read about them, but I never stopped to consider that they were real. Now that I've seen one, I realize there are worse things than the Nothing.

"You said you could feel its mania and fixation with this place," I continue. "Shades are spirits that are tied to an object or a place, literally made into just a shade of who they once were by their obsession. That one must have died here. Instead of moving on, it stayed, and now it can't leave." I shoot a meaningful look toward Jay. He stares back at me, gray eyes like still pools of water, the hint of his skull beneath his paper-white skin.

Maren is the first one to understand. "So you're saying that if Jay doesn't move on . . ."

Even if moving on means being sucked into the Nothing—it's better than this new alternative. "He'll become a shade," I say grimly. "Nothing but a visceral obsession with his grave."

And Scary Road will have earned its name.

CHAPTER 10
BEYOND THE VEIL

I'm awake long past midnight. For the first time in almost a year, I can't quite make myself turn out the light, so I just lie on my bed in the harsh glare of the LED bulbs. It's not the light keeping me up. I got pretty good at sleeping in a brightly lit room after my brush with death two years ago, because for months afterward, I'd go off on a crying jag every time I was in the dark. I told Mom and Dad that I was staying up late to do homework and it was easier to just fall asleep with the light on when I was done. Now that I think about it, that excuse doesn't make a whole lot of sense, but Mom and Dad were just pleased that I was taking my algebra book to bed with me.

I stare at the ceiling without blinking for so long that my eyes cross. Double vision. Everything blurs and is edged in amber, spots of light that burn until I'm forced to squeeze my eyes shut and rub them with the heels of my palms to soothe the ache.

After my foray into the world of the dead, I thought there couldn't be anything worse than the Nothing. An eternity spent alone in the dark? No thank you. It wasn't until Mrs. H's dying exhalation—*Mom*—that I started questioning what happened when my heart stopped, wondering if there was something else after death . . . something better.

I never considered that there might be something worse.

But the shade at Seymour House, tethered by its misery, burning with obsession like a dark flame? That's definitely worse.

And it's what will happen to Jay if the shadow spreads before we can find his grave and help him move on.

I can barely breathe around the knot in my throat. If Jay becomes a shade, it will all be my fault. My stupid made-up spell woke him from his never-ending half rest, but it also woke the shadow that lurks within him.

If I needed something to motivate me to find Jay's grave—as if the timeline imposed by the Desert Heights groundbreaking wasn't enough—seeing what's going to happen to him if we fail has definitely done the trick. It might mean sending him into the Nothing, but even that would be preferable to his fate as a shade.

I fall asleep with Mrs. H's whisper in my ear. It's like a touchstone that keeps me from spiraling into a bottomless pit of guilt and fear.

Because if there's something worse than the Nothing, wouldn't it stand to reason that—maybe—there's something better, too?

It's even enough for me to be grateful that I'm going to spend the next few weeks working with Maren Seymour.

When I walk into the cafeteria for lunch the next day, there's none of the normal inane talk—gossip about who's hooking up with who, complaints about White Haven's lack of weekend entertainment, an in-depth breakdown of the most important of all teenage rituals, high school football. Instead, everyone is focused on the table where the football players and cheerleaders sit.

Mateo Sanchez and Evelyn Martinez are Ocotillo High royalty—literally. They've been elected to the court for Homecoming, Winter Ball, and Prom every year since they got together sophomore year. Mateo's arm is around Evelyn, who has two bright spots of color on her cheeks and waves her hands as she talks. I catch a bit of what she's saying as I walk toward Davis and Vanessa at our regular table.

"Something started knocking on the roof of the car," she insists. "Mateo moved the car, but a few minutes later, the knocking started again. It was right above us."

"Oh my God, I would have freaked," one of Evelyn's friends whispers. Evelyn nods, before collapsing against Mateo's shoulder theatrically.

"What's going on?" I ask when I get to our table. Vanessa still has the black velvet ribbon that came with the turquoise bracelets looped around her neck. She tugs at it nervously, and Davis tightens his arm around her shoulders.

"Didn't you hear what happened to Mateo and Evelyn last night?" Davis mutters across the table. "They were attacked. On Scary Road."

The grape I just popped into my mouth falls out as my jaw drops.

"Oops." I sweep it back into my lunchbox. "What do you mean, attacked? By what?" Sometimes coyotes wander out of the mountains, but it would be really unusual for one to attack people, especially a big guy like Mateo.

"By *who*," Davis corrects. "They didn't get a good look at him."

"Or her," Vanessa whispers.

"Or them," I add. My appetite dries up like a creek bed in July, and I swivel in my seat to stare at Mateo. His booming voice carries over the murmurs of the crowd as he finishes Evelyn's story.

"I got out to see what kept knocking on the roof of the car, and someone sucker punched me in the back of the head, then went after Evelyn. That's when I grabbed him and threw him into the bushes." Mateo cracks his knuckles. "No one hurts my girlfriend. A man has to protect his girl."

"Talk about toxic masculinity," Vanessa says, but she doesn't shake off Davis's possessive arm over her shoulders. Puffy scratches with ragged edges show under the collar of his shirt when he shifts closer to Vanessa, lips brushing her hair. I wrinkle my nose at the thought of Vanessa's nails raking across his skin.

"Maybe it was the shade," Vanessa continues. "The thing you saw at the asylum. Maybe that's what attacked Mateo and Evelyn."

I shake my head. "A shade is tied to something from its life that stopped it from moving on after death. The one I saw at Seymour House is trapped there. It wouldn't be able to leave the house and go into the woods. But Jay . . ." My voice trails off in a whisper. I'm afraid if I speak any louder, my thoughts will slip out in a jumble of guilt and fear: *It was Jay, I summoned him and told him he was dead and that was enough to release the shadow lurking inside of him. He's becoming a shade like the one in Seymour House, and it's all my fault.* There have been rumors of the vanishing hitchhiker on Scary Road for as long as I can remember, but as far as I know, this is the first time anyone has ever been attacked. The timing can't be a coincidence. Jay has been wandering those woods for a hundred years, but it wasn't until I bound his spirit here that he became aware of what he really is.

"No way," Davis argues. "We just saw him yesterday, and he seemed completely harmless." He frowns. "Except for sending a pool of blood rolling across the floor."

Vanessa shudders. "I need something to take my mind off everything going on—meeting Jay and looking for the ledger in the asylum and everything. Do you have plans on Friday night, Olive?"

"What?" I try to force Jay and his shadow-dark eyes out of my thoughts. "No, not really."

"Would you like to come to a slumber party at my house?"

"Um . . ." *Slumber party.* It's a childish expression, something I haven't said in years. Truth be told, I was never really a fan in the first place. "I don't know. I'm not really the sleepover type."

Vanessa leans across the table and plucks at the bracelet around my wrist. "It'll be fun," she promises. "We'll do face masks and eat way too much chocolate and play—"

Ouija.

"—truth or dare. And we'll have blood orange French toast for breakfast. I need some girl time with my best friend. Besides, I went with you to look for Jay."

I bristle at the words she leaves unspoken—*so now you owe me.* If she really considers me her best friend—which, yikes—then looking for Jay shouldn't be a bargaining chip to get me to do what she wants.

Right?

It's been so long since I've hung out with people that now I can't remember how it works. Maybe this give-and-take is normal. She does something I want, then I do something she wants. Maybe I really *would* owe her, if this was a normal friendship. But it's not. We've been hanging out together while we're helping Jay, but we're not friends. I can't be friends with Vanessa. I can't be friends with anyone.

"Come on, Olive," she coaxes. Her bow-shaped mouth twists into a smirk. "Maren's coming."

"Maren?" I stumble over her name. "I didn't know you guys are friends."

Truthfully, I don't think Maren *has* any friends. She's too busy bossing everyone around, and her demanding personality hasn't exactly made her popular. The only people I ever see with her are sycophants using her to move up the ranks of high school achievement. But I doubt any of them would consider her a friend.

"We're not *not* friends," Vanessa says. She leans back against Davis like the matter is settled. "I thought this would be a fun way to get to know her better."

"I guess," I say. I mean *I guess it's a fun way to get to know her*, but Vanessa takes it as an answer to her invitation.

"Great!" she squeals. "Oh, I love slumber parties."

The staccato tapping of heels bounces off the tile floor of the cafeteria. Maren makes a beeline for our table. I can tell by her expression that the old Maren is back: all business. Whatever passed between us as we searched Seymour House for her great-grandfather's ledger is gone, buried deep inside with the real Maren—self-loathing, vulnerable—that I got a glimpse of.

For some reason it doesn't bother me. Maybe because I know that this is just the hard shell she wears to protect herself, just like I protect myself by acting like nothing matters and like I don't need anyone.

That's not the real Olive, and this isn't the real Maren. I can give her that.

"Hi, Davis. Hi, Vanessa," she says, before snapping at me, "Olive—I told you to do it right or I would make you do it again." She thrusts one of the Sock Hop posters at me; the edges are bent, and there's a dirty shoe print right in the middle. "Half the posters you hung fell, and the other half are crooked. Come on."

"Can I at least finish my lunch?" I grumble, but she's already halfway to the door.

When I catch up to her, she's tucked in an alcove under the stairs, one wall dominated by a huge bulletin board. Her hair is woven into an elaborate braid like the trim on the afghan that Mrs. H kept folded at the foot of her bed.

"Did you hear about—" I start.

"Mateo and Evelyn? Of course I did. Everyone did. They won't shut up about it. Self-obsessed fools." Maren's voice is as sharp as her fingernails. "So we don't have any time to waste finding the ledger and the grave if we want to keep Jay from going after anyone else. I'll talk to my mom today. All of the old Seymour family records and stuff are in our attic. No one's been up there since my dad died, but maybe my mom has heard about the ledger."

My jaw drops. "You think it was Jay, too?"

Maren rolls her eyes. "Who else? That would be quite a coincidence if someone else was hiding in the woods attacking our classmates."

"That's what I said! But Davis and Vanessa think I'm being paranoid." I grin at Maren. It feels good for someone to take me seriously, especially someone as no-nonsense as Maren Seymour. The knot of anxiety that's been twisting in my gut ever since I heard about the attack loosens. Maren gets shit done. If she's determined to find the ledger and the grave, it will be found. "Thanks for helping me."

She shifts her stack of posters from one arm to the other. "I'm helping Jay, not you."

Her face is aloof, with a stuck-up smirk I know so well. The one that reminds me every time I see it how she has it all together while I'm unraveling at the seams. The one that tells me that she has better things to do than try to put me back together.

"Right," I say in a brittle voice. "I know you would never waste your time on me."

She looks like she's about to say something, but the bell rings and a flood of kids presses past us before she can. She grabs her backpack, her eyes sharp and gleaming, and taps one of the Sock Hop posters I hung in the middle of a mess of fliers. "This one is crooked. Do it again."

CHAPTER 11
GIVING UP THE GHOST

Between my encounter with the shade at Seymour House and my impending sleepover at Vanessa's, I'm feeling all anxious and overwhelmed, so as soon as the last bell rings, I head to my favorite place to clear my head: the cemetery.

My dad is a memorial stonemason, and he sculpted most of the headstones in the cemetery from the past twenty years. Walking among them is almost like flipping through an old family album: there's the weeping stone angel he did when I was seven, there's the obelisk from the year I got braces, there's the stone with the engraving of the calla lily that he worked on when I was learning to ride a unicycle.

His favorite pieces to do are the ones that incorporate old gravestone iconography, mostly winged skulls or hourglasses. Those are the kinds of symbols that you find in really old graveyards, like the burying grounds in New England. Obviously none of the graves in White Haven are four hundred years old, but when White Haven was really embracing its dark tourism side, it became the fashion to copy historic headstones. People will pay astounding amounts of money for my dad to carve a brand-new headstone, then crack and mottle it until it looks like it's been there for centuries. Some people even have theirs installed at a tilt.

I'm examining the clasped hands etched under John and Helena Carver when I see a washed-out shape hovering over a marble angel a few rows over. The figure is so indistinct that it's almost like a smear in an eyeglass lens. Surprise jolts through me when I realize it's Jay—here, in the city cemetery instead of wandering aimlessly through the woods. Looks like Maren's permission for him to leave did the trick.

Ducking behind John and Helena, I track him as he drifts among the headstones. He's so pale that he almost shimmers in the fading light. So far there's no sign of a shadow possessing him, but I can't see his face from this angle. I creep forward, silently urging him to turn toward me so that I can double-check that his face hasn't been blotted out by a malevolent shade.

"Come on," I mutter. I stuff my hands in my pockets to stop myself from drumming them on the nearest headstone in a nervous beat. I remember the feel of Jay's chest under my hands, hard as stone and twice as cold. He's definitely corporeal enough to pound on the roof of a car like Evelyn described.

If Maren were here, she wouldn't be cowering behind this headstone, waiting to catch a glimpse of his eyes. She would stride right up to him and demand that he tell her the truth about what happened with Mateo and Evelyn.

Just as I'm imagining the exact expression in her eyes, Jay turns and makes eye contact with me over the stone I'm crouched behind. His eyebrows rise.

"Olive?" His voice echoes among the headstones.

"Just hold on a minute." I squint to make out the color of his eyes from ten feet away. They're gray, but is it the color of stone or of oily, belching smoke?

"What's wrong?"

I move a little closer. "Something happened in the woods. A couple of kids from school were attacked." I'm close enough now to see that his eyes are clear and light, but I haven't forgotten the shifting shadows in their depths. The potential to become a shade is in there with him; what if it rises without him realizing?

"Attacked?" Jay's eyebrows draw together, and he frowns. His face looks like it's been carved from stone, like one of the dark angels my dad sculpts to mark a grave. Spiderwebs of cold form on my arms as he takes a step toward me. "Attacked in the woods."

His voice is as cold as the icy waves flowing from his body. My pulse quickens, and I take a step back, but Jay stumbles closer.

"Bad things happen in the woods, Olive. I should know." He groans, and his breath rattles in his chest. The hairs on the back of my neck lift, and I force myself to lock eyes with him, searching for a hint of the coiled shadow that I know lurks just below the surface, biding its time until—

Wait. Breath rattling in his chest? Jay's dead. He doesn't have to breathe.

The tension leaks out of my limbs, leaving me loose-jointed and weak. That son of a—

I stab a finger at Jay. "You're messing with me."

He doubles over in laughter. "If messing with you means that I'm having a gas at your expense, then yes, I am. But can you really blame me? One pair of lovers is attacked in the woods, and you immediately question the dead fellow."

My cheeks flood with heat. "I didn't mean—"

Jay stops me with a wave of his hands. "Don't dwell on it. I'd be suspicious, too. But I swear it wasn't me. The only thing I've done since Maren freed me is look for my grave. When I couldn't find it, I decided to come here to visit my mother. Better late than never, right? Although I'm not even sure she's buried in White Haven."

That's true; he never got to say goodbye. If I didn't get closure even though I was *with* Mrs. H when she died, I can't imagine how Jay feels about his mother.

It doesn't make up for accusing him of being a creepy stalker, but I can at least help him find his mother's grave. I pull my phone out of my pocket. "There's a whole app for finding graves in the White Haven Cemetery. We use it all the time in Junior Reapers."

"What's an app?" he asks, his eyes wide in curiosity as he studies the sleek shape in my hand.

"Um . . ." I glance at the phone. How do I explain what an app is without explaining phones, or computers, or the internet? "It's kind of like a map. Just tell me her name."

"Mary Henderson. She was born in 1880."

"Mary . . . Henderson . . ." I repeat, typing in the name and date and pushing *search*. "Found her. She's buried in the Park section." My shoulders relax; the grave is on the opposite side of the cemetery from Mrs. H's.

The paths through the cemetery are crushed pea gravel that grinds under our feet. I glance at the map on my phone a few more times before stopping in front of a rough stone that reads *Mary Henderson Luna*. Jay runs his fingers over the name as I crouch down to read the back of the stone: *Beloved mother of Diana.*

"She got married again after I died," Jay says. "Had another child . . . a whole other life."

I look up at Jay when I realize his name isn't there. He must know what I'm thinking, because he says, "She was really young when I was born. Just fifteen. And then I died, and maybe it felt like a bad dream. Maybe it was like her life hadn't really started yet."

"Or maybe she didn't have anyone to help her mourn," I say. "People thought it was better to just move on back then. Like if women had stillborn babies, the doctors just took them away and no one ever mentioned them again."

I gaze at Jay as he kneels at the grave and plucks clover from the grass. I've only been thinking of him in terms of the shade: worst-case scenario. And yeah, finding his grave and freeing his spirit before he loses his soul to never-ending misery is urgent, but that's not all Jay is. There's this whole other person in there with the shadow—someone who can actually relate to me when I talk about death. That's something I can't get from anyone else. When I think about telling Jay about the Nothing, I don't feel all sweaty or like I ate too many chocolate-mallow-ghost-fun-pops. Opening up to him isn't risky the way it is with Maren or Davis, because I know, one way or another, he'll be moving on soon.

I sink down in the grass next to him. "What was your mother like?"

"My mother . . ." His voice trails off, and then he grins. "She used to tell me fairy tales before bed. She did different voices for all the different characters." He picks another clover. "It was like she turned into a different person when she told stories. She could be an evil queen or a witch or a werewolf. Sometimes she got so into it that she didn't even notice I was so scared that I was crying."

"Show me," I say.

Jay's thin fingers twist the clover into a crown that he sets on my hair. "How?"

"Like in the office at Seymour House when you showed us the ledger."

Jay closes his eyes and lays one hand on the cool stone of his mother's grave. His skin ripples, shadows shifting.

And then there's a cackling laugh. Jay smiles, and his cheeks are flushed and healthy. The laugh turns into a woman's voice, low and throaty. I can't make out what she's saying, but it must be funny, because a little girl giggles like a peal of bells. The sound is in the air all around us, in the motes of dust that float in the sunlight, in the clover Jay laid on my head. In the empty chambers of my heart.

Jay's eyes pop open, and the voices and laughter are gone. His skull flickers into sight. "Who was that with my mother?"

I glance at the names on the headstone. Something blooms inside my chest, like the first flames that gild the edges of a piece of paper before catching.

Diana was Mrs. H's first name.

"Diana," I murmur. "Your half-sister. Your mother must have told the same stories to her. You remember your mother's voice, so we could hear it . . . and I remember Mrs. H's laugh, so we heard that, too." Warmth floods through my body. Jay and I are linked together by a double chain now: the locket, and Mrs. H.

Jay stares at me and then reaches back for the headstone. The sound is clearer this time, his mother's voice simpering and then booming and then scratching like nails on a chalkboard as she tells the story of Snow White.

And Mrs. H squealing with laughter.

We listen to the end of the story, and then Jay takes his hand off the headstone and lies back in the grass. My clover crown slides off as I settle beside him. The sky's the color of faded forget-me-nots.

"That's why Mrs. H had the locket. Your mother was her mother, too." My heart aches, but in a good way—a way that I don't completely want to stop.

Jay fishes the locket out of his pocket. "Here. You should have this. Your friend—Diana—must have given it to you for a reason."

"She didn't give it to me at all," I admit. I cover my face with my hands. "I stole it. When she died. I wanted something to remember her by."

Jay laughs, and I peek through my fingers at him.

"Still. Take it." He holds it out to me.

I shake my head. "No. Maybe you were meant to find it again." I leave out the part about the locket swinging over the flame as I sprinkled the salt and spoke the words: *to bind the spirit.*

"Is that why you're helping me? So you can find out where your friend is?"

I clasp my hands over my belly, feeling it lift and fall with my breath. It feels like showing off next to Jay.

"That's how this started," I admit. "I thought if I could summon a spirit, it would be able to answer all my questions about death. But I didn't think about what that would be like for you." My cheeks flush with shame. "Now it's more than just finding out what comes next," I say, and with every word, I mean it more. "I want to help you move on. I can't just let you become a shade."

Jay rustles in the grass next to me. "Thank you."

We fall silent. The sky is turning pink and rose, and the leaves are edged in gold. Lying in a cemetery at dusk seems symbolic somehow: the sun setting on the day like it sets on our lives, the darkness coming to take me home. One day I'll lie down and the sun will set and when it rises again, I won't be here anymore.

"When I died," I say. "I felt like I was floating."

Jay props himself on one elbow to look down at me. Deep circles smudge the skin below his eyes like bruises, and his mouth hangs open. "What do you mean, when you died?"

"They brought me back," I explain. "I had an allergic reaction. My heart stopped. I was dead for five minutes. But then the doctors restarted my heart, and—" I hold up my hands like I've just done a magic trick. "Here I am."

Jay settles back next to me. "It was like floating?" he prompts.

"Floating on a black sea. I could feel it lapping against my body, carrying me somewhere. And then everything went still. It was empty. Quiet. I was alone." I shudder as chills sweep through my body. I don't think it has anything to do with Jay lying still as stone next to me. "I think of it as the Nothing."

"The Nothing," Jay repeats in a soft voice. "Is that where you think your friend is? Diana—my sister?"

"I hope not."

—oh Lolly, oh Lolly—

"She said something when she died," I continue. "She said 'Mom,' like she could see someone. Waiting for her. And that's when I started to wonder . . . maybe there's more than the Nothing after all. That's why I went to Seymour House that night to find you."

"I should have been there when my mom died." Jay's voice is tight with bitterness. "I should have been there to welcome her. Instead, I'm stuck here." Darkness flashes in his smoke-gray eyes. The shadow is stirring in the depths of his soul, twisting, fighting its way to the surface. Every day that Jay is here, it will get stronger. If he wants to see his mom again—if she still exists on some kind of cosmic scale—we have to hurry.

"Not for long," I promise. "We're going to find your grave, and then you'll be free. You'll be able to move on."

To whatever kind of afterlife comes next.

CHAPTER 12
YOUR COFFIN OR MINE?

The sun is hidden behind the trees and the streetlights are flickering on as I drag myself down Blood Orange Street on Friday night. I huff out a breath, blowing a wisp of hair off my forehead, and shift my overnight bag to the other hand. I can't believe I'm doing this. Mom danced around the kitchen for an hour when I asked if I could spend the night at a friend's house. I purposely didn't clean my room all week, hoping she would ground me, but no such luck.

I need some girl time with my best friend, Vanessa said. That term makes my skin twitch, like a major case of pins and needles. When Vanessa started sitting with me at lunch, I figured we would be just friendly enough to talk at school but completely forget about each other as soon as the bell rang. Even when we went to Seymour House, I didn't think things would go this far. But now she's involved with everything going on with Jay and I'm on my way to a sleepover at her house like a character in a Raina Telgemeier novel.

Light pours out of the windows of Vanessa's black house, illuminating a twisting path through a maze of waist-high lavender bushes. Even though I can see over the bushes to the front porch and the leaded glass door, it takes me a good five minutes to make my way through the maze. I keep hitting dead ends and having to backtrack. I finally push my way through a thin spot in the bushes, only trampling a few flowers on the way, and stumble up the front steps.

White, gray, and corpse-green pumpkins stand in piles on either side of the door with cuttings of dark flowers from the garden tucked here and there. Purple-black ivy creeps along the banister of the porch. A wooden plaque swings from the porch roof: *The Lenore,* written in such curly cursive that I can barely read it, with the silhouette of a raven just a suggestion in the white space between the letters.

Vanessa opens the door before I can push the doorbell.

"I was watching you." She giggles. "You made it much harder than it really needs to be, Olive. Just go right at every intersection."

"Now you tell me," I grumble. Then I gesture at the sign. "The Lenore?"

"Like the Edgar Allan Poe poem," Vanessa explains.

Inside, the wallpaper is red watered silk. White pillar candles fill the windowsills. There's a heavy, claw-footed wooden desk with a huge bouquet of black roses overflowing a vase.

"My mother won't be home until late," Vanessa says, taking a tarnished candelabra from the desk. "Let's go up to my room—Maren's already here."

She leads me up the stairs, past a baluster topped by a polished wooden skull that could fit in the palm of my hand.

Framed portraits line the wall, most of women with the same high cheekbones as Vanessa: posed on the running board of an old-fashioned car . . . wearing a fur-trimmed coat outside Radio City Music Hall, pillbox hat set at a saucy angle on her head . . . posing with a daisy and huge, round sunglasses.

"Is that your mom?" I ask, pointing at the girl in a picture that looks like it's from the nineties. She has the same flaxen hair as Vanessa. The photograph is faded by time, but the girl looking out at me could be Vanessa's twin.

"Hmm?" Vanessa stops on the landing and looks back. "Oh, those are all family pictures." She tugs me down the hall and into her room.

A marble fireplace dominates one wall of the room, the mantel lined with black taper candles, all aflame. Puddles of wax dot the rich wood of the mantel. Crystals tucked between the candles catch the light from the flames, covering the walls and floors with refracted light: deep purple from the amethyst, rainbows from the prisms. Maren is sitting in a stiff armchair. She looks as uncomfortable as I feel. I wonder if she's ever been to a sleepover before. Somehow I have a hard time envisioning a row of sleeping bags laid out in her posh house, and being a Seymour is enough to guarantee that no one has ever invited her over. I'm sure she never thought her first sleepover would be with me.

"Hi," I say. "Can you believe *we're* going to spend the night together?"

Maren raises her eyebrows slightly, and my face grows hot. I turn toward the mantel to try and cover my awkwardness.

"Aren't these a fire hazard?" I examine the pillars of wax.

"They're fake," Vanessa explains, pinching the flame from one of the candles. "See? It's an optical illusion."

When she moves her fingers, the flame is gone and the wick is clean and white, the wax that runs down the candle dry. Her fingers brush the top of the taper again. I don't see what she does, but the flame is back.

"Let's go ahead and get comfortable before we eat," she says, passing around matching silk robes. She is determined to check off every box on the quintessential slumber party checklist.

After we're all wearing the robes—mine is inky black, while Maren's is bloodred and Vanessa's is the deep purple of a bruise—Vanessa brings up a pizza from Van Helsing's ("Guaranteed extra garlic!") and a tray with drinks and an arrangement of fruit on it—pomegranates, black cherries, blood oranges.

Vanessa sets the tray on the dresser by the bed and pours us each a drink.

"It's just sparkling grape juice," she explains. Then she pulls a tiny glass bottle from the pocket of her robe. "But I have something to make it more interesting." She adds a splash to our glasses and then hands one to each of us. "To new friends and old grudges!"

Maren and I glance at each other. If she thinks Vanessa's toast is as weird as I do, she doesn't let on. I sniff at my drink, wrinkling my nose at the sharp scent. I'm not really a fan of alcohol. Maybe I've never gotten buzzed enough to make up for how awful it tastes, because I definitely don't see the appeal.

Vanessa doesn't even hesitate. She tosses her drink back in one swallow, then sets the empty glass on the tray and wipes her mouth. "Come on," she urges us. "I thought you wanted to have fun."

Maren's eyes are fever bright as she studies the amber liquid. At first I think there's no way Vanessa will get strait-laced Maren Seymour, Ocotillo High's unofficial designated driver, to drink anything stronger than Diet Dr Pepper. But then I remember the bitter longing in Maren's voice when she told me she's never been invited to a party. This is a rite of passage for her; this is what she's wanted. She takes a tiny sip, coughing and spluttering, then squeezes her eyes shut and downs the rest. "Wow," she chokes out. "That is not what I expected."

Vanessa gives a little cheer, then turns to me.

"Ehh, I don't know," I say, trying to hand the glass back to her.

"What?" She laughs. Her eyebrows rise so high that

they almost disappear into her hair. "But you can't be the only one not drinking tonight. That takes all the fun out of it!"

"She doesn't have to," Maren says, eyeing me. "I'm sure Olive is just as much fun sober as she is drunk." I can't tell if it's supposed to be an insult or not, but it makes me feel better to have Maren brushing off my reluctance to drink like it's nothing. Vanessa just tilts her head to the side, eyes wide in an expectant gaze that makes me squirm. This must be what peer pressure feels like.

"I expected you to be the life of the party," Vanessa says, taking another swig. Laughing, she chants my name under her breath until I take a sip and make a face, choking on a cough.

"Face masks!" Vanessa says when I can finally breathe again. She pulls three packages from behind her back, and she and Maren pile onto the bed.

If you've seen any teen movie, you can imagine the next few hours, so I won't bore you with the details. We do face masks and paint our nails; we eat popcorn and have a pillow fight; and we play—

"Truth or dare?" Maren asks, pointing one perfectly manicured finger at Vanessa before tipping her head back to take a swallow from the tiny bottle. She's not wincing at the burn anymore.

Vanessa hugs a pillow to her chest. "Truth."

"Hmm . . . tell us a secret from your past."

"A secret?" she squeaks. "I don't know . . . I can't think of anything except . . ." She shakes her head, her cheeks flushing. "I don't think I should tell you."

Maren rolls her eyes. "Well, now you have to! Spill."

"That's the game, Vanessa," I add. "If you don't answer Maren's truth, you have to do a dare. And *I* get to choose what."

"Okay, okay." A shy smile spreads across her face. "I'm

the love child of a forbidden romance." She giggles, glancing up at us to take in our reactions. I just shrug. I've never been into soap operas, and this sounds like it came directly out of a script for *Riverdale*.

Maren cocks one eyebrow. "A forbidden romance?" The words are like honey in her mouth. "Do tell."

"Okay." Vanessa crosses her legs and settles into the nest of pillows on the bed. She definitely doesn't seem hesitant to tell the story now. "My mother, Willa, had the most tragic love affair. She emigrated from Germany when she was the same age we are now, all alone, and got work as a maid in a prominent family's home. The son fell in love with her. She knew she would lose her job if she was caught with him, so at first she tried to resist her feelings. But he begged her to be with him, showered her with compliments, and won her over. They started seeing each other in secret, sneaking around the house and meeting in the woods on the family's land. She was so in love with him. She told me that he was the most handsome man she had ever seen, with dark blue eyes and full lips. For a while they were very happy, even though they could never be seen together. But then my mother told him she was pregnant—with me. He promised to make things right, but when it came down to it, he denied their relationship and swore that he wasn't the father. The family threw my mother out when I was a babe in arms."

Vanessa's flair for the dramatics makes me roll my eyes, but Maren presses her hand to her mouth. "Oh my God. That's terrible! What did she do?"

"She was devastated. Not only did she have nowhere to go, but she was truly in love. She pined for him for years. Eventually she took me back to meet him, hoping that if he saw me, he would recognize what he had done and welcome us both back home."

"Did it work?" I ask, but I think I know the answer.

Vanessa shakes her head. "Sadly, it didn't, and he died soon after. But things got easier for me and my mother after that."

"What a dick," Maren mutters. "I never knew my father or his family, either. He died when I was three and then his parents passed away a few years later, so my mom raised me on her own. But even though it was just the two of us, it never felt like it. There's a painting of a Seymour ancestor in every single room in our house. All eyes on Maren, all the time." She raises the bottle in a mock salute, her face twisted in a bitter smile. "Being a Seymour—rich, powerful, important—is a huge deal to her. Sometimes I think she married my dad just for his name."

My skin prickles with insight. There are so many more layers to Maren than I ever realized. She tries so hard to be perfect to escape her family name, but her own mother won't let her move past it.

Maren deserves more than to be judged for being a Seymour. She deserves to create her own legacy. She deserves to be loved for who she is.

"I definitely didn't get any perks from my father's name," Vanessa says. "Did you know 'Fitz' was used by British kings to identify their illegitimate children? Why do you think my mother chose it for our surname? But I'm better off without him."

"Amen to that," Maren says grimly, passing the bottle to her. "Okay, Olive, your turn. Truth or dare."

"Dare."

Vanessa groans. "Olive, you don't get this game. Only little kids choose dare."

"We want dirt," Maren adds. "We want to hear your deepest, darkest secrets."

I shrug. "I'm more of a dare person."

"Fine." Maren giggles. "Then I dare you to tell us if you and Davis ever—you know. Hooked up."

My cheeks flood with heat.

Vanessa looks at me with eyes so wide I can see myself reflected in them. She reaches for the ends of the ribbon around her neck, tugging at the velvet. It's starting to go threadbare under her constant touch. "Did you? You can tell me. I won't be mad."

"No," I insist. "No way."

"But he says he used to spend the night at your house."

"When we were kids," I say. "He slept on the couch. Davis and I have only ever been friends, I swear. He's like my brother."

Maren and Vanessa glance at each other with raised eyebrows. It's clear they think I'm lying, and their silent exchange sours my mood. Maren looks pitying, but it's the expression on Vanessa's face that makes my blood curdle. She looks both wounded and satisfied, like she's just waiting for me to admit that I want to be with Davis. Like she *wants* me to tell her how Davis and I used to hook up so she can be all hurt, and graciously forgive us for doing something before we even knew her, and get some weird high from playing the martyr. A hot swoop of anger fills my stomach.

"Davis and I have never been a thing," I repeat, staring at Vanessa.

"Okay, sure." Maren rolls her eyes. "You guys spent every waking moment together for years. Don't tell me that you *never*—"

"It's fine if you and him used to have a thing," Vanessa cuts in. "I'm confident in my relationship with him now. But I don't want to be lied to, you know? Just tell us the truth."

"I am!" I snap. My voice echoes off the high ceiling. "Believe it or not, Davis Wills is not the god among mortals that people make him out to be. We never hooked up because I'm not attracted to him. Because I'm not into him.

Because—" I clamp my teeth closed and catch the very tip of my tongue. Tears spring to my eyes, and that makes me even more mad because they'll think they made me cry when really my tongue feels like it got sliced off by a hot knife.

"Okay," Maren says, bemused. "I'm sorry. We were just messing around."

"Yeah, sorry if you got upset," Vanessa adds, brow creased. "I didn't think it was such a big deal to ask my best friend if she used to sleep with my boyfriend."

Thick silence falls over the room like the haze of wildfire smoke that drifts into town every summer. My cheeks are still hot, and my heart pounds so hard I can hardly catch my breath. There's a bitter taste in my mouth, like I've been chewing on lemon peels. Half of me wants to storm out and walk home, but the other half knows that if I do, Maren and Vanessa will spend the rest of the night giggling about me, calling Davis and telling him about my overreaction and speculating about what I meant but didn't say.

This is why I hate sleepovers.

"Umm . . ." Maren yawns. It sounds fake. "It's five to midnight. Maybe we should—"

"We can't go to bed yet," Vanessa interrupts. "What kind of sleepover would that be? Besides, I have another game—Olive, turn out the lights."

"The lights? Why?"

Vanessa sweeps across the room and takes three tarnished candlesticks from a sideboard. The flames sputter as she hands one to each of us. "This game is played by candlelight."

Huffing out a sigh, I hit the switch by the door. The room plunges into darkness, broken only by the three points of light from our candles. My shadow swoops across the floor as I join Maren and Vanessa in front of a huge, ornately framed mirror leaning against the wall. It's as big as a doorway.

Vanessa lowers her voice to a husky whisper. "The legend of Bloody Mary says that if you stand in a room lit only by candlelight and gaze at your reflection in a mirror, she will appear after you chant her name three times. And what better way to summon her than with three girls and three candles?"

This is just another one of those silly sleepover games that teenage girls do to feel edgy. I roll my eyes, but there's something eerie about the way our reflections float in the mirror. We look like ghosts, like Jay, like we've already summoned something. Morbid curiosity bubbles up in my chest. If Jay answered when I lit that candle, who will answer when we call Bloody Mary's name?

All my weight drops into my feet, and I sway slightly between Vanessa and Maren.

"Bloody Mary," Vanessa says. Her voice is low and soothing.

"Bloody Mary," I repeat in a whisper.

"Bloody Mary," Maren finishes, just as the clock strikes twelve.

As soon as she speaks the name for the third time, her reflection's long hair turns to blood, spilling down her robe, running in rivulets down her neck, dripping to the floor like bright pennies. When the blood rains on my feet and the air smells of copper, I look away from the mirror to see Maren covered in blood.

Her eyes weep tears of red. The drops hug the curve of her cheeks and fall to the shoulders of her robe, where they sizzle like water in a hot pan. A bubble forms at the corner of her mouth, then pops with a little spray of fine mist. She holds her hands up to me, like she did outside her family's mausoleum, in supplication, in admission of her guilt.

Horror blooms in my chest like blood spreading from

a wound. This is the blood of generations of people like Jay, inmates of Seymour House trapped in misery by Maren's family. She told me, that day in the cemetery, that it doesn't matter what she does; she'll always be covered in their blood. And now I see the tangible proof of that. *She* is Bloody Mary, the girl from the urban legend, and everything she touches turns to blood.

I stumble back, dropping my candle. The flame sputters but doesn't go out, and it casts long, wild shadows across the room. A pool of blood on the floor rolls closer and closer to the candle. When it touches the flame, the candle goes out.

The room goes dark.

And Maren begins to scream.

CHAPTER 13
THE GRIM REAPER

It takes me longer than it should to stumble to the wall and hit the light switch. I stub my toe against the bed frame on my way, so when light fills the room again, I'm hopping on one foot and cursing.

Maren stands in front of the mirror, screaming, her fingers twisted into claws in front of cheeks ruddy from fear. She yanks at her hair, examining it for any sign of blood. There's a sharp rip as she pulls the silk robe from her back and balls it up, before hurling it into the fireplace, where it smolders among the flames.

My heart pounds. The blood is gone, but I can still imagine it running down Maren's neck in thin streams. I hobble to her side and wrap my arms around her, pinning her hands against her chest so that she can't pull at her hair anymore.

"Stop, stop, stop," I whisper against her cheek. "It's okay! You're okay. There's nothing there."

Vanessa watches us with wide eyes, her breath fluttering in little gasps. And now I remember the way the candles flickered to life at her touch. *An illusion*, she said.

"Did you do something to the mirror?" I ask over Maren's shoulder. "Like the candles? Somehow make us see all that blood?"

"What blood?" Vanessa stoops to pick up the candle I dropped. Flames leap from the wick at one touch of her fingers. "I didn't see anything. Maren just started screaming for no reason. She scared me to death."

I blink back at the mirror. The glass is foggy and

tarnished, clear in places where the mirror's silver backing has rubbed away. There's no sign of blood. Was there ever? Now I'm not sure. A trick of the light . . .

Maren stops crying and struggles away from me. "You—you didn't see it?" she gulps.

"There was nothing to see, Maren," Vanessa says gently, setting the candlesticks back on the sideboard. "We've all been drinking . . . you're seeing things that aren't there."

My head spins as I try to figure out what's real and what isn't. Shadows cast by the flickering candles, or shadows seething just below the surface? Maren covered in blood, or Maren sobbing in my arms? My heart racing from fear, or to keep pace with hers?

Maren staggers and presses one delicate hand over her eyes. "My head," she moans.

"I'll take her to get some aspirin and a drink of water," Vanessa says, slipping an arm around Maren's waist.

"Wait—" My lips feel numb, and the word comes out garbled. I don't want to be left alone in this room with the hint of blood hanging in the air like a ghost; I don't want to let Maren out of my sight.

"It's just the alcohol," Vanessa says. She's holding Maren up with one hand; the other is fingering the ribbon around her neck. "She just needs to sleep it off."

My mouth still tastes bad from whatever was in Vanessa's little bottle. I don't drink often, so the few sips I had were enough to make my head fuzzy and my thoughts disjointed. With the pressure to find the ledger before Jay becomes a shade, it's no wonder that the combination of alcohol and our overwrought nerves made us see something that wasn't there. Maren's long coppery hair, trailing over her shoulders, turned to blood in the candlelight.

The coiled knot in my chest loosens, and I nod as Vanessa leads Maren out of the room.

I stare at my moon-white face and dark lips in the mirror until I'm ninety-nine percent convinced.

But then I step in something wet and warm and sticky. A drop of blood.

I lie awake long after Vanessa's breathing has turned slow and even. Maren's air mattress is right next to mine, and she isn't asleep, either—I can tell by the hitch in her breath every few minutes as she suppresses another sob.

"Are you okay?" I finally whisper after the moonlight has moved from one side of the room to the other.

Maren sucks in a sharp breath. She must not have known I was still awake, listening to her cry.

"I shouldn't have had so much to drink," she says. Her voice sounds raw and scratchy.

"I mean the mirror and the candles—"

"I *know* what you mean." She rolls onto her side to face me. "I'm embarrassed, okay? That was my first time drinking and I didn't know my limits. Vanessa's right, there wasn't anything to see. I was freaking out about nothing."

"But I saw it too." My heel pressed into the drop of blood like a promise. "Do you ever think Vanessa's kind of . . . I don't know . . . manipulative?" I turn onto my side, and Maren and I are nearly nose to nose in the dark. "I think I like her, but then she does something to make me feel like anything I decide is stupid and she's the only one who's right. I end up doing whatever she wants. Like drinking tonight. I don't like to drink."

"And that's fine. You shouldn't feel pressured to drink by anyone. No explanation needed." Maren's breath tickles my face, and I shiver. "But I know what you mean. I didn't want to come to this sleepover, and somehow she convinced me."

"I didn't want to come, either."

Maren snorts. "I don't know why she thought having

the two of us over at the same time would be a good idea."

"She thinks we're friends," I say. "Ever since she saw us working together at the Festival of Death."

"God, and I thought she just wanted to host the world's most awkward slumber party."

I burst into giggles, then stuff my hand into my mouth to muffle the laughter. Maren's air mattress shakes next to mine as she laughs silently with me. Every time one of us starts to catch our breath, the other sets us off again. Finally, I hiccup my way back to silence.

"It's almost morning," I say. "I guess we should try to get some sleep."

"If you would just stop making me laugh," Maren accuses. "So irresponsible."

"So uptight," I shoot back. "Goodnight, Maren."

"'Night, Olive." She rolls to her other side and is snoring within five minutes. Actually snoring. I can't wait to hold this over her.

Vanessa is gone when I wake up in the morning, but Maren is still lying on her back with one arm flung over her eyes and her red hair in a tangle around her neck like a noose. It looks uncomfortably tight, so I reach over to try and loosen it. Her eyes flicker open just as I touch her skin, and she sucks in a sharp breath with a hiss.

"What are you doing?" she cries, flailing backward and slipping off her bed in a heap of sheets.

"Sorry, sorry!" I hold up my hands in a placating gesture. "I was just trying to fix your hair so it wasn't wrapped around your neck!"

Maren claws at her hair, glaring at me. She has dark circles under her eyes, and her skin is ashen under her freckles. "My hair is fine." She grimaces, blinking and pressing a hand to her forehead. "God, my head. Where's Vanessa? I need aspirin."

We wander downstairs together, following a hallway

lined with floral oil paintings to a kitchen with a scarred wooden table set for three. Vanessa is already seated in front of a plate heaped with French toast. My stomach growls at the scent.

"So," she says in a brittle voice as she drops a few pieces of French toast on each of our plates. "You're up. I thought I better let you sleep. You know. After your late-night talk."

I freeze, midreach for a glass of orange juice. Maren bites her lip, shooting me a look twisted with guilt. My chest tightens as I race through the conversation from last night, going over everything we said. God, we were laughing about Vanessa while she was lying awake listening. Blood burns in my cheeks. What's wrong with us?

"We shouldn't have been gossiping," I say. "That sucks. I'm sorry."

Vanessa crosses her arms and leans back in her chair, looking at Maren and waiting for her to apologize as well. The satisfied set of her mouth takes me back to last night when they were asking me about Davis, and suddenly I realize that she likes this. She *wants* us to feel bad. She wants to hold this over our heads so every time we do something she doesn't like, she can bring it up and remind us of how we wronged her. She's manipulating us right now, without either of us even realizing it.

"Yeah, I'm—"

I interrupt Maren before she can finish. "You know what? No. Vanessa, you do manipulate people. You're doing it right now. It's not healthy, and it's not okay. What happened last night with the mirror was really fucked up."

"I didn't do anything," she says. Her hand strays to the velvet ribbon around her neck. She's worn it every day since Davis bought her the bracelets at his mom's diner, though I haven't seen the bracelets since that night.

"You gaslit us," I retort. "You manipulated both of us into coming when we didn't want to. And you didn't listen when I said I didn't want a drink."

"Your exact words were 'Ehh, I don't know.'" Vanessa's voice is cool. "And thanks for telling me you didn't want to come, that makes me feel great."

"We're not trying to make you feel bad," Maren says. "But you can't always control what other people decide."

"I'm not *trying* to control anyone." Vanessa looks away, her cheeks a splotchy red. "It just happens sometimes. I can't help it."

Wait a second.

"What do you mean, it just happens?" I fold my arms over my chest, narrowing my eyes. I have to admit, I'm still a little pissed about the ambush during truth or dare last night, and it feels good to push back and question Vanessa about something that clearly makes her just as uncomfortable. "You just *happen* to manipulate people? To control us? That's what you're saying. You *are* controlling us, aren't you? Just admit—"

"I'm an empath!" Vanessa shouts. The light bulbs above us flare as an electrical current surges through the room; the hairs on my arm stand up. Vanessa closes her eyes for a moment, breathing slowly through her nose. "I'm an empath, okay? It's just who I am. I can't help it."

Maren and I glance at each other, and I can tell that I'm not the only one who has no idea what Vanessa is talking about. Could it be that there's actually a vocabulary word that even Maren effing Seymour doesn't know?

"It means I can read energy," Vanessa explains. "I can sense what people are feeling when they're around me. And that allows me to . . . influence their perceptions." She sighs and presses her hand to her face. "It's hard always being the new girl. My mother and I are always moving around. When I realized what I could do, it made it easier. I try not to abuse it, but sometimes I lose control. I just . . . want to be liked."

The way she pushed her way into my life when no one else has been able to for two years . . . that was all part of Vanessa's manipulations? We're not friends. We're not anything. We're Nothing.

"This is such a violation," I say. "What gives you the right to make someone feel something—"

Vanessa shakes her head. "It's not like that. I can't make people feel things that aren't already there. I can't make someone hate someone that they love—or love someone that they hate. But if there's just a little bit, just a little inkling . . . I can take that and magnify it. It really doesn't have to be a big deal. It doesn't change who I am, or our friendship or anything."

How can she believe that? That we would just sit back and let her change how we feel? Is she so used to controlling everyone around her that she has no idea how weird it is?

"I don't know, Vanessa," I push my chair back with a scraping sound. "How can I ever trust what I'm feeling when I'm around you? And last night—you did that, didn't you? You manipulated our fear until we saw that blood. That's sick."

"I can't make you see something that isn't there," Vanessa insists. "Whatever you saw last night, I swear that wasn't me. I would never do something like that." She reaches across the table, clutching at my hand in a death grip. Her lower lip trembles. Tears cling to her eyelashes like dew on a spiderweb. "Please, Olive, I'm sorry. I don't know what I would do without you."

"You'd find someone else to lie to and exploit." I yank my hand out of hers and turn to go.

Vanessa lets out a soft cry like I hit her. It's enough to send a ripple of shame through my chest, but it's Maren's response that actually stops me in my tracks.

"That's enough, Olive!" she snaps. "Just drop it, okay?"

I spin around to see Maren with her arms around

Vanessa. She glares at me over Vanessa's shoulder. "You don't know what it's like. You don't even care if people like you—"

"I care," I say, stung. "Just because I don't go around manipulating everyone—"

"You shut everyone out. I don't know why—it's your business—but it's different for me and Vanessa. I would do anything to be seen for who I really am and not for who my great-grandfather was. And Vanessa's mom has been dragging her around her entire life. If she has something that makes it easier, no wonder she relies on it."

I'm stunned into silence. Maren's cheeks glow with bright spots of color, and her eyes flash. She still has an arm tucked around Vanessa, protective, but Vanessa has stopped crying. Instead she's watching me out of the corner of her eye, as though trying to read my response.

"That's not—" I splutter. "You're missing the point. She can change how we feel, and she said herself that she can't always control it! Doesn't that creep you out?"

"Olive," Vanessa says in a quavering voice. "What can I do to make you trust me? I'll do anything. Just tell me what it will take."

"Really?" I cross my arms. "There's not a single thing—" The words die in my throat as something dawns on me.

I drop back into my chair at the table, mind racing. I close my eyes, and I'm back in Seymour House, the phantom voices ringing in my ears, dread creeping over my skin as Jay told us what happened to him there. The tension twisting in my gut as I knelt in the center of my chalk pentacle. The sparks rising from the candle as I searched for a spirit.

Seymour House is heavy with energy.

If Vanessa wants me to trust her, despite the fact that she admits she can't always control her gift, she's going to have to prove her intentions. And I know the perfect way.

Opening my eyes, I lean across the table. "How does it work? Can you do it with a place? Read its energy?"

Vanessa slides out from under Maren's arm, hope blooming on her heart-shaped face. "I've never tried. But theoretically, yes. Places have energy, too."

That's what I thought. It's pretty much the basis of dark tourism: that places associated with death hold on to that energy. Whether it's a ghost tour in New Orleans or visiting the catacombs beneath Paris, tourists seek out that energy left behind.

"If you can read the energy of a place," I continue, "maybe you would be able to learn its secrets. Or find things that are hidden."

"You're thinking of the ledger," Maren says in a voice as sharp as the tapping of her heels on the cafeteria floor.

I nod, pressing my mouth into a grim line. "Vanessa, you said you would do whatever it takes for me to trust you. Here's your chance. Read the energy at Seymour House, and help us find the ledger."

"That's not fair, Olive," Maren protests. "You can't put that on her. Bad things happened at Seymour House. I could feel it when we were there, and I'm not even an empath. You don't know what might happen to someone vulnerable to that kind of energy."

"The shade didn't seem to bother her," I mutter, re-membering the heavy, creeping sense of dread that it brought with it.

"She wasn't actively seeking it out," Maren points out. "She wasn't opening herself up to all that negative energy."

"What do you call trying to summon Bloody Mary? If it's so dangerous for her to seek out negative energy, chant-ing the name of a spirit by candlelight probably isn't a good idea."

Maren stiffens when I mention Bloody Mary. There's something unnatural about her stillness. It's like she's afraid that any sudden movement will summon back the blood that cascaded over her skin last night.

I feel a sharp pang at the expression on her face, but maybe after we find the ledger and help Jay, the blood that Maren thinks stains her will wash clean. If I can free Jay from his misery, it will free Maren, too.

So I don't back down.

"And besides, she can decide for herself," I add. "So Vanessa, what do you say? Are you in or are you out?"

Vanessa has been silent during our exchange, chewing on her bottom lip and twisting her ribbon around her fingers. She drops it when I say her name, looking up with her deep blue eyes swimming in her face.

"Maren's right," she says. "That kind of energy can be dangerous. But I can do it. I will do it, if that's what you need me to do to make you trust me. The asylum should have everything I need to find the ledger. But it will take time . . . preparation. We should go there today so I can feel it out."

I lean back in my chair. I should feel satisfied, but instead I just feel bloated, like I'm one of those swollen, sluggish flies that swarm around roadkill.

CHAPTER 14
CURTAINS

As soon as we make plans with Davis to go to Seymour House later this morning, Maren disappears into the bathroom, leaving me alone with Vanessa. I pretend to focus on a very important round of Candy Crush, but really, my thoughts are racing. It's unsettling to know that Vanessa can feel every undercurrent of emotion in the room. Electrical impulses carried on unspoken words. Silences that say more than conversations. I know she can't read my mind, can't reach into my brain and unspool my thoughts, but if she can feel my emotions, it comes down to the same thing. She knows what I want, maybe even before I do. She knows how I feel about Davis and Maren.

Like Maren's bloody reflection last night, I'm suddenly not sure what's real and what isn't. Hints of my old friendship with Davis reemerging as soon as Vanessa moved to town . . . the complicated tangle of feelings I have for Maren, part exasperation, part admiration, part something else that I'm not ready to name yet . . . is that all Vanessa?

Finally she looks up, one side of her mouth lifted in a smirk. "You want to ask me something. I can feel it in the air. It's like a taut wire, the tension growing and growing. It's going to snap if you don't ask me soon."

I fold my arms and lean back in my chair. "Does Davis know?"

I know that I have no right to worry about him, not after the years I spent ignoring him, but my palms go clammy at the thought of Vanessa manipulating him. He's had enough people in his life who only pay attention to him as long as he's serving their purpose. His dad, for example.

If Mr. Wills didn't have delusions of expanding the family business, I don't know if he would ever notice Davis. And I know his mom loves him, but she's spent more time at the diner than with Davis over the past few years. It took all of her energy to get things running, and now that she has a little to give back to Davis, it's like neither of them know how to be in each other's lives anymore.

Then there's me, pretending I wanted to hang out so he would take me to Seymour House.

A knife of guilt twists in my chest. I'm no better than Mr. Wills, using Davis and everyone I care about to get what I want.

"Yes," Vanessa says. "I told him that first night we went out, after the asylum. We were laughing about you believing in ghosts—"

I scowl at the memory.

"—and then I told him there were some elements of the paranormal that I knew were real. I wanted him to know what I can do, but that I don't do it to him. I've never changed how he feels about me, Olive." She fingers the ribbon around her neck, her eyes brimming with tears again. "I don't have to."

I can't decide if I believe her or not. Why should I, when I know very well that she can manipulate everything I feel?

Davis picks us up an hour later, not questioning why we want to go back to Seymour House or the tense silence that envelops me and Maren. Vanessa tells him about our sleepover—leaving out the uncomfortable interrogation about our supposed past romance, and the way Maren's hair turned to blood—and he drives with his hand on her knee. We're bumping into the woods before I know it.

I catch sight of Jay fluttering among the trees. He's wispy and insubstantial, and the sun seems to pass right through him. Davis slows to a stop, waiting for Jay to drift closer and get in the back seat with me and Maren.

"Any luck?" I ask Jay, but I know he'll shake his head. He would have told us right away if he had found his grave.

"No," he answers. "What are you doing here?"

I purse my lips. "I have an idea."

Davis parks at the top of the hill. Seymour House rears above us. The porch sags; the doors are swaybacked. The paint is dingy and gray and peeling in long swaths, like bandages on a horror movie mummy. Possibly condemned; *definitely* haunted.

Vanessa paces along the iron fence, trailing her fingers through the rusted balusters so that they sing. She faces the house and tugs at her ribbon, muttering under her breath.

"It's Vanessa," I tell Jay. "It turns out that she's really sensitive to emotions and what people feel. She can read energy and even manipulate it. It's called—"

"She's an empath," Jay says. "Mysticism was very popular when I was alive. Seances and psychics. Empaths. I've heard of them before." His face twists. "But how will that help me?"

Vanessa strides over to us, shaking back her hair. "Olive suggested that I try to read the energy at the asylum, to find out where the ledger is. And she's right; this place is swimming in energy. The things that happened here left a mark that time and disrepair can't erase. If the ledger is inside, I'll be able to tell."

She places one hand on the gate and the other on her ribbon, closing her eyes. For a moment nothing happens. But then she speaks in a low husky voice. "Hundreds went in but few came out. Their cries echo through the years. This is a place of death and anguish, secrets and lies. The gates are bound in blood, the house is bound in blood— Seymour blood." She opens her eyes and fixes them on Maren. "I need Maren."

My stomach plummets like Vanessa said my own name.

This isn't what I expected. I thought she would just close her eyes, do her thing, and bam, know where we should look for the ledger. I didn't know Maren would have a part to play. A bitter taste fills my mouth. I keep getting Maren sucked in deeper and deeper.

Maren fidgets, her face draining of color. "What do you need from me?"

Your blood, I think I hear, like a whisper coming from the house itself.

"I just need you with me," Vanessa says. "In the asylum. The house will try to hide its secrets, but it won't be able to keep them from a Seymour."

I'm relieved that Vanessa isn't planning on draining Maren's blood or something, but Maren looks like the thought of entering Seymour House is just as bad. It *is* like being in a tomb. But a tomb that holds the information we need to help Jay—to free him from the dark destiny that I've trapped him in.

"When can we do it? Tonight? Now?" Maren twines a strand of hair around her wrist.

"Next week," Vanessa declares. "When the moon is full."

"We can't do it sooner?" I ask.

Vanessa shakes her head. "The ledger was here long ago, long before any of us. But the moon was here, watching, witnessing. It will testify for me."

That doesn't make any sense to me, but Vanessa seems confident.

We shuffle our feet in the dirt for a moment before Davis shakes off the tension in his shoulders and says, an edge of sarcasm in his voice, "Well, what are we supposed to do now?"

I don't know if it's the fact that now we have a plan, or if it's something Vanessa is doing, but my heart rate slows until my blood is the lazy brown water of the Rio Grande in the heat of the summer, slow and meandering. Maren lets out a short laugh. Jay hauls himself up on the crumbling stone column that supports the fence and crouches like a gargoyle. There's a playful grin on his face that looks out of place. I don't think Jay's spent much time messing around or goofing off like a normal teenager.

To be fair, I haven't done a lot of goofing off, either. We have that in common. Only, Jay actually has an excuse. He didn't have much opportunity during his wretched life, and his death has been filled with desperate attempts to escape the woods where he died.

"Is there anything you wish you had done?" I ask him. "You still have some time."

"Well . . ." Jay draws the word out. "I never did make it to the pictures, what with dying of consumption and all."

"There's a scream queens marathon at the Silver Screen tonight," Davis says. "*Friday the 13th. Halloween.* Seems like a good place for a twentieth-century ghost to have some twenty-first-century fun."

"I'm in," I say. "Maren? Want to come?"

She twists her hair into a knot on top of her head and tucks the ends under into a neat bun. It would take witchcraft to make my hair do something like that. "I don't know. I should work on stuff for the dance."

"Oh, come on," I cajole. "Take a night off from over-achieving and *under*achieve with the rest of us."

I'm surprised to realize that I really mean it. Going to the drive-in theater will be the most normal thing we've ever done together. I want to see what it's like to hang out with Maren when there isn't a malevolent shade bearing down on us, or phantom blood dripping from her hair. I want to see if we'll go back to bickering without the urgency of impending doom, or if things have really changed between us. I want to see if there's something there.

"Maybe I wouldn't be so stressed about the Sock Hop if

I had a little more help," Maren says pointedly.

"Fine. If you come to the movie with us tonight, I'll help you with the Sock Hop next week," I promise. My stomach flips.

She almost smiles at me. "Deal."

Davis insists on him and Vanessa driving to the movie separately, even though admission is by the car and it makes more sense for us all to ride together. I think he's trying to guarantee that I can't crash his date again. Jay says he wants to see if he can live up to his reputation as the vanishing hitchhiker, and he'll meet us there.

Which leaves me and Maren alone in her car that night, climbing the hills behind town, winding into the mountains over White Haven. The town is just a collection of lights in the valley between the sanitarium and Seymour House. The stars are dull in the sky above us, brassy and washed out from the pink glow of Santa Fe and Albuquerque to the south.

I can't think of anything to say. The only thing in my head is a meme of a girl saying "Basically I don't have any interests or any talents," under the caption *Me on a first date*. Only this doesn't feel like a first date; it feels more like a job interview. One that I'm blowing.

"So do you—"

"I was wondering—"

Awkward pause. Maren fiddles with the rearview mirror. I stare out the window.

"Do you have any plans for next summer?" she asks.

Next summer? It's October. I don't have plans for next *week*.

"I'm going to try to get an internship at a nonprofit in Albuquerque," she continues. "It's an organization that utilizes dead space in the city to build micro urban farms.

Like park strips and alleyways and things."

I've always been super aware of the wasted space along city bike trails or between buildings. Maybe because sometimes I feel like a waste of space myself. Filling those in with something useful, like fresh produce, is a great idea.

"That sounds really cool. Do you like to garden?"

Maren frowns. "I suck at it. I can't even keep a cactus alive, and we live in the desert."

I try to choke back a laugh, but it bursts out in an embarrassing splutter. "Then micro urban farming might be hard for you."

"I was hoping I could just help with the administrative stuff." Maren's voice is cool. I've never seen someone grip the steering wheel so hard, or keep her hands so rigidly at ten and two. God, I've offended her again. Looks like we can't get through even one conversation unless there's a backdrop of terror to distract us from how much we annoy each other.

"I could help you," I suggest. "My mom has a huge garden that I work in during the spring and summer. I'll show you the basics."

She keeps her eyes on the road, but the corner of her mouth hitches up into a smile. "Really?"

"Sure. We'll start with something easy, like zucchini. Everybody can grow zucchini."

"Okay. Thanks." She glances at me. "What were you going to say? Before I interrupted you. You were wondering something?"

It takes me a second to remember. "Oh, right. I was just wondering what other kind of music you like, besides Saves the Day."

The half smile turns into a grin. "Oh, I don't even know where to start. The Get Up Kids. Dashboard Confessional, but only his acoustic stuff. I used to love Brand New, but Jesse Lacey turned out to be a creep, so that kind of ruined it for me."

"I don't know any of those," I confess. "I only know Saves the Day because my mom plays it when she's cleaning the house."

It dawns on me that a lot of the music my mom listens to is kind of dark for her soda pop personality. She ties her hair up in a bandana, dances as she's mopping, and sings along to lyrics about death and destruction like it's a love song. And maybe to her it is. After all, she *was* a teenager in the age of emo, and those ridiculous, angsty songs have stuck with her for twenty years. They must mean something to her.

Maybe she would understand my existential dread more than I think.

"You teach me how to grow zucchini, I'll teach you about the best pop-punk bands of the late nineties and early aughts," Maren says.

I grin. "Very niche."

Maren answers by pulling up her Spotify playlist and turning the music up. She throws her head back so that her voice reaches up to the stars. I don't know the words, but when she looks at me in the moonlight, I can feel them in my bones. My heart stutters to a stop, and for a moment only the pounding of the bass keeps my blood pumping.

Everything is still spinning when we get to the turnoff for the Silver Screen and Maren turns the music off. There's already a long line of cars twisting through the woods to the parking lot, and it takes forever to get our tickets. Davis's car is parked in the back row when Maren and I finally pull in. He and Vanessa are curled together on a huge beanbag chair under a blanket.

Maren and I drag a pair of camp chairs next to Davis and Vanessa's beanbag. I shiver and pull a scratchy Navajo wool blanket that Davis's mom gave me for my tenth birthday around my shoulders, tucking it under my legs.

October nights in the high desert are cold.

Maren nudges me and nods at a cluster of girls setting up their own chairs in the row ahead of us. I recognize a few of them from my gym class. They're talking about a hitchhiker they picked up by Scary Road. I overhear Sally Romito panic-whispering about how he disappeared from the car after a few miles—just vanished into thin air.

"I can't get warm," Sally insists, rubbing her shoulder with one hand. Her voice is high and tight with fear, echoing over the cars. "He was so cold sitting next to me. I can still feel it."

"Jay." I snort. "I guess part of his fun tonight is leaning into the whole ghost identity. Out of all the things he could do."

Davis folds his arms over his chest, the beanbag crackling as he shifts. "I would haunt my dad's office. Scatter important contracts. Scare away the young, pretty secretaries he always hires. Knock his diploma sideways so that it never hangs straight. That would piss him off."

"I would dump all of Ms. Hunter's fundraising ideas in the trash," Maren says. "She has the worst ideas."

"I would take revenge," Vanessa says. Her voice squeaks a little and her cheeks flush, but she sets her jaw when I look at her, surprised.

"On who?" I ask.

"Everyone who's ever wronged me."

Yikes. Remind me not to get on Vanessa's bad side. She's definitely the kind of girl who could paint your nails one day and then claw your eyes out the next. I might as well be friends with Regina George.

The first sign that Jay is here comes fifteen minutes into the movie when the horn in a Ford Taurus two rows up from us starts blaring. It's not the measured blaring of a car alarm; this sounds like someone is laying on the horn with both hands. A kid in a hooded sweatshirt scrambles out of his lawn chair, fumbling in his pocket for his keys. He dives into the front seat, and the trumpeting changes to staccato pumps, like the car is wheezing. Laughter ripples across the rows of cars, and a few kids call out to the unlucky driver.

"Can it, Bobby!"

"Save it for Scary Road!"

But when the honking doesn't stop after Bobby gets behind the wheel, the laughter turns to boos. Bobby finally drives away, handfuls of popcorn showering the still-honking car as he goes.

The rest of the movie is riddled by outbursts of honking cars, headlights dancing across the movie screen, blasts of static from the speaker boxes mounted on poles at each parking spot. A few other cars leave early, but the parking lot is still pretty full when the first movie ends.

"Gus swears that he wasn't flickering the lights."

"Dude, did you hear what was coming from the speaker? It sounded like a demon."

"Ramon doesn't even want to stay for the second movie!"

I have to admit Jay's shenanigans are pretty funny. I press my hand to my mouth to stop from laughing as I stand in line to get a refill on my drink. No one watched the movie, and for once it wasn't because they were hooking up or drinking.

"Hello," Jay breathes in my ear, appearing out of the shadows. I jump, sloshing half-melted ice and watered-down Coke all over my feet.

"Don't do that!"

"This is my thing now." Jay cracks his knuckles. His shock of corn silk blond hair flops over a bone-white forehead. "This is what I do, Olive. I haunt people."

"Not me," I gasp, swatting at his arm. "Hey, how does this work, anyway? Shouldn't my hand go straight through?" I prod at his chest, but it's solid. Cold and hollow and dead, but solid.

"If I'm here, I'm here. If I'm not, I'm not."

"That doesn't make any sense." The line inches forward, and it's my turn. I pass the empty cup across the counter and ask for a refill.

Jay shrugs. "Just because I'm dead doesn't make me the authority on ghosts."

"So have you gotten your fill, or should we expect more during the second movie?"

"You haven't seen anything yet," he says, rubbing his hands together.

The girl behind the counter hands back my drink.

"You coming?" I ask Jay.

He shakes his head and puts a finger to his lips. "I got a ride with those guys," he says, nodding at the cluster of boys in letterman jackets. They're at the back of the line, wrestling and crushing empty cans. "I don't want them to recognize me."

"How many times did you pull that hitchhiking ghost routine?"

"Five or six. Uh-oh—" One of the jocks is staring straight at him. "Gotta go."

And just like that, Jay blinks out.

Friday the 13th starts with lots of honking. At first it's just disorganized blaring, but then Jay starts picking up on the score of the movie and being more deliberate. Soon the movie is playing to a chorus of the horns and alarms of half a dozen cars. Most of the audience is on their feet, laughing and waving their phones around as they record the cacophony. It's weirdly cool, listening to the different tones of car horns mimicking speech patterns and creepy background music.

I'm just as startled as everyone else when the sound cuts out and static pours out of the speaker boxes. It's loud enough that I can still hear it with my hands clapped over my ears: the roar of a jet from an Air Force base, the rush of the ocean, the race of the blood coursing through my veins. It's the sound of a thousand wasps burrowing into your skin, forcing their way into your mouth and filling your throat.

My teeth go loose in my gums as the hiss grows in intensity. The taste of blood seeps through my mouth, like I've been sucking on pennies. The sound is inside my skull, drilling into my brain until I think I'm going to scream. Next to me, Maren's face is screwed up in pain. I don't think I can take much more when the sound suddenly falls away.

The absence of the bone-numbing hum takes me by such surprise that I drop my hands from my ears. On-screen, the camera pans across one of the camp counselors pinned to a door with arrows. The blood is technicolor red, splattered across the scene. There's something clinical about watching without the sound. Here's the camp, here's the storm, here's the body, here's the arrow.

My heart pounds. I feel fear all around me, creeping across the ground like a low-hanging fog. If it's this intense for me, it must be unbearable for Vanessa. I sneak a glance at her—she has her face buried in Davis's shoulder.

At first Jay's pranks seemed so silly, so innocent, like going to the local haunted house and recognizing the brain-eating zombie as the kid who always falls asleep in math class. It's fun being scared when you know you're safe, when you know the monsters can't really claw their way out of the movie screen. When you know monsters don't exist.

But monsters *do* exist. I've seen them myself. Why the hell did I think this was funny?

A girl in the row ahead of us shrieks. There's a shadow on the screen, a slump-shouldered shape that looms larger and larger until it blocks out the movie and the screen goes dark. Whispers fill the parking lot. My breath shudders out, and cold claws its way into my chest. I clamp my jaw down until my teeth ache, a jolt shooting through my body like I'm biting on tinfoil.

A low, muttering voice joins the crackling. It's the whisper that you hear when you're walking home alone after dark, the one that you tell yourself is just dry leaves blowing across the street but still chases you up the stairs and into your room, the one that you try to block out by hiding in bed and pulling the blankets over your head.

I try to cover my ears and block out the whisper, but my arms are frozen at my sides. At first, I think I'm so scared I can't move, but that's not it. I can still draw breath, I can still turn my head to lock eyes with Maren, I can still shift under my blanket. The fear hasn't seized my body. No, I don't cover my ears because there's a part of me that wants to listen to the whisper, as terrified as I am to hear what it says.

Because I recognize the voice.

The whisper reaches out to caress me, curling tendrils of hair off my neck so that I shudder.

"Lolly," it says in Mrs. H's voice. "Lolly, I'm afraid . . . it's dark, and I'm alone. Are you there, Lolly?"

The voice sends a jolt through my body. I want to cry out, but my jaw is locked shut. My bones grate against each other. The movie screen is shifting, bulging out as something presses against it: the round dome of a skull, the hollow of empty eye sockets, a grinning jaw.

The monster is escaping the movie.

Tiny silver clouds, puffs of panicked breath, dot the parking lot. I'm not the only one held spellbound by the palpable fear in the air. Maren, Vanessa, and Davis don't move, pressed back in their chairs, their heads tilted to the side as they listen to the whispers issuing forth from the speakers.

"I don't want to be alone . . ." The voice drops off into a soundless moan, an empty hum filling the frozen air. A whimper escapes my tensed jaw. I squeeze my eyes closed, but behind my eyelids it's dark, so dark, as dark as Mrs. H's casket in the ground, dirt and rocks and worms piled on top of me.

Fear coils in my belly, holds my limbs tight and stiff, keeps my jaw clenched against the scream that's trying to escape. It twists tighter tighter tighter as the skull swells out of the screen, mouth yawning open, pressing, pressing, pressing—

The screen bursts. The shadow of the skull is gone, and the only hint of a ghost is the way the white screen, split down the middle, flaps in the breeze. I collapse forward, hugging my knees, my muscles shaking as the tension releases, and gulp in a great, shuddering breath.

"What the hell?" I mutter. "What the hell? What the hell?" My voice is a scratched record; my shoulders shudder like I'm shaking off cobwebs. "Did Jay do that?"

—*Oh Lolly, oh Lolly, I'm afraid*—

Maren lets out a sound like a sob. "Oh my God. What was that? What happened? Was that him?"

Vanessa squirms closer to Davis under their blanket. "I could barely breathe," she whispers. "I wanted to scream when that skull started swelling out of the screen, but I couldn't."

"Did you guys hear something coming from the speakers when the sound cut out?" I lean forward in my chair. "I thought I heard someone talking to me . . . someone who's dead."

"Static," Davis says. "And then—" He hesitates, pressing his lips together in a grimace. "Something else."

"I heard a voice telling me that Seymour House is my legacy." Maren's hair is tangled around her wrist.

"I heard my mother whispering to me," Vanessa says.

That grating mockery of Mrs. H's voice . . . like she's been devoured by the Nothing and someday I'll die and I will be, too.

I read once that it used to be so common for people to be buried alive that they started tying a string connected to a bell above ground around the corpse's finger. That way if you went to sleep in your bed but woke up under six feet of dirt and rocks, the bell would ring as you scratched at the top of the casket. And hopefully someone would notice in time to dig you up before you ran out of air.

I've never considered myself claustrophobic, but that's got to be the most terrifying thing that could ever happen to a person. The smell of dirt and worms. The close, suffocating darkness. The quiet.

That's what it felt like listening to Mrs. H's voice coming out of that gravelly speaker. Like I was trying to claw my way out of the Nothing all over again.

"We all heard something different," I say. "He got in our heads, made us each hear what would scare us the most."

I don't mean scare us like a slasher movie or a monster come to life—no, he showed us each the thing that's rooted deep inside our chests, the nameless thing that we pray we'll never have to face, but we know is waiting for us in the end. The dread. The disquiet.

The end of everything.

White flickers at the corner of my vision, and then Jay steps out from between the rows of cars. I shiver as a high desert chill washes over me. His face is shrouded in shadows. Something is different about him. I can't put my finger on it, but it makes the hairs on my arms stand up and my heart wither in my chest. Even with the glimpses of the skull that flicker in and out of my vision, I haven't seen Jay for what he is until tonight.

The four of us stare at him, faces blank, but he either doesn't notice our fear, or he takes it as a compliment.

"Thank you, thank you." He takes an exaggerated bow. "I decided to go with a more playful personality than your typical haunting. A poltergeist rather than a revenant."

"What the fuck?" I hiss. "It started out funny, but you went too far."

"Why would you make us hear that terrifying voice coming from the speakers?" Maren adds in a shaking voice.

Jay freezes halfway through his mock bow. "What voice coming from the speakers?"

Maren and I glance at each other.

"The one we all heard telling us what we're most afraid of," I say. "How did you do that, anyway?"

"I didn't do any voice. Just the stuff with the cars." Jay's eyebrows draw together in bewilderment, casting his face into deeper shadow. He glances around the parking lot, frowning at the tattered screen flapping in the wind. "Hold your horses . . . what happened to that?"

The beanbag rustles as Vanessa sits up. "Come on, Jay, we're already in on the joke. How did you get in everyone's head like that?" She straightens her ribbon so it lies like a gash across her throat.

"I'm telling you, I didn't do that," Jay insists. "At least . . . I didn't mean to." He looks worried now, like he's unsure of what actually happened. He presses a bone-thin hand to his forehead, and his face slips away for a split second, leaving just the high smooth dome of his skull. And suddenly I know what's different about him, I can see what's changed:

His eyes are black craters in the white moon that is his face, hard and round and empty. They seize on mine, and for a moment I feel like I'm falling—like I'll never be able to stop looking into those dark holes.

I stumble back, a shadow of the fear I felt during the movie rising in my chest. Davis mutters a curse behind me, and Maren gasps, a sharp hiss. My stomach sinks. I know what this is. I know what this means.

"Your eyes," I say. "It's starting."

The shade within him is getting stronger.

Tonight was just a taste of what he'll do if we don't find his grave.

CHAPTER 15
GAME OVER

turns out, we're not the only ones who figured out what really happened at the Silver Screen. By the next morning, #whatdidyouhear is trending, and everyone in White Haven is using an anonymous app to share what they're most afraid of:

The thud of a body hitting my car and the squeal of the tires as I drive away.

My boyfriend telling me he never loved me.

The crackle of flames engulfing my house and my family screaming for me to come back and help them escape.

I'm sitting under the apple tree in the backyard, scrolling through the feed, when Davis comes outside. He's still wearing his clothes from last night, and his face has a grayish tinge that makes me think he got less sleep than I did.

I swallow, blinking and looking away. Last night was so raw and unsettling. I've never let Davis—or anyone—see me so afraid or unnerved. It almost feels like he saw me naked. Half of me wants to pretend I don't notice him, to stare at my phone until he gives up and goes back inside. But the other half wonders what he heard. Was it his father?

Was it me?

Before I can haul myself to my feet and retreat inside, he kicks a few rotting apples out of the way and sits down next to me. "Hi."

"Hi."

"So last night . . . pretty scary shit."

I grunt, closing my eyes.

Mrs. H's voice still bores into my skull, ringing with

the echoes of what I heard last night.

It's dark, and I'm alone.

The world is vast and empty, and even with Davis right by my side, I'm alone. I've been alone for two years now, and last night was just a reminder of how utterly meaningless all of this is.

Davis's presence next to me sends sharp, static electricity racing across my skin. There's a stitch in my side when I breathe in, like I've been running for years. Running from the Nothing, running from Davis, running from anything that could hurt me.

All that running has left me exhausted.

Davis taps at his phone screen, fingers battering like raindrops against a window. He's adding his own #whatdidyouhear confession. He shifts to the side, holding the phone between us so I can read the screen as he types.

My father telling me I'm dead to him. It's what I've always been most afraid of. That if my life doesn't go exactly as he planned it, he'll just drop me and want nothing to do with me.

His thumbs hover over the keyboard, and then he adds one more line, slowly and deliberately, like my dad carving names into stone meant to mark the dead.

Just like Olive did.

At first I think I misread it. The words don't make sense. Davis thinks I want nothing to do with him? The complete opposite is true. How could he—

Then he hits submit and the message appears on the screen, just as permanent as the headstones in the cemetery. More, even, because wind and rain and time will fade the headstones, but the internet is forever.

The words blink on the screen, settling into my bones and twisting in my heart like knives. It hurts so much I can barely breathe. My chest tightens as the air leaves my lungs in what feels like a dying gasp. All of a sudden I might as well be back in the Nothing, the world dimming like a cloud passing in front of the sun. Mrs. H's words echo in my head.

Are you there, Lolly?

But this time the moaning voice sounds like Davis.

For the past two years, all I've been able to think about is the fact that everything ends when we die. Love and relationships, the things that are meaningful during life—they all blink out. There's so much pain for everyone left behind, and for what? In the end, we're left with Nothing.

I didn't want that for me. I didn't want that for the people I loved. I thought I could protect us all by pulling away, by shutting down before it was too late. I spent those first few days after I came back from the Nothing lying on my bed, staring at the ceiling and ignoring my phone buzzing across the room. Pretending to be asleep whenever my mom came upstairs to tell me Davis was there. It never occurred to me that for him, it would be just one more person leaving him with no explanation. It had only been a year since his family had fallen apart. His parents split up and all but disappeared from his life, both consumed with work. And then I was gone, too. Without any explanation, I stopped texting him back, I stayed in my room during dinner every night, and I became one more person who left him trapped in his own personal Nothing.

It takes everything I have to unclench my jaw. Adrenaline pumps in my veins, my body tingling with the urge to push him away again. But the words on Davis's phone are the only thing I see. As much as it hurts, as lost as I feel, I think the only way to drag myself back from the edge is to talk to him.

"I died," I say in a low voice. My throat hurts as the words scrape out. "Remember? When I found out I was allergic to shellfish, back in ninth grade? I died, and it scared me. It made me . . ." I struggle to find words that can describe the endless sea, the panic that consumed me. "It made it hard for me to care about anything and anyone. I thought it would be easier to stop caring. I didn't mean to hurt you." The words come out strangled, and my throat feels like it's closing up again. "I'm sorry."

Davis stares straight ahead, then puts his arm around me. "I'm sorry, too, Lolly. I never thought about what it was like for you."

In Davis's voice, my childhood nickname with all its innocent, syrupy sweetness doesn't sound like it's mocking the dark mess that I've become. He says it like I'm still the little girl with pigtails climbing the apple tree in the back-yard with him. He says it like there's still hope for me.

"Is that why you want Jay to tell you what happens after we die?"

I nod. "If there *is* something after this life, maybe knowing that will be enough for me to care again." The words come out brittle.

He leans his head against mine. His arm is tight around my shoulder. "I didn't know, Olive. I thought there was something wrong with me. Something I did that pushed you away. I had no idea that you were going through that by yourself."

"You didn't push me away." I pull back so I can look Davis in the face. "I have issues that have nothing to do with you. What I did has nothing to do with you. If I had let you, you would have been there for me."

"I still want to be there for you." His voice is tight, like he has to force the words out. "I love you, you know? But I can't—" He shakes his head, pressing his lips together. "I can't handle someone else dropping me."

His words are a flare of light in the darkness of the last two years. The back of my throat aches as I hold back everything I never said to him, and I wrap my arms around my chest, shrinking back against the knobby bark of the tree. I don't think *I* can handle losing someone else. If I let Davis back into my life and something happens—how would I ever claw my way out of the Nothing again?

I clench my hands into fists. My palms tingle at the memory of Maren's hand in mine as the shade was bearing down on us at Seymour House. The darkness had been closing in on me, threatening to swallow me whole, but then I took her hand and light sprang back into the world. Her hand in mine was the only thing that saved me from being devoured by the shade.

As scary as it is, maybe letting Davis back in will protect me from the Nothing that I've built around myself.

"I love you, too," I whisper. "So much. And I swear, Davis—" I draw in a deep, hitching breath that feels like it's going to crack my chest wide open. "From now on, you're stuck with me."

He snorts.

"And—" I continue, because this is important, and I need him to know this. "If your dad is so caught up in life going exactly how he wants, that's his problem. You're not his puppet. You shouldn't have to work for his approval. You should have it just because you're you and you're fucking amazing. Coolest guy I know."

"Yeah, right."

"What do *you* want to do with your life?" I press. "Screw your dad and Wills and Son and law school and everything he has planned for you. What do *you* want?"

Davis leans back on his elbows. His mouth pulls into a twisted smile. "It's silly. I haven't ever told anyone before."

"Think about who you're talking to. Olive Morana, whose life ambition is to develop a cookies-and-cream flavored Oreo. *Cookies-and-cream.* That's what Oreos already are." I flop back in the grass and look up into the yellow-orange leaves of the apple tree. There's one right above me that is edged in red, like a blush spreading over a face. "There's no such thing as a silly dream."

"Okay. I'll tell you if you promise not to laugh." Davis draws in a deep breath. "I want to buy a bus and renovate it to live in. My cousin Jacy in the Navajo Nation has one he'll sell me cheap. I'm going to go out there this summer to work on it and spend some time with my grandparents." He snorts. "My dad would lose his shit if he knew that. He always talks about how hard it was for him and Mom to get the opportunity to leave and how he doesn't understand why my grandparents still live there. It pisses me off that he thinks his way of life is the *only* way of life. But I don't want what he has. I don't want to go to law school. After high school, I want to travel around the country and see everything."

I can imagine Davis going wherever the wind takes him, leaving on his own terms. Free in a way that he isn't here. "Where will you go?"

Davis pulls a small atlas out of the back pocket of his jeans. It's curved from being in his pocket, and the corners are bent and worn away. He drops it on the grass between us, grinning. "Everywhere."

I pick up the atlas and open it. The first few pages are a simple map of the continental United States, just an outline of the states and their capitals and the tangled arteries of the major highways. Davis has traced a line in yellow highlighter that starts in New Mexico, winds along Route 66 to California, then climbs the West Coast before heading back east. It's a sprawling, winding route that takes him through every single state in the lower forty-eight.

"The individual state pages are more detailed," Davis explains as I flip through the pages. "I have a lot of national parks on my itinerary. A lot of cities, too. Big ones, like New York and Chicago and Atlanta. And I want to spend some time on the coast."

"This is incredible," I say, studying his route through South Dakota. I never thought I'd want to visit South

Dakota, but Davis's trip makes it sound fun. A corn palace? I want to go to a corn palace. "How long have you been working on this?"

"Years," he admits.

"It sounds great," I say. "You should go."

He hesitates for a second, then says, "You could come with me. Be my sidekick, like the old days."

My mind goes back to Vanessa's masklike face, insisting that she wouldn't be mad if Davis and I had been something before she moved to town. "I don't think Vanessa would approve of that."

It's like she knows what we're talking about, because Davis's phone buzzes.

"Vanessa," he mumbles, glancing at the screen. "I'm supposed to meet her so we can spend the day together."

"Go," I say. "I'm glad you have that." Something swoops in my stomach that might be jealousy, but might also just be indigestion. I wish I had what Davis and Vanessa have—someone to share my life with. Someone that makes me feel something.

He stands up, then glances down at me in the grass. "I'm glad we're friends again. I missed you."

"Me too," I say. And I mean it.

CHAPTER 16
AT DEATH'S DOOR

I first hear the rumors when I'm in the bathroom between classes. A couple of girls I only know by sight are huddled around someone's phone when I come in to touch up my lipstick. The white noise of a poor-quality phone recording fills the small room, bouncing off the tile walls. It's like standing inside a radio stuck between stations. I'm leaning close to the mirror with a tube of matte Red Dahlia when a tinny scream rises from the phone. I glance in the mirror at the knot of girls; their faces are serious and drawn. One chews her bottom lip; another has tears gathering in the corners of her eyes.

Whatever they're watching, I get the feeling it's not the newest TikTok trend.

The girl holding the phone sees me looking and beckons. "You have to see this—Minnie and Hugo were attacked Saturday night on Scary Road."

Jamming the lipstick back in my pocket, I join the group of girls staring down at the phone. One of them starts the video over. The screen is dark, full of shifting shadows and a flash of white teeth when Minnie speaks.

"Hugo thinks I'm imagining things," she says defensively. Someone snickers beside her: her boyfriend, Hugo. "But after what happened to Evelyn, I'm not taking any chances. We came out to Scary Road, and everything seemed normal, but then something started scratching at the door, like sharp nails on glass, that screeching noise that gets in your head. I convinced Hugo to go somewhere else. But before he could get back in the driver's seat, something started tapping on the roof. Here, listen."

There's a muffled roar while Minnie shifts the phone, holding it up so her spectral reflection flashes in the dark window. "Hear that?"

She goes silent, and at first all I hear is the empty noise of a video without any talking. But then something catches my ear. I lean closer to the phone, and the girl holding it turns the volume up.

It's not the irregular sound of a tree branch blowing in the wind or the erratic, wet sound of raindrops. This is a slow, measured beat: the sound of fingers drumming on metal.

Goose bumps erupt over my arms as I remember the shade reaching for me from the doorway in Seymour House, the waves of bone-chattering cold that washed from it, the coiled darkness in Jay's eyes.

What he'll become if we don't find his grave.

Hugo murmurs something out of frame: *Dios te salve, Maria, llena eres de gracia.* Minnie's huge eyes swim in her heart-shaped face. "It's right above us." Her gaze flicks up toward the ceiling of the car. "We can't see anything outside the windows, so it must be on the roof." She lets out a little squeak of fear as the car shifts, the roof groaning as something scuttles across it. Hugo curses and reaches for the door.

"Enough of this shit," he snarls. "I'm going out there."

Minnie clutches at his sleeve, her voice high with panic as she begs him to stay in the car, but Hugo shakes her off and crawls out of the back seat. The screen goes dark; it looks like the phone has fallen between the seats. We listen to Minnie hyperventilating for at least a minute before there's a loud crack, a muted thud, and a scream like shattering glass.

The video ends. I look up, blinking, at the other girls.

"What was that?" My voice shakes, and I take a deep breath. "Where did you *get* that?"

The girl who motioned me over answers. "Someone added it to the whatdidyouhear account last night. The caption just says 'the Scary Road stalker.'"

"It's a joke." I'm trying to convince myself as much as them. "Right?"

They exchange a look, but the bell rings before anyone can answer.

The latest attack is all anyone talks about all morning. According to the White Haven gossip mills, Hugo has a concussion and Minnie's face was sliced to ribbons. I heard that she had to get over a hundred stitches.

"It's like one of those old slasher movies, with the couple in the car on Lover's Lane and an escaped criminal with a hook for a hand stalking them," I say to Davis and Vanessa at lunch. "I hate those movies. All the characters make such stupid decisions."

"That's the point of slasher movies," Davis says. "The characters always run toward danger instead of away, and they always overlook the knife in the very obvious killer's hand. But this is real life. No one's getting gutted by Ghostface in White Haven."

"You don't know that. Maybe we're making the same bad decisions as Casey did at the beginning of *Scream.* Maybe instead of trying to help Jay, we should be trying to stop him." The legs of my chair screech against the floor as I shift backward. I'm not hungry anymore. Maybe the attacks on Scary Road aren't just a matter of wrong place, wrong time. Maybe Jay has been there all along, watching, waiting, straining at the chains that Mr. Seymour put in place to hold him back. And when Maren broke those chains, maybe it left Jay free to do more than just leave the grounds. I keep imagining him wandering the woods, his face blotted out by the shadow. "He must be the one attacking people."

My cheeks are hot. If Jay has taken to haunting others,

if he attacked Mateo and Evelyn, Hugo and Minnie, it's my fault. I drew him out of the in-between place where he existed for so long. Unleashed him on my classmates. Woke the shadow lurking at the back of his eyes.

Vanessa shrugs. "Or maybe the killer in this story isn't the most obvious one."

"If it is Jay—" Davis lowers his voice so that we have to lean in to hear him. "The only thing we can do is find the grave so that he can move on."

Before the shade takes him completely, I finish in my head. Luckily there are only two more days until the full moon, because if what happened at the movie and the attack on Hugo and Minnie are any indication of what Jay is capable of, we don't have any time to waste.

Today our Junior Reapers meeting is in a little courtyard behind city hall, kind of hidden away where no one can stumble across it. There are rosebushes that bloom almost all year long, paths lined with bells that tinkle in the wind, and a plaque that reads *White Haven Home for Foundling Wraiths and Spirit Children.*

The Foundling Home is so macabre and bizarre, it could only happen in White Haven. It's basically a ghost orphanage. A hundred years ago, the childhood mortality rate was so high that almost every family lost at least one child. Living in White Haven with the sanitarium and Seymour House just compounded that. Wealthy children have their own section of the cemetery, and let me tell you, that is the *one* part of the cemetery I've never liked to go. All the headstones are shaped like puppies and kittens with huge sad eyes. People used to leave lanterns lit all night so that the children wouldn't be afraid of the dark, but the city switched to solar lights a few years ago. Energy conscious.

Anyway, life was good and death was okay if you were a

rich kid in turn-of-the-century White Haven, but the poor kids had it pretty bad. Most of them ended up orphaned, their bodies unclaimed and their spirits restless when they died, so the city opened its Home for Foundling Wraiths and Spirit Children. They could have just, like, made sure kids weren't dying alone in the streets in the first place or whatever, but the Foundling Home was good, too, I guess.

It's not a cemetery—there are no graves or bodies buried there—just a place for the spirits of those kids who were unable to move on and be at peace because of all the emotional baggage from their wretched lives. Rich women mourning their own children could go to the Foundling Home and visit with the spirits, and it was supposed to bring comfort to both sides.

It must have worked, because I've never seen a ghost at the Foundling Home, much less a shade, which means that all the spirits of the children trapped here broke free and moved on a long time ago.

I know this sounds absurd, but seances and spiritualism were all the rage in the early 1900s. This kind of thing wasn't that unusual, especially in White Haven, which had already begun to lean into its reputation as a dark tourism destination.

It's actually really nice. Peaceful. I sit on a wrought iron bench tucked away under a huge, drooping rosebush toward the back of the courtyard while I wait for everyone else to show up. I'm the first one there—shocker, I know, but I did ask for a library pass during my last period and then promptly left campus.

"Olive." Ms. Hunter props the door to the courtyard open with a stack of buckets and drops a bundle of work gloves to the ground. "I'm surprised to see you here so early. Want to give me a hand with the rakes?"

By the time we've lugged the rakes and pruning shears and weed spray from her car to the courtyard, everyone else has arrived. Ms. Hunter passes out the tools and steers pairs of Junior Reapers toward the overgrown rosebushes, the weeds that creep over the benches, the gravel kicked from the path into the flower beds. Soon everyone has chosen a partner, leaving Maren standing by herself next to a stack of buckets.

"Guess it's you and me," I say to her. She tightens her mouth and pulls on a pair of gardening gloves.

I glance around at the rest of the Junior Reapers. Everyone is busy with their own piles of weeds; no one is paying attention to us. Maren and I haven't talked since Saturday night, and after what happened at the movie and then the most recent attack, all I can think about is how badly we need to find the ledger.

"So . . . are you freaking out as much as I am?" Doubtful. Maren can hold herself together way better than I can.

"I'm just trying to focus on other things," Maren says. "Like getting ready for the Sock Hop. I have to meet with Poppy to finalize the menu." She viciously yanks weeds out of the ground. "It's coming up so soon. Want to come with me?"

"To the Sock Hop?" I cover my flushed cheeks by wiping a bead of sweat off my forehead with the back of one hand.

"What?" Maren reaches for a clump of dandelions. "To Poppy's. You said you would help out more, remember?"

Right. I did say that. "Oh yeah. I guess I can go with you, if you really need me to. But I still think you're taking this all too seriously. It's just a dance."

Just a stupid dance.

My stomach feels all twisted inside. For half a second, I thought Maren was asking if I wanted to go to the Sock Hop with her. I've never gone, but this year I'll have to. One of the many important duties of a Junior Reaper. Drinking ice cream sodas out of old-fashioned glasses and doing those dances with the ridiculous names—the mashed potato, or the boogaloo, or whatever—doesn't fit the aesthetic I've carefully curated over the past few years. But it could be fun with the right person. And believe me, I see the irony in suddenly thinking that *Maren Seymour* is the right person. A month ago, we couldn't stand each other. But things have changed. Maren has changed.

Regardless of why or how, Maren and I are kind of friends now. Friendly. Friend adjacent. I don't even feel that panicky about it, because we haven't ever been close. There aren't years of history there waiting to undo me. But now I realize we have more in common than I thought. I don't even mind her hard shell or how bossy she can be, because I know that's just a cover. She's as broken inside as I am.

Maren blows a loose strand of hair out of her face with a tiny puff of air. She doesn't seem aware of the tumult inside me. At least I'm still as inscrutable as ever.

"The Sock Hop is on the same night as the Desert Heights groundbreaking," she reminds me. "I want the dance to be perfect, so it can be a distraction from the groundbreaking in case . . ."

"In case we discover bodies buried on your ancestral land," I finish for her. The words send a shiver racing over my skin. It feels wrong to think about it like that, like Jay's remains are part of some twisted scavenger hunt. I wonder if he's as disturbed as I am at the idea of finding his own grave, standing over it and knowing that's where his body rotted away, where his bones will lie until they're nothing but dust.

Then again, lots of people do just that when they buy cemetery plots. Walk around admiring the view, checking out the neighbors, like any of it will matter when they're dead and gone. Dad carves lots of headstones for the living, filling everything in except for that one final piece of information that no one can know ahead of time. I think

I would have a panic attack if I had to walk past my own grave every time I passed the cemetery.

But that was where Maren fled when she caught me researching her family, and it occurs to me that her name is probably already carved in stone.

"Is it weird knowing where they'll put you after you die?" I blurt out. Ms. Hunter raises an eyebrow as she passes. I duck my head, scrabbling at the dirt again.

"That's a strange thing to ask," Maren says.

"I know," I say, but what I really want to ask is, *Where do you think we go?*

"I guess I don't think about it," she admits. "I doubt that I'll care after I'm dead."

"Jay cares," I point out.

"Jay's different," Maren says. "He has, like, unfinished business. I'm not going to let that happen to me."

Unfinished business. That's one way of putting it. Or you could say that something has bound him here, trapped him so he can't move on . . . first Maren's own great-grandfather with his edict that Jay couldn't go back to visit his mother, and then my stupid charm.

"So you won't care where your body is. What about everything else?" I press. "Do you think you'll still care what people think of you or who comes to your funeral or how often your family brings you flowers after you're gone?"

She narrows her eyes at me. "I'll be dead. I won't know any of that. I won't *be* anymore."

"You don't think there's anything after this life?" I don't know why Maren's opinion is so important to me—maybe because she's the smartest person I know. Or maybe there's another reason—maybe it's because I care what Maren thinks, about me, about life, about death. She makes me feel something. If she feels hope, she'll make me feel hope. If she feels despair, mine will wrap itself around me and drag me down.

As I wait for her to answer, my heart pounds the way it always does when the dark edges of the Nothing are trying to creep across my eyes. It's as if it's afraid of stopping again—one last solid thump before falling silent forever—and so it races to stay ahead of the fear.

"No," Maren says. "That's why it's so important for us to fix things while we can. I don't think we get second chances."

I guess my normal resting bitch face looks disappointed or upset or something, because Maren actually puts down her trowel, peels off her grimy gloves, and hugs me. I startle back, rocking on my heels, before relaxing into the hug. Even after grubbing in the dirt for half an hour, Maren's skin is as soft and fragrant as a rose.

"You okay?" she asks.

I let out a shaky laugh. "Yeah, of course. Why wouldn't I be? You just told me there's nothing after we die, and there's no point in life, so—"

"That's not what I said," she protests. "I don't believe in an afterlife, that's true. But that doesn't mean I think life is pointless. In fact, I think the complete opposite. I want to give life even more meaning because it's all there is. It's all we get. I'm not going to wait until it's too late to let people know I care about them."

We're still tangled together, our faces just a breath apart. The thrum of my heart marks time with hers in a moment that seems to last a lifetime.

Then Ms. Hunter claps her hands to get our attention, and I fall away from Maren, heart pounding. I think she sees me the way I see her, but it's dark in the Nothing and after we die, I won't be able to see her at all.

CHAPTER 17
THE ULTIMATE SACRIFICE

the next day at school, Vanessa's eyes are bright and hopeful when she tells me her plan for reading the energy at Seymour House.

"I've been studying," she says, falling into step with me and linking her arm through mine. "Reading everything I can find from other empaths, and I think I'm ready. The meridian is at 1:11 a.m., so you, Maren, and Jay should be at the asylum by one. Davis and I will get everything set up—"

"One a.m.?" I slow, and Vanessa drags me out of the middle of the hall so the crowd behind me can pass. "I didn't know we would have to be there in the middle of the night. And what is the meridian, anyway?"

"When the moon is at the highest point in the sky," Vanessa says. She twirls the ends of the ribbon around. "This will work, Olive. You don't have to do anything—just make sure Maren is there."

Davis and I walk home together after school. Things are still a little awkward between us—there are pauses in conversation that weren't there before, and we keep having to fill each other in on little details from our lives that we missed out on—but being with him feels as natural as slipping on a favorite sweater that was packed away in storage because the colors were too bright. At first the cuffs feel too tight, or the collar itches, but after a while all you notice is how soft the sweater is and how warm it keeps you. And then you start to remember the smell of the bonfire or the way the leaves crunched under your boots the last time you wore it. All those good things come rushing back, and it's like the last two years never happened.

And maybe, in the grand scheme of things, they didn't. What's two years when Davis and I have a lifetime ahead of us? Maybe the awkward edges of our friendship will soften and stretch until the fit is perfect again.

Maybe I really will go with him when he leaves White Haven after graduation.

"What do you think Vanessa is going to do at Seymour House tonight?" Davis asks when we turn onto our street.

The smile slides off my face like an oil slick. I'm actually a little worried about tonight, but humor is my way of dealing with uncomfortable things, so I say, "Probably a few blood sacrifices and some ritualistic sex."

"Be serious."

"She's *your* girlfriend."

"She won't tell me anything," Davis admits. "She doesn't like when I ask questions about her being an empath. I think it makes her worried that I don't trust her."

"*Do* you trust her?" I ask, but I'm really asking myself. Finding the ledger is out of my hands now, but that doesn't mean I trust Vanessa. I just don't have any other choice.

"Of course I trust her," he says, but he's not looking at me and it sounds like a rote response. "And really. What do you think she's going to do tonight?"

I shrug. "I think she'll hold Maren's hands and try to read her grandfather's energy through her. And the truth will finally come out."

In more ways than one. Yeah, the most immediate consequence will be finding what's really in the woods behind Seymour House. Everyone in White Haven will finally know about Jay and all the other forgotten victims of Seymour House. And if Vanessa helps us find the ledger, there will be no reason not to trust her.

But I'd be lying if I say I'm not still thinking about what

will happen when Jay lies down in his grave and moves on.

Maren doesn't bother with music as we drive to Seymour House. I can feel her shaking in the driver's seat. I want to grab her hands and press them between mine, shake the fear out of her and shout, "You're Maren fucking Seymour!" Instead I sit poker straight, my skin alight with sparks.

The moon is a silver coin in the sky above, and it's so bright that I can see the rust on the pitted metal gate outside Seymour House. But behind it, it's like someone took a pair of shears and cut the shape of a house out of the world, letting the void of the Nothing gape through.

A knot twists in my stomach, and I swallow hard. I can feel my heart fluttering like a moth in a spiderweb, hear the blood racing through my veins—a dull roar that's almost as loud as the silence that comes from Jay's chest. I take a deep breath and hold it until my temples throb and my vision goes spotty, then let it rush out of my mouth like a howling wind.

"What happened to it?" I whimper. "Why's it so dark?"

"It's the middle of the night," Maren points out. She kills the headlights, and the dark shadow that is Seymour House rears over us like a monster awakening in its lair. I don't understand why she's acting like there's nothing strange about us pulling up to a dark vacuum—

Then I remember the bones and the shade. Those things I see that no one else does. Tonight, I see Seymour House for what it truly is.

Jay is perched on one of the stone balusters that support the gate. If he's nervous, he doesn't show it. He sweeps his hair back off his forehead and drops to the ground.

The porch floorboards creak as we move in a group to the back of the house. I feel the walls under my trailing hand, an unpleasant scratch like sandpaper. The house is so dark that I might as well have my eyes closed. It's like moving through deep space. *Nothing, Nothing, Nothing* pounds through my veins with every heartbeat. My windpipe feels like it's shrinking and I concentrate on taking deep breaths, steady breaths, breathing like it's effortless. But soon I'll be gasping if I have to stay next to this vacuum much longer.

When we reach the broken doors that lead into the office, it's suddenly so bright that I have to blink and shade my eyes with my hand. It's like all the light that was left in Seymour House was sucked into this room, where it swirls, fleeting and effervescent, around Vanessa. The tightness in my chest eases up, and oxygen floods my brain in a sudden rush.

Vanessa's kneeling in the middle of a circle made up of candle stubs, bundles of dried herbs and flowers, and crystals reflecting the ever-moving light. Woven through them all are ribbons, silk and gossamer and grosgrain and velvet. Her eyes are closed. The candles flicker slightly as we slip, one by one, through the broken window and take our places along the wall where Davis already stands.

Inside it smells earthy and wild: a deep, rich scent that seems to come from the light itself. There are dozens of lit candles—long, slim black tapers, melting wax puddling around them like dark shadows; stubby white pillars that bleed red; tea lights that are nothing more than dishes of clear wax and flame—but the light in the room isn't dim and flickering. It pulses around Vanessa like a heartbeat, drawing away from the shadows on the wall and the corners of the room so that if I look away from her for too long, the rest of the room is like the dark void of the house from outside. The light clings to Vanessa like an aura, clear and faintly pink.

My ears buzz with a low hum. At first I think the sound is just the thrumming of my own tightly wound nerves, but when Davis and Maren reach for my hands, it grows in intensity and I realize it's coming from the crystals placed in the circle. There are spires of crystal quartz, domes of rough-cut amethyst, a polished chunk of black tourmaline the size of a skull. Whispers fill the room, murmurs from the stones, overlapping in a wild chorus that sets my teeth on edge and makes my bones rattle.

And we wait.

Vanessa, eyes still closed, turns her palms open to the room. The light rushes down her arms and across her hands, bursting from her palms and rippling across the room. It pools around Maren, and Vanessa's eyes open.

"Maren," she says. "Come into the circle." She rises to her feet and reaches for Maren, guiding her past a stem of dried lavender, over a black silk ribbon, near a piece of citrine. Maren steps in a blotch of red pooled next to a candle, her heel pressing into the soft wax like a seal, like she's signing a confession, like she's settling a score. That night at Vanessa's house when I stepped in the drop of blood, sticky and warm—what was I promising then?

When Maren reaches the center of the circle, Vanessa twitches a silky red ribbon from her sleeve and twines it between Maren's fingers, then fits her fingers into Maren's. The ribbon standing out against their skin, twisting them together.

"Seymour," Vanessa says. Her voice is low and discordant, fingernails on a chalkboard, and the buzz from the crystals grates through the room. I clench my teeth and want to clap my hands over my ears, but Davis is holding one hand and the other is waiting for Maren.

"Seymour," Vanessa rasps again. "Your blood pools in this room, where you built your fortune. It is eager, cunning, desperate, and hungry. You're bound by the blood of those who died at your feet."

The pitch of the hum intensifies. My blood is electric in my veins. People died in this house; maybe in this very room. I'm suddenly thinking about Mrs. H and how one hundred years ago—hell, maybe even fifty years ago—she might have ended up in a place like this instead of Evening Bell.

The light rushes to Vanessa, swirling around her so that her face is all at once beautiful and terrible.

"Your secrets are written in blood," she hisses, pulling her hand away from Maren's, yanking the ribbon out from between their entwined fingers. The light rises up, pressing me back, a weight on my chest that makes me gasp for breath. Vanessa raises her hands like a conductor, and the thrumming of the crystals and the pulsing of the light grow and grow until—

Maren weeps on her knees, one hand pressed to her chest while the other cups it protectively. My heart flutters as the tinnitus dies away, leaving the air around me heavy and thick. The room is draped in shadows, flickering shapes cast on the walls by the flames of the candles. The orderly chaos of the circle is gone, and now the crystals and herbs and candles and flowers and ribbons are nothing but a tangled mess with Maren in the middle.

I push through the disorder, crushing a sprig of sage under my heel, and throw my arms around Maren. She falls against me, crying, and holds her hand out to me. Blood drips from her knuckles.

"What did you do?" I hiss at Vanessa, smearing the blood across the back of Maren's hand as I grab it. "You said you could find out where the ledger is!"

"I did," Vanessa says, straightening her ribbon. "It was written in blood." She nods toward Maren's bleeding hand.

I press Maren's hand flat against my knee. Davis and Jay crouch over me as I brush the drops of blood away from her long, slim fingers. The blood seeps out from deep cuts between the first and second knuckles of each finger, letters carved into her skin.

"C, R, Y, P, T," I mutter. "Crypt."

"My family's mausoleum?" Maren asks, sniffing and brushing the tears from her cheeks with her other hand.

"Is William Seymour buried there?" Vanessa asks. Maren nods. "Then that's the first crypt we should check."

Davis curses under his breath and I leap to my feet.

"Of course!" I groan. "Of course his secrets would be buried with him."

Why didn't we think to check there? It's so obvious now, with Maren bleeding at my feet. Regret ripples in the air, passing over my skin like one of Vanessa's charms. I should have thought of looking in the mausoleum.

I could have spared Maren from Vanessa, held her hand tight and safe in mine.

"So how do we get into the mausoleum?" Davis asks Maren. She struggles to her feet. I swallow a knot of relief when I notice that the marks on the back of her hand are already fading away, obscured by the drying blood.

"My mother has a key," she says. "I haven't been inside in years, but sometimes she goes in and lays flowers on my father's crypt."

"Can you get it?" Jay asks. "The key?"

Maren examines her hand, running her fingers over the smooth skin of her knuckles. Her fingers are unblemished again. If I hadn't just seen the word carved in her skin, I never would have believed it. "I know where the key is," she says. "I can get it tonight while my mother is asleep. She'll never know it's gone."

"Tomorrow, then," I say. "Right after school. We'll meet at the cemetery gates."

Maren grits her teeth and nods. The hollows under Jay's eyes grow more pronounced, and Davis bites his lip. Vanessa's the only one who looks unruffled at the thought of going into the Seymour mausoleum.

Seymour House is gritty silver again in the moonlight as we creep back through the window and across the grounds. All the light that Vanessa stole has washed back over the house, leaving pockets of dark, creeping shadows behind doorframes and around corners. I force myself not to look back, not to let myself see what could be hiding among them.

CHAPTER 18
LIGHTS OUT

Jay is waiting at the cemetery gates after school the next day. He trails after us like a shadow, pausing every now and then to examine crumbling, lichen-covered headstones.

The Seymour mausoleum is the same glowing white as Jay's skin. Davis hits the flashlight on his phone, and the five of us stand shoulder to shoulder at the gate as he sweeps the narrow light across the crypts inside.

Growing up as the daughter of the region's preeminent monument stonemason makes the difference between mausoleums, crypts, tombs, and catacombs common knowledge to me. The building itself—in the Seymours' case, a miniature Spanish-style mission with rough-hewn timbers and white stucco—is the mausoleum. Inside, there are separate burial spaces; these are the crypts. Some mausoleums only house one crypt. The Seymour mausoleum looks like it has at least a dozen. Then you have tombs, which are usually openings in rocks or caves, and catacombs, which are like a honeycombed cave filled with bones.

I'm glad there aren't any catacombs in White Haven.

"Can you see anything?" Davis mutters.

"A dead mouse," I say, and it's true: there's a tiny carcass just inside the gate, shriveled and desiccated.

"I mean the ledger."

I peer into the dark. Dead leaves are piled in the corners, and a few white pillar candles weep wax in niches.

Jay raises one long, thin hand, his flesh rippling, pale bones flickering in and out of my eyesight.

"There." He points into the darkness at a narrow space between the stone crypts where Maren's ancestors rest. The corner of a leather book pokes out of the gap. "Next to those—"

His words cut off with a hiss. He drops his hand and balls his fists at his sides. His skin tightens until he's just a skull with yawning, empty eye sockets staring into the mausoleum—staring at a dark figure crouched over the book.

My mouth falls open, trying to scream, but all that comes out is a strangled wheeze. The iron bars under my hands are frosted with delicate lace. My hands go numb from the cold that washes out of the mausoleum. Fear rolls off Jay in waves, creeping with stealthy fingers up my spine and wrapping me in a never-ending embrace. I feel like I'm watching a drop of ink spread through clear water, polluting it, and I'm helpless to stop it. The darkness spreads, and soon it's going to pull me under.

The figure puts out one grasping hand and wraps fingers like creeping tendrils of pale smoke around the corner of the ledger. It makes a noise like dry leaves skittering across a dirt road as it disappears deeper into the gap. The cold wasteland that spread from it lifts just enough for me to jerk away from the gate, leaving my fingerprints seared in the cold metal. Jay stumbles back as well, his skin taut against his skull.

"It's a shade," I say. My voice wavers, and I swallow a lump the size of a peach pit in my throat. "In the mausoleum."

Davis narrows his eyes and peers deeper into the darkness. "I don't see anything. Are you sure?"

Damn right I'm sure. There's no mistaking the bone-chilling cold or the feeling that I'm teetering on the edge of a bottomless pit. I grit my teeth and nod, rubbing my arms to try to bring back some of the day's fading warmth. The sun is already dropping below the horizon, and the trees stand out, black and skeletal, against a blaze of color in the sky. The shadows cast by the other mausoleums are already long. In the maze of the dead, darkness has fallen.

"But what's it doing here?" Davis asks. "Is it the same one that you saw at Seymour House?"

"No," I say. "Shades are trapped here by an obsession with something from their life that wouldn't let them pass through. The one we saw at the asylum probably died there . . . and this one . . ."

"Is my great-grandfather," Maren says in a brittle voice. "He's in there with the ledger. He didn't move on because he didn't want to leave his secrets unguarded." She steps closer to the iron gate, jaw clenched as she looks deeper into the shadows where the shade lurks. If that dark entity really is William Seymour, then Maren is connected to it by blood. That must be why she can see it, when the one at Seymour House was veiled to her eyes.

"He's still thinking about the asylum," Jay says in a hoarse whisper. "Filling it with more bones and blood. It's all he thinks about." He shudders, folding in on himself. "I don't want to go inside. If he sees me, he'll make me go back." His pleading eyes bounce between us. "If I go in there, I don't think I'll be able to come back out."

My stomach twists. As terrifying as I find the shade, I know it must be even worse for Jay. He's facing his greatest tormentor—his worst nightmare. Jay stepping into the mausoleum would be like me stepping into the Nothing.

And there's a part of me that's afraid of what will happen to Jay himself if he gets too close to the shade. The shadow in his eyes rose and twisted when we faced the one at Seymour House. Shades are like black holes: They suck away everything good, leaving you with only the worst parts of yourself, the parts that are like slimy creatures under a stone. And the worst part of Jay is the shadow spreading deep inside his mind. Every time he gets close to a shade, that shadow gets stronger. Confronting the shade of William Seymour might be enough to destroy Jay altogether.

"You don't have to go in," Vanessa says. "Just me and Maren. He'll recognize her as a Seymour and won't realize she's a threat right away. I can't see the shade, but I can manipulate the emotions tied up in the ledger long enough for her to take it."

Maren blanches. The shade at Seymour House didn't seem to affect her, but that was a different shade—different circumstances. This is her great-grandfather, the part of her past that brought so much suffering to the poor of White Haven, the man who is responsible for everything Maren hates about herself. What if the pain and shame that runs through her veins turns out to be too much, and she wades into the darkness to find the ledger and can't find her way back out?

The only thing that saved me at Seymour House was taking Maren's hand—that spark of light that leapt between us.

"And me," I blurt out. "I'll go in with you. I don't think it can hurt us if we're together—holding hands."

"Are you sure?" Maren asks, pulling a strand of hair from her ponytail and wrapping it around her wrist.

"No," I admit. "But that's the only thing that helped me at Seymour House."

"Maybe I should go instead." Davis shifts his feet. "I saw the book when Jay pointed. I can just go in and grab it—"

Vanessa shakes her head. "That won't work. You can't take the book, only Maren can. It's her legacy. And Olive is right. If we hold hands, we'll be fine. She's sensitive to spirits and shades. That can be scary, but it keeps her safe because she knows what to watch out for. You'd be helpless in there. Unable to see to what's happening."

Davis tenses his jaw and nods, stepping back beside Jay.

"Maren, you go in first," Vanessa decides. "A Seymour should be the first one through the gate." She puts her hand on Maren's arm, her lips curved in an earnest smile. "It'll be okay. Olive and I will be right behind you."

My hands, empty and shaking, twist around each other. I'll be right behind her.

Maren lets the hair around her wrist fall away. She's wearing the key on a long silver chain around her neck, and she fishes it out of her sweater and hands it to Vanessa. It's old-fashioned, a skeleton key with the same fancy swirls as the mausoleum gate.

Vanessa puts the key into the lock and turns it.

The gate opens soundlessly. I was expecting it to creak or groan or clang or make some other ghostly noise, but the silence is even worse. It's the way a gate would open in a nightmare.

A breeze from inside the mausoleum lifts Maren's hair off her neck as she steps through the gate. For a split second I'm sure Vanessa is going to slam the gate closed behind her, turn the key, and throw it into the shadows. I'm about to leap forward, heart in my throat, but Vanessa just slips the key into her pocket and reaches for my hand. I give it to her without meeting her eyes, and together we slip through the gate into the damp mausoleum.

A candle flares to life. Vanessa drops my hand and leans over another, left behind from a previous mourner. A flame dances from its wick as well. She picks it up and touches it to the other candles in the mausoleum: set into niches, lining the floors between the crypts, grouped together in the corners. Their flickering light illuminates Maren from below, casting her face into shadow.

Vanessa stands with her back to us, fingers spread

and palms placed flat against one of the crypts. She hums, low in her throat, muttering words under her breath every now and then. *Secrets,* I hear, and *whispers* and *vespers* and *charms. Scarlet* and *violet* and *crystal* and *dreams.* Maren stands in the middle of the narrow aisle, shoulders hunched and shaking. I reach for her, and she jumps when I touch her on the back.

She turns, clasping my reaching hand between both of hers. I wrap my fingers around her palm, anchoring her to me. The air seems to ripple, the hairs on my arms standing up suddenly before settling back down. A wild shriek of laughter builds in my throat and I swallow it, choking on it as I force it down into my chest. Anger flashes through my veins, then despair and fear and grasping—always below everything else—grasping, seeking, searching.

"Maren," Vanessa says in a low, guttural voice. "This is your legacy. Take it."

The shade uncoils itself from the tight space between the crypts. Cold, the kind of cold that makes you gasp for breath and sticks your eyelashes together, sweeps out over us as it straightens up. Its face is a whirlpool of black that seems to suck every bit of light into the swirling vacuum.

The shade crooks one finger at Maren, beckoning. She inches forward, clinging to me with one hand while searching with the other hand for the book. The shade plucks the book from the mists of darkness it wears like a shroud. The book is just like Jay's memory: handsome and bound in leather, the initials *WS* embossed on the cover.

I suck in a breath and hold it tight in my lungs. The ledger. Maren just has to take it from the shade that used to be her great-grandfather, ease the book out of its hands before it realizes—

But as Maren reaches for it, the shade cocks its head at an unnatural angle and draws back. Cold billows out from it, dark clouds that are almost solid. My fingers immediately cramp, and I almost let go of her hand. Gritting my teeth, I squeeze harder, and the darkness recedes just a bit, just enough for me to make out the flickering light of the candles on the stone walls and the human-shaped void that is bearing down on Maren. Her hair whips through the air, a tangled frenzy in snarling wind.

"Take it," Vanessa commands. She's standing in the middle of the cold, dark fury, but her clothes hang still and untouched. The bracelets on her wrists, the bow looped around her neck . . . all motionless, unruffled by the howling wind.

"Take your legacy, Maren. He won't give it freely, but it's yours just the same. Take it. Take it from his hands and his blood."

Maren shrinks back, folding in on herself, her fingers slipping away from mine. And suddenly I know that if she lets go, she'll be devoured by this darkness.

I do it without thinking—tighten my grip on her hand and stiffen my arm to force her back, then step in front of her. A rhythmic beating fills the air, pounding in my veins and rattling the bones in their marble beds. It's a liquid sound: the hot, wet blood of the Seymours coursing through the thinly veined marble of the stone house.

It's a heart, I think. *The Seymours keep their secrets close to their heart.* The walls of the mausoleum bellow in and out as the heart pumps. Blood seeps out of the veins that crisscross the floor and the crypts.

The shade tucks the ledger into its dark shroud and disappears into a crack at the back wall. Blood runs down the walls of the crypts, pooling in the timeworn grooves and names carved into the stone: *William Seymour. Edward Seymour. Maren Seymour.*

I spin on my heel when I see her name, my breath frozen in my lungs. The metallic scent of blood fills the room, cloying and bitter, and the flickering light of the candles turns Maren's hair to blood, streaming down her back, blooming like red flowers on the white lace of her blouse.

Pain cleaves my head and rattles my bones. The darkness invades my mind, shock jolting through my entire frame, grating, gnawing, needling.

There's a voice in my head, and it sounds like Mrs. H. Only this voice is bitter and mocking instead of afraid.

It is Nothing—you're right, Olive. Look at them and see. So much blood and shame and pain and secrets and love carried around for such a short time. And for what? You see how it ends, don't you?

Darkness blooms across my vision, black spots that meet and grow until I can't see anything. Until I see Nothing.

It's dark and cold. I'm alone. There is no stone floor below me, no stone walls around me. My heart thuds erratically and then stops. It grows cold in my chest, like a dead knot of wood. My lungs stop drawing breath; my blood stops flowing. Everything is still. I try to move, but my arms are held in place. By the shade's power over darkness or by my mind or by some betrayal of my body, I'm not sure. All I know is, when I try to reach out for Maren, I find Nothing. I can't touch her, but I also can't *feel* her. There is no sense of the girl I'm falling in love with.

If my heart were still beating, this thought would have stopped it. Falling in love isn't something I do. I'm physically incapable of the kind of vulnerability that love requires.

But I stepped toward the shade for her.

It dawns on me slowly, the way the sun sinks toward the horizon on an autumn evening. Then the night rushes in, and I know that I love her. My body recognized it before my heart did. My feet stepped between Maren and the shade.

My heart flares, one solid thump that sends blood

coursing through my veins. It's not much, but it's enough for the darkness to fade just enough for me to lift my hand and see my fingers still twisted around Maren's. I stretch, trying to step toward her, and this time I can sense her, just on the other side of the darkness. Her hold on me is like an anchor as she reaches for something hidden between the crypts and the wall.

The ledger. She clutches it to her chest and yanks on me, reeling me out of the darkness, away from the shade's power. I can feel my heart gaining strength, even as the darkness threatens to close over me again. The charged air ripples as the shade lets out a noiseless shriek that rattles my bones. The sound is in the air all around me, in the motes of dust that swirl off the crypts, in my clenched teeth and pounding head. The shade rears back, wispy arms clutching at the empty air, the fog that makes it up swirling tighter and tighter until it shrinks down into a squall of fury. Its sound, the one that makes me want to claw out my eyes and bash my head on the wall, grows to a fever pitch.

And then the shade bursts into a kaleidoscope of darkness, a supernova of rage that throws us to the ground.

CHAPTER 19
WORM FOOD

A pair of hands yanks me to my feet none too gently. Davis crushes me against his chest before releasing me so fast that I almost fall back to the ground.

Jay is on his hands and knees, scrabbling under the stone bench for the book. It must have flown out of Maren's hands when the shade knocked us to the ground. Everything spins. I squeeze my eyes closed, willing my muscles to relax. My arms are tight against my sides, and my jaw aches from holding back a scream.

Vanessa stands by the gate, locking it with the skeleton key, her eyes wide and swimming in shock. She reaches out to brush a cobweb from my hair. Her touch is like ice, the cold from the mausoleum and the shade still clinging to her skin.

"Are you okay?" Maren asks, running a finger down my arm; I shiver and loosen at her touch, letting my head loll forward on my neck.

My pulse thrums in my wrist where Maren touched me, reassuring me that we broke free with the ledger that we came for. All the tension in my body leaks away, and I press a hand to the space between my eye and my temple.

I let out a shaky laugh. "Can we please go? I don't want to be here any longer than I have to."

"Where?" Vanessa asks.

I need lots of people, bright lights, music, chocolate—

"Poppy's," I say. "I want a Mexican chocolate malt."

Davis's jaw tightens in a brief grimace, but he glances at me and adds, "And green chile cheese fries."

"Won't people see?" Jay says, running his fingers over

the embossed initials on the cover of the ledger. The gold flake is rubbing off.

I shrug. "See what? Friends looking at an old book? If anyone asks, we can tell them it's something for Junior Reapers that Maren and I are working on."

"A history of the town's cemetery bylaws," Maren says immediately. "How long decorations can be left up after holidays, and the appropriate space left between graves, and—"

"Oh my." Jay holds up his hands in surrender. "You're right. That's terribly dull. Anyone who asks will lose interest in us immediately."

I laugh. I'm still rattled—it feels like the little discs of jelly that pad the joints between my bones are gone, everything grating together when I move—but laughing helps. And I have a feeling that a chocolate shake will, too.

The neon lights are already on when we get to Poppy's, and the parking lot is full. Dinner rush. Poppy's face lights up when Davis walks through the door, and to his credit, he reluctantly smiles back. But even with the owner's son, we still have to wait for a booth, and I can tell Jay is anxious. He keeps fidgeting, patting the ledger to be sure it's still tucked under his arm, his face flickering to bones and back again. Poppy finally points us to a corner booth in the back by the jukebox. Jay lays the book in the center of the table as soon as she takes our order and walks away.

I glance at Maren; her eyes are fixed on her great-grandfather's initials in the bottom corner of the cover.

"Open it," she says. "Just open it. I need to know how deep this goes."

Davis reaches over Jay and flips the cover open. The pages are yellowed, the handwriting old-fashioned and slanting, but each page has a name at the top, followed by a column of numbers and dates and a few short addendums.

Davis turns the pages slowly, looking for Jay's name.

He's two-thirds of the way through the book when he stops.

"Jay Francis Henderson," he reads.

Jay sucks in a sharp breath. "Does it—"

Just then, Poppy comes back with a tray loaded with food. Davis leans over the book to take his burger and green chile cheese fries, and Vanessa passes around the rest of the food. I can't even wait—I'm plucking fries from the greasy paper cone while she's still reaching across the table, dipping them in my Mexican chocolate malt before it's even set in front of me. The fries are crispy on the outside and mealy on the inside, and my tongue burns from the bite of ancho chile pepper in the malt.

"God, Olive, don't forget to breathe," Davis says. I cross my eyes at him and grab another handful of fries. He's not the one who faced a shade earlier tonight.

"Okay," I say around a mouthful of chocolate malt. "Now we find out—now we know."

Davis runs his finger down the column of numbers on Jay's page. There are a few notes written in fading ink here and there, but at the bottom of the page is a longer paragraph.

"*Died October 31, 1914. Front porch. Cause of death: consumption related. Buried November 2 with ten others in gravesite VII, south of the house, marked 137.*"

"Consumption. Goldarn," Jay mutters. "I was run down and left to die in the woods." The skin on his face is tight, the ghost of the bones peeking through. "At least they bothered to give me a number."

My stomach jolts. A number. I grew up playing in my father's workshop, wandering through half-finished projects and examining the custom memorials he carved. Some people went all out when it came to choosing something to mark their loved one's final resting place: lambs and weeping angels and Celtic crosses, shiny slabs of marble engraved with a favorite photograph. It makes me sick to think of Jay's remains decaying under some faded rock, like he was nothing.

"There's no point in looking tonight," Maren says. "It's way too dark to try to find it."

"Tomorrow afternoon?" Vanessa suggests, but Davis shakes his head.

"I can't tomorrow. My dad's making me go to a Wills and Son board meeting."

"And we have Junior Reapers," Maren says.

"Friday, then," I say. The words are already out of my mouth when I realize it's Friday the thirteenth. In October.

Perfect day to help a ghost find his final resting place, right?

CHAPTER 20
KISS OFF

I should be mentally combing the hill behind Seymour House. I should be mulling over every rock I've seen in the woods, mapping a course in my mind for when we go back to look for the grave.

But all I can focus on is Maren.

Mom and Dad were eating dinner when I got home, but I was still stuffed from my French fry feast, so I told them I had to do homework and went up to my room. Now I've been lying on my bed for an hour, staring at the ceiling and trying to understand why it took me this long to recognize how I feel about Maren.

I've never had a girlfriend. Never had a boyfriend, either. And I've never been obsessed with boys or giggly and flirty. Maybe that's how I didn't notice, how I didn't even realize that it's not the boys I'm interested in anyway . . . it's Maren.

I love her passion and intensity. I love that she pushes everyone to be better, even a lost cause like me. I love how she shows her vulnerability every time she reaches for her hair, and I love that she has no idea she does it. She would think it's a weakness, but I know it shows how strong she is. That her insecurities don't hold her back.

Most of all, I love how she makes me feel something again.

My face warms as I think about how she drew her finger down my arm in the mausoleum. I can still feel it, a trail of cold flame from my shoulder to my elbow. I close my eyes and we're standing in the dark together, silver white sparks leaping from our linked hands to our lips.

It's raining when I wake up. The wind gusts over the roof and tears the last remaining leaves from the cottonwood tree in the front yard. Hank the skeleton slouches on a soggy hay bale next to the mailbox, rain running down the long thin bones of his arms. Mom has propped a fishing pole in one of his hands, and he's wearing my old yellow rain boots.

I pull on an oversized black sweater that droops over my hands and jam my feet into a fuzzy pair of socks that barely fit in my combat boots. Mom is leaning over the morning newspaper and eating a piece of peanut butter toast when I get downstairs.

"Raining," she remarks as I reach around her for a bowl of cereal.

"Yep," I say. "Can you drive me to school? I really don't want to swim to class."

Mom looks up, brushing a strand of strawberry-blonde hair off her forehead. It's shot through with veins of silver. "Honey, I'm sorry, I can't drive you. Dad went to work early this morning and took the car."

The rain streams down the window. I already feel clammy. "I'll just walk."

But before I can find a raincoat, a red blur fills the window as a car pulls into the driveway.

Maren Seymour. She never fails to surprise me. I chuckle as she ducks under an umbrella and dashes up the front steps.

I open the door to her raised hand, poised to knock. "What are you doing here?"

"I thought you might need a ride to school. You usually walk, right?"

"Olive? Who's at the door?" Mom pokes her head in the hall. "Oh, do you have a ride? That's so nice of you, Maren.

Thank you."

"Let me just get my stuff." I open the door wider. "Come on in."

Maren shakes her head, the umbrella bobbing with her. "I'll wait out here. I love rain."

I leave the door open a crack in case she changes her mind and stuff my books and computer into my backpack, grabbing a granola bar and an apple for my lunch. Maren is facing away from the house, head tilted back and face turned to the sky, when I open the door.

"Thanks," I say, hesitating in the doorway. She tilts the umbrella slightly back, pulling me under with her. I'm huddled so close against her that I can smell the desert storm on her skin: the sweet and earthy fragrance of the creosote, the clean scent of powder-fine dirt, the sharp, bitter aroma of broken sage. I'm suddenly aware of the whistle of my breath in my lungs. Maren shifts the umbrella into her other hand, her arm brushing against mine, and all the blood pumping through my veins flows toward her.

"Ready?" She doesn't wait for me to answer before pulling me down the steps and through the curtain of rain to her car. Shrieking with laughter, she opens the passenger door for me and pushes me in, then races to the other side of the car. Damp strands of hair cling to the curve of her cheek.

"So yesterday," I say. "It was . . ." My voice trails off as I look at her out of the corner of my eye and try to read the expression on her face. There are circles under her eyes. From reading through the ledger until late into the night? Or from lying awake thinking about me?

"A good thing," she says firmly. "It's time for the truth to come out. Everything looks better in the light."

I shake my head. "You're brave."

"So are you." A sheet of water sprays over my window as she steers the car through an overflowing gutter. "You stepped in front of that shade for me. I don't think anyone else would have done that."

My cheeks go hot, flushing like the clouded windshield. "No big deal."

"Thank you." She slows to a stop at the corner by the school, red from the stoplight blurring the windshield. Her pinkie trails off the gearshift, brushing my hand with a touch like fire. We don't even notice the light shifting to green until there's a chorus of honking from the cars behind us.

Maren yanks her hand away and the car jerks forward. I crack my window to let in a gust of fresh air.

The rain slows as she pulls into a spot at the back of the parking lot, and when I open my door, it's just a fine mist.

"Guess you could have walked after all," Maren says, slinging her backpack over her shoulder and clutching the books that don't fit into it against her chest.

"I like riding with you, Maren."

"I like driving you, Olive."

We stare at each other with the car between us. Maren bites her lip. My stomach swoops in a way that makes me regret eating Count Chocula with chocolate milk for breakfast. I feel it every time Maren looks at me from under those long eyelashes, her green eyes so wide I can see the whole world reflected in them. And when she says my name . . . God. It makes me feel like a marshmallow over a bonfire, all hot and melty.

I open my mouth, but before I can decide if I'm just trying to get enough oxygen to my brain or if I'm actually going to say something, the bell rings. I feel it in my bones, reverberating around the hollow, empty spot in my chest where my heart used to be. It's like an alarm going off right in the middle of the best dream, shocking me out of sleep and back to reality.

Reality: Maren and I have nothing in common, and

when we're done helping Jay, we won't have any reason to spend time together.

Reality: We annoy each other to no end, and not in a quirky-cute rom-com way, but in a way that is completely incompatible with any kind of relationship.

Reality: If I tell her how I feel, she will break my heart.

The echoes of the bell fade as Maren works a tendril of hair free from her braid. "Olive—"

"Gotta go," I squeak, taking off toward the school building. I shoulder my way through the crowd and make a beeline for the nearest bathroom. Inside, a group of cheerleaders are patting their hair dry and passing around a tube of waterproof mascara, but they ignore me as I lean over the sink, gulping water straight from the tap. The chipped porcelain is cold against my cheek. The door swings open, letting in a burst of shouting and laughter and lockers clanging shut, then closes again behind the cheerleaders.

I straighten up and stare at myself in the mirror. My hair stands out in a wild halo around my face, frizzy from the rain. I clutch the sink in both hands, lean toward my reflection—deep purple lips slightly parted, black-rimmed eyes wide—and tell myself not to do anything stupid.

Like fall in love with Maren effing Seymour.

Or fall in love at all.

I stay holed up in the bathroom until the second bell rings and I can be reasonably sure that Maren is in class and I won't have to face her. By the time I poke my head out, the halls are empty.

Dammit. I'm going to be late for math again, and yesterday Ms. Leroy hinted strongly that we would be having a pop quiz today. If I miss another quiz, my parents will have to meet with my counselor about my grades. And while *I* don't really care if I pass eleventh grade math or not, it would be a huge hassle to have to listen to all the same concerned clichés that I've been hearing for two years: *apply yourself,* and *not meeting your potential,* and *Olive, are you paying attention? This is serious.*

I hurry toward the stairs, but before I start to climb, I hear voices arguing in the alcove tucked below. My breath hitches to a stop as I strain to hear what they're saying. Vanessa, murmuring too low for me to catch her specific words; Davis, his voice low and tight with tension. I admit it, I linger on the stairs longer than I should. Long enough to hear Davis growl, "I just don't want to do it, okay?"

The stairs clang like something hit them from below and I jump, scrambling up the last few steps with the ringing reverberating behind me in the stairwell.

He doesn't want to do what? Maybe Vanessa is trying to convince him to go to the Sock Hop. He used to call the kids who went dorks and squares, and believe me, the irony of using fifties slang to make fun of them was utterly lost on him.

Ms. Leroy is already handing out sheets of paper when I get to class. She purses her lips at me and points at my seat.

"I shouldn't let you take this quiz," she says. "But since we haven't started yet, I suppose you made it just in time."

I'm too distracted by what I heard to be relieved. I thought Davis would do pretty much anything Vanessa wanted him to—he followed her to my lunch table, after all. And that was before I even knew she's an empath.

But he's definitely pushing back against something.

With the Sock Hop in less than three weeks, Ms. Hunter's productivity levels are in overdrive at our Junior Reapers meeting after school. She starts handing out assignments: go to city hall to ask about stringing lights for the dance, meet with the geriatric swing dance team to discuss their performance, order black-and-white checked paper straws for the milkshakes.

"Olive, you help Maren sort the records she collected from residents of Evening Bell," she finishes, before scurrying away to break up a fight between two members of the decorations committee over black versus purple balloons.

My stomach is a knot of snakes as I cross the room to where Maren crouches next to a cardboard box stuffed with vinyl records in paper sleeves. She heaves the box into her arms, trying to lift it to the folding table, but the box bulges, the flaps threatening to open and spill the records across the floor. I dart the last few feet and help her hoist it onto the table before it breaks apart.

For a few seconds, it's like that moment under the umbrella at my house this morning. My heart forgets that it's cold and dead, and it skips a beat when our eyes meet. Then I manage to drag my gaze away from her, praying to Edgar Allan Poe himself that she can't see all these new *feeling*s slapped across my face.

Maren clears her throat. "So I haven't ever seen you at the Sock Hop before."

"That's because I've never gone." I slide a record out of its paper sleeve and pretend to examine it for scratches, while in reality I'm trying to catch my breath. Maren's presence alone is enough to knock me off balance and send me spiraling.

"Yeah, I didn't think so." I can feel rather than see her on the other side of the box, pulling out an armful of records and settling on the floor. "I know you think you're too cool for it, but it's actually really fun. There's always good food, and everyone just dances together in a big group. Of course, you can go with a date if you want."

I look up and catch her smiling and biting the corner of her lip. It's not the normal hard smile she pastes on her face when she's bossing everyone around at school; this smile looks like she's asleep and dreaming.

"Oh yeah?" I ask, suddenly knowing that she could undo me with one question.

But she doesn't ask. Instead she just nods and bends over the records, her hair swinging forward over her face like a curtain. I force myself to think of the sheet the nurses pulled over Mrs. H's face after she died. I thought my heart would stop beating when she disappeared under that dingy white sheet. The fact that my lungs still pumped air in and out, my blood still raced through my veins, and my brain still fired electrical impulses to my fingers and toes was a cruel joke.

I swallowed my love like a bitter pill and tucked it deep inside a secret place in my heart, safe behind bars made of bone and guarded by blood.

But now my defenses are splintering before Maren, and I can feel my heart struggling to break free.

CHAPTER 21
FADING FAST

The sky on Friday morning is fragile blue wreathed in gold—the kind of blue that looks like it will crack in the wind. The skeletal branches of the cottonwood tree, bare after yesterday's rain, scrape the sky like fingers clawing at the silk lining of a coffin.

Today's the day we're going to look for Jay's grave. If it were up to me, we would blow off school and go straight to the woods. But when I suggested that, Maren looked at me like I was blaspheming the dead, so after school it is.

But as soon as I get to school, I realize that nothing will go according to plan today.

The overhead speaker crackles to life after the first bell rings. "All students please report to the auditorium for an assembly before continuing to class."

I catch up with Vanessa and Davis by the auditorium doors. Davis's eyes are bloodshot and puffy, like he's been drinking. But he's never been much of a partygoer.

I bite my lip, trying to catch his eye. A pit in my stomach grows, a feeling that something isn't right with Davis. What were he and Vanessa arguing about yesterday?

Yesterday . . . the Wills and Son board meeting. My heart sinks as I realize that I didn't ask how it went. I should have texted him, maybe even gone over to his house after dinner to check on him. But with everything going on with Maren, I completely forgot.

"You okay?" I mutter out of the corner of my mouth. "How did things go yesterday with your dad?"

Vanessa slips her hand into his and frown-smiles at me, like she'll be the supportive girlfriend and let him tell me, but she really doesn't think it's any of my business. My temples twinge with irritation, but I clench my teeth and ignore her.

"Fine," Davis mumbles. "My dad created a new internship for me. It starts after Christmas and goes through graduation. Twenty hours a week during the school year, then forty hours a week all summer long. The board approved it at the meeting."

I draw in a sharp breath. "But what about spending the summer with your grandparents? And working on your bus?" That must have been what he meant when I overheard him saying he didn't want to do it. He and Vanessa weren't arguing after all—Davis was just upset about his dad trying to force more responsibility on him instead of asking what *he* wants.

And now Davis will be stuck working at Wills and Son instead of preparing to leave town the second he gets a chance.

"We're going to try and work something out so we can still go on the trip Davis is planning," Vanessa says, squeezing Davis's hand and steering him into the auditorium.

The words feel like a pinch on the back of my arm, that spot where you can really dig in and leave a bruise. I haven't given too much thought to going with Davis on his road trip, but it's been in the back of my mind ever since he suggested it. Vague pictures keep forming in my head: sitting on the roof of his bus and watching the stars come out over Monument Valley, the desert sky so big and full of light that it drives away all my fears of the Nothing.

That moment could never happen with Vanessa there.

Maren joins us as we follow the shuffling crowd, shooting me a quick smile that I barely see through swelling anger. It's not that I'm jealous of Vanessa; I don't want to *be* with Davis. Not like that. But one thing is clear by the way she's gripping his arm: Vanessa wants me to see that

Davis belongs to her. Not me.

The four of us sit down together in a row of moth-eaten seats. Principal Tsinnajinnie stands on the stage flanked by two police officers.

"What do you think this is about?" Vanessa asks.

I shrug, but my stomach is twisted in knots. I have a bad feeling about this.

Principal Tsinnajinnie waits for everyone to settle down before stepping up to the microphone. It whines with sudden feedback, and she fumbles with her phone before speaking. "Thank you, students, for being so orderly this morning. I apologize for interrupting your school day, but we have a serious matter to discuss. As some of you may know, two of your peers were attacked in the woods last night."

My stomach drops and I have to close my eyes to stop the world from spinning. *Another* attack on Scary Road? I flash back to the dark holes of Jay's eyes, and the memory seems to open up and swallow me whole.

"This is the third such attack on White Haven students in the last few weeks. While the first one ended up being relatively harmless, this attack was much more serious. The students involved were both injured, and one of them may not return to school for several weeks." Principal Tsinnajinnie frowns, gripping the microphone. "Officer Dawes and Officer Hodson from the White Haven police department are here to talk to us about the severity of this situation." She motions to the police officers and takes a step back.

"Thank you, Ms. T. I'll keep this brief." The police officer who speaks is shorter than the principal, and he keeps breathing directly into the microphone. It's the same sound from Minnie's video. "If anyone has any serious information about this attack, we invite you to come forward. What may have been intended as a joke has had serious consequences, and the White Haven police department is taking it—er, seriously," he finishes lamely.

His partner leans over to speak. "This is also a good reminder that the woods surrounding Seymour House are private property and trespassers will be prosecuted. There will be extra patrols in the area while we investigate this crime." She presses her lips into a tight line and surveys us, as if expecting the culprit to leap to their feet and confess.

The crowd buzzes as Principal Tsinnajinnie dismisses us to go to class. I catch snatches of gossip from every direction as we file out of the auditorium.

"Mikey's shoulder is broken, he'll never play football again—"

"My little sister is friends with Ava's brother, and he said she's in the hospital—"

"Yeah, she wouldn't stop screaming and the doctor had to sedate her—"

"They should have stayed out of the woods." Vanessa swallows hard and rubs the ends of her black velvet ribbon between her fingers. "After what happened to the others."

"You can't blame the victims," I protest. We draw to a stop outside the auditorium doors, forming a huddle by the trophy cases. "Nothing like this has ever happened before."

"I'm not blaming the victims, but it's clear that Scary Road is dangerous now," Vanessa says. She sets her jaw and takes a deep breath. "Now that Jay is turning into a shade."

"So we have to find the grave," Maren says. Her long hair fans over her shoulders and she brushes it out of her face, her expression hard. "That's the only thing that will stop the attacks."

"The woods are bound to be crawling with cops," Davis says. His voice is rusty, like he's been shouting. I look at him in concern, but he won't meet my eye. "There's no way they're going to let a bunch of kids into a crime scene."

"But we have to talk to Jay anyway, let him know why

we can't look for the grave today," I say. "Maybe he can tell us what happened, or we can figure out a way to keep him from attacking anyone else."

"Then it's settled," Maren says. "We'll go out there after school, just like we planned."

Davis is right; Scary Road *is* crawling with cops. Maren slows down as the main road curves toward where Scary Road breaks off the highway and winds into the woods. The Desert Heights billboard stands sentinel over the clearing—and half a dozen police cars parked in a semicircle. The red convertible rolls to a stop, lingering long enough for us to scan the woods for Jay. I catch sight of his pale shape just inside the tree line right when one of the cop cars' sirens chirps at us, warning us to keep going. I raise my hand, pointing up the road, in what I hope looks like an apologetic gesture to the police but still gets my message across to Jay: *Follow us.*

Maren presses on the gas, and the red convertible purrs as we pass Scary Road and twist higher into the mountains. She pulls onto a wide, dusty shoulder around the bend, and we all climb out to wait in the purple brush that lines the road.

The sun breaks through a bank of clouds and illuminates Jay like a shaft of moonlight. He stands in the middle of the road, his form wavering in the light. He takes a few steps toward us, but keeps his head bowed, his wispy blond hair a shining silver cap.

"What's going on?" he asks, bemused. He half turns, facing away from us. "There are policemen in the woods."

"Change of plans," Maren says, all business. "We can't look for your grave today. Something happened at Scary Road last night."

"Kids from school were attacked there," Vanessa says.

"Again," Davis adds in a mutter.

"Was it you?" I say bluntly. I shiver as a gust of wind lifts the hairs on the back of my neck. What have I unleashed on White Haven? Jay may be the one turning into a shade, but I'm as responsible for those attacks as if I had cracked Mikey's shoulder myself. The only way to make up for that is to ensure Jay moves on before he has a chance to attack someone else.

"I don't know," Jay mutters, still looking down so that his hair falls like a shroud over his face.

"What do you mean, you don't know?"

"I mean I can't remember everything. Sometimes when I'm not with you, I'm in the woods, looking for my grave. But sometimes things are . . . dark. I don't know where I go when that happens. The dead don't mark the years the way the living do, in heartbeats and breaths, but time is running out for me."

He shakes back the shock of hair that droops over his forehead and reveals his face to us.

Poison leaks from the corners of his eyes like oily black tears. The shadow bleeds from those black holes in his moon-white face. Delicate branches trace across his temples and disappear under his hair.

The shadow is spreading.

My stomach rolls. I can feel my chest caving in, a hollow dead lump in place of my heart. It's like the shade is spreading from Jay to me, and soon I'll be consumed by it.

"Shit," Maren says.

"So we have to find the grave as soon as possible," Davis says. "Police be damned. They'll be hanging around tonight and tomorrow night, keeping kids out of the woods, but if we get up early tomorrow, no one will be around. We'll meet at Scary Road just after sunup."

CHAPTER 22
SIX FEET UNDER

the next morning, there's a knot in my stomach that's all twisted up in the question that brought me to this point:

What happens after you die?

Now I'm sure there are two possibilities after death—the Nothing and becoming a shade—but is there something else? If we find Jay's grave today and he's able to "move on," what will that mean? Will we be sentencing him to an eternity of darkness when he sinks into the Nothing, or is there something else on the other side, a place where his mother is waiting for him?

I keep going back to Mrs. H's last word: *Mom.* For nine months, it's been a lighthouse in the dark sea of my life, giving me hope when memories of the Nothing threatened to drown me.

Jay is standing by the gate when Davis pulls up to Seymour House, his corn silk hair flapping across his face in the wind. I force myself to follow Maren past the house and into the woods.

The leaves are piled knee deep, and instead of crunching underfoot as we walk, they ooze like half-rotted sludge. Branches smack me in the face, and I have to stop twice to free my hair from thorn bushes. I sense voices all around us, whispering and following us as we wander. Calling to Jay? Guiding his way to the grave he wandered away from so long ago?

"Do you recognize anything?" I ask him.

He stops to look around, then shakes his head and presses deeper into the woods.

After a few minutes, we come to a clearing. The border is too defined for it to be natural, and there are stones here and there among the leaves and bushes and along the tree line.

I can just see Seymour House through the trees. Jay crouches down to look at the rocks that line the circle; Vanessa walks into the center and looks up.

"There's something here," Maren says, tapping a birch tree. She's clutching the ledger, one finger marking the page with Jay's records. We crowd around her, and she scuffs her sleeve over a mark carved deep in the white bark of the tree:

I

The edges are smooth and dark against the papery bark; it's been here a long time.

"I?" Vanessa says. Maren shakes her head.

"Not I; *one*. Look, in the ledger—" She lets the ledger fall open. "*VII*—gravesite seven. They used Roman numerals to number the gravesites."

"So this clearing," I say. "It's gravesite one."

Maren nods and snaps the ledger closed. "And all those rocks scattered around"—she motions at the clearing—"must mark the individual graves. Or they did at one point."

"One down, six to go," Davis says. "Come on." He tromps back into the woods.

Now that we know what we're looking for, it's not hard to find the other gravesites. They're all marked by a Roman numeral carved on a white birch tree and rocks lining the edge of the clearing. It only takes us another hour to find the tree marked VII.

Jay runs his fingers over the number and steps into the clearing. The ground is slightly sunken in places.

"Is this it?" I ask. "Is this where you . . . er . . . woke up?"

Jay closes his eyes. A breeze rattles through the trees, and a few leaves still clinging to their branches drift down before getting caught in the wind. They swirl around the edge of the circle. I don't realize what Jay is doing until it's already happening.

Leaves and sticks and brush spin around us, a whirlwind of the woods, and a roaring, rushing sound fills the air. I open my mouth to shout but nothing comes out. It's like the wind has snatched my voice. And now something else swirls in the tangle around us: the clacking of bones.

The whirlwind stops, and everything falls to the ground, but the clearing is different now. The trees are younger, closer together, and the edges of the clearing are ragged and less uniform. There's a pile of rocks next to me in the center. Something lumbers toward us through the underbrush. I can see Maren out of the corner of my eye, deathly still as two figures break through the trees.

A man and a woman in old-fashioned clothes. They're wispy and shadowy, their outlines blurring slightly as they move. The woman weeps, clutching her elbows like she's trying to hold herself together. The man carries a limp shape wrapped in canvas slung over his shoulders.

"Edward," the woman whispers. Her voice is muffled by time. "Let's go back. Please."

Edward leans forward and lets the bundle of canvas fall from his shoulders. A hand spills out. I stumble back, yelping.

"I have to dispose of this first. You go back, Mina. It will be better if my father doesn't see us together." Edward grabs a shovel from where it's leaning against a tree and begins to dig. The hand emerging from the canvas twitches, and the woman gasps.

"He moved," she says. "He's still alive. Edward, he's alive!"

"Not for long," Edward mutters. He seizes the end of the shroud and pulls it into the shallow hole. The canvas catches on a root, bunching so that Jay's face is visible. His wispy blond hair stands out against the black dirt. He struggles to sit up, and red blooms bright against his torn shirt, a rivulet seeping out of his nose and coating his chin. I hear the death rattle in his chest as a bubble of blood forms at the corner of his mouth. Edward shoves him down, wrapping the canvas tight over Jay's face.

Mina is frozen in place, tears streaming down her heart-shaped face. She lets out a soft cry as Jay screams, the sound muffled against his canvas shroud.

"Help me, you dirty little gold-digger," Edward snarls. Mina falls forward on her knees, sweeping armfuls of dirt and rock onto the flailing figure as Edward holds him down. Finally, Jay stills. Edward's and Mina's figures disappear, and the clearing snaps back into focus. The trees tower over us once more, the stones line the edge, and the ground is pockmarked with the hollows of a dozen graves.

My breath comes in short gasps, wheezing through a stitch in my chest. I gag on the phantom taste of dirt and grit pouring down my throat and filling my lungs like it did to Jay all those years ago. He'd told us what he remembered about his death, but seeing it hits differently. How can Maren be related to that monster?

I sneak a glance at her. Her mouth is twisted in a grimace, but she stands ramrod straight, staring at Jay.

"This is it," he says.

"No shit," Davis says wryly. Vanessa gives a little moan, pressing her trembling hands against her mouth to muffle the sound. Her nose is wrinkled in disgust at what we just saw. "But we still have to find the actual grave. 137, right?"

We all bend down, shuffling through the leaves and peering at the stones dotted around the clearing. The paint is faded, and the rocks are half-buried in mud or missing altogether.

"You know that expression—someone walked over my grave?" I call out. "Jay, let us know if you start shivering for no reason."

"Haha," he says, but I wasn't joking.

"I think I found it. Oh, wait—" Davis holds up a fist-sized rock. "This lichen looked like a seven, but I think it's really a one."

My eyes leap from stone to stone—129, 140, 133—and my hands shake. I'm starting to worry that 137 is long gone when I trip over something and fall to my knees.

I can see Jay look up out of the corner of my eye as soon as I pick up the rock. It's smooth and round on one side, rough and chipped on the other, like something broke it in half. But under the gray-green lichen that covers everything out here, I can make out a number in fading white paint: 137.

My palms are slick with sweat, and my heart leaps inside my chest. This is all there is to mark Jay's final resting place. This, and the paragraph scrawled in the ledger, are all that is left to prove that Jay really lived, that he was here, that he deserved more than a few short years of misery and an eternity of being forgotten. For now, the only people who hold memories of Jay are me, Maren, Davis, and Vanessa, and someday we'll die, and those memories will disappear and Jay will cease to exist.

"You found it," Jay says over my shoulder, and I jump, dropping the rock. It narrowly misses my toes. "Was it right here?"

I nod, pulling aside a tangle of vines and leaves. Davis, Maren, and Vanessa gather around us as I work. Finally, I rock back on my heels over a rectangle of hard-packed dirt: Jay's grave.

"Now what?" I ask, looking up at him. For a split second, I can see the blood that coated his face and chest when he died like an afterimage on the back of my eyelids.

"I guess I, uh—" He crawls into the center of the grave and lies down, clasping his hands over his chest.

This is it. This is what I've been searching for. My heart races as I stare down at Jay's opaque figure, waiting for his face to change the way Mrs. H's did when she died. My eyes water, but I force myself not to blink. I don't want to miss it. Maybe if I focus hard enough, I'll be able to catch a glimpse of the other side when Jay goes.

Darkness or light? Will he drift into the Nothing that I floated in during my brush with death, or is there something more?

Nothing happens.

The threads of black that twist from the corners of Jay's eyes pulse slightly in the breeze, but they aren't knitting together into a shroud of darkness. He isn't turning into a shade, but he isn't moving on to the Nothing, either.

I finally clear my throat. I can't wait anymore.

Jay opens one eye. "What, Olive?"

"Sorry, not to interrupt, but I was just wondering if you see anything. Like a light at the end of a tunnel, or like—" My voice catches in my throat as I remember being caught in the Nothing. "Like darkness?"

Jay sits up and buries his face in his hands. "This isn't working."

"Maybe it's not the right grave," Davis says, striding off through the underbrush and digging through the mound of stones we've already uncovered. "Maybe you should try in another spot."

"No, this is the right one," Jay says. "I felt it when Olive found the stone. It was like she said, like someone walking over my grave. I could feel it in my bones."

My heart shrinks until it feels like the shriveled rubber plant I never remember to water. After everything I've done to free Jay's spirit—sucking Maren into this whole mess, going to Seymour House for Vanessa to read its energy, and confronting the mausoleum and its terrifying truths—what went wrong?

"Um—I have an idea. Of why it isn't working," Vanessa offers. She bites her lip, eyes darting toward Maren and then away like she wishes she didn't have to say this in front of her. "Jay, you say that you want to move on. But maybe the way to do that isn't by trying to be at peace. Maybe it's by taking revenge."

"Revenge?" Jay's brow draws down until his face is a skull, shining white bone in the dim light under the trees.

"On Maren."

CHAPTER 23
ERASED

Maren sucks in a sharp breath as I step forward, blocking her from Vanessa. My hands twist into fists, tight so that my rings chatter against each other and my nails dig into the soft skin of my palms. Jay stands shoulder to shoulder with me, and Davis's gaze flicks between us and Vanessa.

"What did you say?" I hiss. A knife twists in my heart, painting the edges of the world in a red mist. I can sense Maren's quick, shallow breath behind me. Whatever Vanessa says, I won't let Maren pay for what her family did.

Vanessa grimaces at the danger in my voice and reaches to tug at her ribbon with trembling fingers. Her eyes catch on mine, wide and pleading.

"It's just that, Maren is the last surviving member of the Seymour bloodline. She's the last one responsible for what happened to all of these people." Vanessa sweeps her hand over the clearing. "It's not fair at all, and I know Maren didn't choose it, but she's benefited her whole life from what her family did." Her voice speeds up, tripping to stay ahead of my arguments. "She needs to lose everything, just like the people who died at the asylum did. Jay needs to expose the truth about the Seymours if he wants to move on."

"I don't think—" I start to say, but Maren elbows her way past me.

"She's right. I have to make things right for you and the others." Jay's eyes are bottomless-pit black, but Maren holds his gaze. "And that can't happen until everyone in White Haven knows what my family really did here."

"Pictures," she says, yanking her phone from her back pocket. She starts taking shots of the tree with *VII* carved on it, the cluster of rocks with their fading numbers, the odd uniformity of the clearing. "We'll take pictures of the gravesites and bring some of the rocks to show the mayor."

"That won't be enough," Davis says grimly. He hesitates over Jay's grave, then lumbers away to one on the other side of the clearing. There, he finds a sharp, pointed tree limb.

It takes me half a heartbeat to understand what he means. When I do, the bile rises in my throat so quickly that I barely manage to duck behind a bush before losing everything in my stomach. I rub at my mouth, my shoulders heaving as Davis stabs the limb into the ground. This isn't what I meant to happen—disturbing the graves, waking the dead. My legs itch to turn and race through the woods to get away from what we're about to do. The only thing that stops me from running is Maren standing frozen, her phone still pointed at the pile of rocks. I got her into this; I can't leave her here.

Vanessa crosses the clearing to help Davis dig.

"He's right," she calls over her shoulder. "We need to make sure there are really human remains here."

Maren moves first, pushing past me and sinking to her knees next to Davis. I force myself to follow as she plunges her hands into the ground.

The dirt is fine and powdery, ochre dust that clings to my skin. Maren's red nails break almost immediately, leaving jagged stubs that crack and bleed with every handful of earth she scoops out. The ground is hard and full of rocks. Every time my hand brushes against a hard, unyielding curve, my pulse throbs in my temples. Time stands still as I scrape the dirt off, revealing nothing more than tree roots. Then the clock resets, and we keep digging.

It takes us over an hour to make a hole eighteen inches

deep. I keep gagging on the dust that coats the inside of my throat. When Davis uncovers the splintered end of something long and thin, everyone falls silent. Even the birds stop singing, and the leaves go still. A sense of reverence falls in the clearing, like we're in a church. And maybe in a way we are. Maybe for the people buried in these woods, these trees are a kind of cathedral, and this dirt is hallowed ground.

"Now what?" Davis asks, gulping air like he's drowning.

Maren's nostrils flare. "We go straight to the mayor, the police, the governor, and the fucking president if we have to."

After we leave the woods, Maren calls the mayor and demands that she meet us at city hall. Luckily, as president of Junior Reapers, Maren has enough credibility that Mayor Perez is waiting for us when we get back. She has a bemused expression on her face when we troop into city hall, shedding dry leaves and tracking mud across the marble floors.

Mayor Perez blanches when Maren tells her that we found human remains in the woods behind Seymour House. Maren pulls the ledger out of her bag, slaps it down on the mayor's desk, and explains how she started reading the ledger when she was curious about family history, and how she started to wonder if the burial records were accurate. Mayor Perez flutters a hand over her heart, refusing to look at the pictures on Maren's phone of the bones in their shallow hole. Her hand shakes as she calls the police department, and she stumbles over her words as she paces around the echoing room. I can tell that she had no idea about the unmarked graves.

Maren's mom and Mr. Wills show up around the same

time as the first detective. Mayor Perez must have called them as well, because none of us did. I guess that makes sense, considering the Seymours and Wills are two of her biggest campaign donors and she's up for re-election. Maybe that's the real reason she was so upset when we told her about the burial grounds. It doesn't exactly look good for her campaign to be funded by blood money.

Mr. Wills has a grim look on his face that he rearranges into a mask of concern. I wonder how much of his worry is for Davis, finding unmarked graves in the woods, and how much is for the hit that Desert Heights is sure to take.

"It must have been terrible for you kids to find this," Mr. Wills says. "I wish you had called me right away, Davis. I could have helped you know what to do."

Davis makes a noncommittal noise in his throat without meeting his father's eyes. He can't exactly say what we're all thinking: that we didn't trust him to take the bones to the police.

"Thanks for bringing this to our attention," Mrs. Seymour says. "We'll take care of it from here." She puts a hand on Mr. Wills's shoulder, steering him back to the mayor.

"Do you think she knew?" I asked Maren in a low voice. "About the graves?"

Maren watches her mother guide Mr. Wills back to the mayor. Mrs. Seymour looks like an older version of her daughter. They have the same sun-kissed skin and long, straight noses. They even wear the same shade of bloodred lipstick.

"Probably not," Maren says. "If she had known, she would have had the remains moved a long time ago instead of risking them being found like this. She'll do anything she can to try and make the Seymours look like a respectable family. Speaking of . . ." She slides the ledger off the mayor's desk and back into her bag, shuddering. "This thing gives me the creeps, but I'm worried it will get 'lost' if I don't keep it."

"Let me take it," I offer. "I can hold on to it for you. Until things are settled."

"Really?" Maren's face sags in relief, and she fishes the leather-bound book out of her bag, handing it to me before I can change my mind. "Thanks, Olive. I really appreciate it."

"No problem." I hold the book by one corner and pretend it doesn't make my skin crawl to touch it. I'm already kicking myself for offering to take it. I must be hoping Maren will dream about me instead.

CHAPTER 24
LONG WALK OFF
A SHORT PIER

I lie awake half of Sunday night, worrying how everyone at school will react now that the Seymour family secrets are laid bare. By some miracle of fate, I get to school on Monday before Maren does. So I'm the one to see BLOODY MARY spray-painted across her locker in dripping letters.

Is this the revenge that Vanessa meant? To shame Maren, pull her down from the throne she built for herself out of A+ papers, awards, and volunteer logs?

A month ago, I would have been snickering with everyone else to see Maren effing Seymour humiliated like this. I would have gotten the same thrill to see her brought low. Serves her right for being so insufferable, for thinking that she's better than everyone.

But now I know that Maren doesn't think she's better than everyone—she thinks she's a monster because of her family. And isn't that revenge enough?

I grab a bucket of soapy water and a sponge from the custodial closet. Maren is standing at her locker when I get back.

"You okay?" I mutter, dropping the bucket to the floor so that suds splash out onto my shoes.

Maren's back is ramrod straight as she takes in the spray-painted words. She lets out a harsh bark of laughter. "Everyone hates me."

"Screw them." I roll up my sleeves and plunge the sponge into the bucket of water.

On Tuesday, someone passes out those little plastic capsules of blood you can buy at Halloween stores, and when Maren walks down the hall, she's greeted by bloody smiles everywhere she looks.

At the end of school on Wednesday, Maren's car is covered in tampons that have been dipped in red dye and corn syrup, like horror movie blood. The fake blood drips down the sides and puddles under the car and leaves a trail when she drives out of the parking lot.

On Thursday, the halls are papered in crude drawings of a stick figure with dripping red hair. They're covered in scrawled insults: SICKMOUR and DEAD BODIES NEVER HURT ANYONE and NECROPHILIAC.

By Friday morning, Maren is a wreck. Her eyes are flat, and her lips are colorless, washed out against the gray of her skin. I'm half expecting someone to dump a bucket of pig's blood on her.

And the worst part?

It didn't even work.

Jay is still here. His eyes are chips of onyx, his face spiderwebbed by fine veins of shadow that swirl beneath his skin. He's gone back to his grave every day this week, but nothing has happened. The curtain between this world and the next is drawn tight.

With every failed attempt, Maren's eyes have sunk deeper and deeper into her skull like a corpse's. I don't think she regrets revealing the truth about her family—Maren is the most sincere person I know, and she genuinely wants to make up for what her family did to Jay and the other people who died at Seymour House—but it's hard to feel like it was worth it when Jay is still skulking around town, the shadow metastasizing and spreading.

As for me, I would be lying if I said the thought hasn't crossed my mind that the reason Jay can't move on is because there's nothing to move on *to*.

Maybe the Nothing is made up of shades just like what Jay is becoming. Those of us who aren't held back by unfinished business in life are consumed by those who were. And when the shade takes hold of Jay, I'll know that he's become a part of the Nothing that's waiting for me after death.

I'm lost in these dark thoughts at lunch on Friday. My granola bar is just a pile of oats and chocolate chips on the wrapper in front of me. Davis eats his cardboard nachos mechanically, chewing and swallowing without even looking at them. There's no sign of Maren in the sea of faces around us; she's been hiding in the office whenever she's not in class.

"It's not that bad," Vanessa says. "So Jay is still stuck here. At least everyone knows the whole truth about the Seymours now. Maybe that will bring peace to some of the souls that suffered at their hands."

"Yeah, but . . ." I try to swallow a chunk of granola bar, but my throat is so dry that I have to force it down. "The point of revealing the burial ground was so that Jay could move on. Now he'll be stuck here as a shade forever, attacking anyone who goes into the woods."

Davis stirs, his eyes tracking Vanessa as she takes a sip from her can of Peace Tea. "You think there will be more attacks?"

Vanessa makes a face and puts her can down. "It seems like it, doesn't it? No one is taking these attacks seriously. As long as people go into the woods, there will be attacks." She seems more bothered by the idea of more attacks than by the fact that Jay—someone she knows, someone she's helped—will be the one lurking in the woods like a shadow.

Maybe it doesn't bother her because it's not her fault, but I don't have that luxury. My throat thickens as I remember the way the shadow rose in his eyes. I spend the rest of the afternoon cringing at the memories of my ridiculous rituals, my clumsy communion with the dead, my make-believe spell work. Summoning a spirit without knowing exactly what I was doing was clearly a mistake; I don't know why I thought I would be able to find a way to free him on my own.

I'm halfway home after school when I finally admit to myself that I need someone who knows what they're doing. And despite Vanessa's claims that she's not a witch, I have a hard time believing it. I saw the light flow to her hands and wreath her face at Seymour House; I felt the white-hot snap in the air as she read the asylum's energy.

I need to tell Vanessa everything. Not just the vague explanation I gave everyone when I convinced them to help Jay find his grave; I need to tell her about the candle, the salt, and the locket. The words I spoke. Maybe it's not too late; maybe she knows a way to undo what I've done, to cut through the snarled web I've trapped Jay in.

My stomach twists at the thought of going to her for help. I can already see the expression on her face. That smug smile as she listens to me admit that I need her. The way she'll draw out her answer, making me wait, making me beg. How she'll hold this over my head until I give her something she wants.

I slow to a stop, closing my eyes and huffing out a breath. Asking Vanessa for help is the last thing I want to do, but I can't think of anything else that might fix this.

So I turn on my heel and head back across town to the tree-lined street where she lives.

When I get there, the wind rattles through the sycamore tree that looks over the house. Three knotholes mar the papery white bark: two yawning eyes and a mouth open in a silent scream.

I lift the hand-shaped door knocker and rap on the heavy wooden door, but there's no sound of movement from inside the house. I shift my weight from one foot to the other and remind myself to breathe.

Still no answer.

"Come on, Vanessa," I moan, banging on the door again.

It clicks and falls open, creaking like a lid sliding off a sarcophagus. I blink as dust rises out of the house.

"Vanessa?" I call into the gloom. "It's Olive."

There's a thud from the end of the hall and a rumble of voices, low and electric like the air before a storm. Vanessa's rises out of the argument: "Come on in, Olive. I'm in the kitchen."

Foreboding clings to my skin like spiderwebs as I step through the door. Weak sunlight casts shadows on the walls: grasping, reaching hands. Like the shade that drummed its fingers on the doorframe at Seymour House. I creep down the hall, freezing against the wall when I hear Davis curse under his breath.

"We're not done, V," he says from the kitchen.

"Yes, we are." Vanessa's voice is cool, almost bored, but then she gasps—a sharp inhale of breath. "You shouldn't have done that."

My eyebrows draw together, and I rush to the doorway at the end of the hall. Davis is braced against the back door, nostrils flared, hands jammed into his pockets. Vanessa's standing on the other side of the room. Her hands are at her neck, but instead of fidgeting with her ribbon like I've seen her do so many times before, she's tying it, hands jerking as she loops it into a bow.

Tying it, like Davis grabbed at its trailing ends and yanked it loose.

My eyes dart back and forth between Davis and Vanessa. What have I walked into?

A ripple of shame flashes over Davis's face when he sees me in the doorway. He looks like my dad when I caught him smoking after he'd promised to quit. Like Vanessa is bad for him and he knows it, but she lingers like secondhand smoke whenever he tries to escape her.

Davis presses his thumb and forefinger to his temples like he has a headache.

"You know what? You're right, Vanessa." His mouth twists in a grimace. "We *are* done. For good." He jerks the back door open and disappears through it, slamming it hard enough to rattle the glass.

Vanessa blinks at Davis's retreating shadow, then gasps and sinks into a chair at the table, her face crumpling.

"Oh my God." I dart across the room and hover next to her, not sure what to do. Should I hug her? Rub her back? Curse Davis and all boys and pour her a shot? I settle for patting her on the shoulder once or twice. "Are you okay?"

"I'm sorry." She looks up at me through eyes swimming with tears. "I'm so embarrassed that you saw that."

I pull out the chair next to her, wincing as it screeches across the floor. "What happened?"

Vanessa gives a bitter laugh, shaking her head.

"We had a fight. It started out so stupid." She buries her face in her hands so her voice comes out muffled. "He asked why I never wear the bracelets he bought me at his mom's diner. I told him that they're not my style, I'd just commented on them that night to break the tension between him and his mom. And then it turned into this big thing about me not respecting him. I don't even know how!" She peeks up at me from between her fingers. "I swear that I never meant for him to feel like that."

"Of course not," I say, but it's a rote response. I remember Vanessa explaining how she can read energy and change how people perceive things. Manipulate emotions. Twist reactions until she controls how people feel.

There's a pit in my stomach as I wonder how often she's been in my head. Did she understand my feelings about Maren before I did? Did she exploit Davis's need to be loved and his fear of rejection? I wonder what she makes him feel, what she makes him do.

That time I heard them in the stairwell at school, he said, "I just don't want to do it." I thought it was Davis venting about his dad's endless expectations, but what if I was wrong?

"Olive," Vanessa says in a steady voice. I look up as she wipes the tears from her cheeks. "You're worried I've been manipulating him, aren't you?"

I flush at how easily she can tell what I'm thinking, but I don't deny it.

Vanessa leans across the table. "If I wanted him to stay, he would. You think I would have let him break up with me like that if I was controlling him?" Her voice trembles again, fresh tears spilling down her cheeks.

I guess not. Suddenly I realize that being an empath is a double-edged sword—you can control how people treat you and feel about you, but you know that if you do, nothing is real. She could make Davis stay with her, but what would be the point if he didn't want to?

"You're right," I say. "I'm so sorry. Breakups suck."

She laughs a little through her tears, then sniffs. "I need tea. Would you like some?"

"Sure."

Vanessa fills a matte black kettle with water and sets it on the stove to boil, then opens the pantry door, flooding the room with an earthy scent—lavender, sage, and something else I don't recognize. The pantry shelves are filled with glass jars of herbs and loose-leaf tea. Ropes of dried blossoms braided with bright ribbons are strung along the ceiling. Vanessa shuffles through tins and apothecary jars, then comes out holding a tray arranged with two delicately veined teacups and a jar of tea leaves as the kettle begins to sing.

"Witch's Brew?" I wrinkle my nose as I read the label.

"That's just the name." Vanessa adds a spoonful of tea to each cup. "It's a mixture of oolong for courage, dandelion for helpful spirits, nettle for protection, mint for purification, and lemon for happiness." She pours the hot water over the leaves, inhaling the steam deeply. The scent swirls around my head, intoxicating and potent. The crisp, clean scent of mint mixes with sharp flowery notes that make my mouth water. Vanessa lifts her cup to her lips, drinking deeply.

After a few sips, she sets her cup down, her breath hitching in her throat. "That's better. Tea always helps me think clearly. And Olive—" She reaches for my hand, squeezing. "I'm sorry. You came here for something, and I was so wrapped up in my argument with Davis that I didn't even ask. But now I can feel it." She closes her eyes, tilting her head to the side as she tastes the air around us. "Shame. Reluctance. Are you ready to tell me why you feel so guilty?"

My stomach feels like it's full of swooping bats. Of course Vanessa knows. She always knows everything I'm feeling, all the private, hidden parts that I barely know myself.

"I first noticed it after we took Jay to the Silver Screen," she continues. "It's been getting worse and worse. It's like a fog around you. Soon it will be so thick you won't be able to find your way out."

A dark fog, like the poison that swirls under Jay's skin. When the shade takes him completely, my guilt will take me as well.

I tell her everything. I tell her about the pit I found myself in after my visit to the other side of the grass, and how I had basically stopped trying to claw my way out when Mrs. H came along. I tell her about the way Mrs. H's face changed when she died and the tiny flame of hope that I felt when she said her mother's name. I tell her how I decided to summon a ghost to tell me what happens after we die.

I tell her about the wildflowers I gathered at the Phoenix Project Pyre and the bells that I rang at the Home for Foundling Wraiths and Spirit Children. The letters I burned and the pictures I tore and, finally, the candle that I lit at Seymour House.

"I sprinkled the wax with salt," I say. "I said 'to bind the spirit.' And I was wearing a locket that I took from Mrs. H when she died. I didn't know it at the time, but it belonged to Jay's mother a long time ago, and there's a lock of his hair inside. I think that's why it finally worked. But it didn't work the way I thought it would. Jay still wasn't able to tell me what happens after we die, and now he's stuck here. If he turns into a shade, it will be my fault because I woke his spirit. I don't know how to release him."

Vanessa nods, tapping the corner of her lip as she thinks.

"There may be a way to undo what you did, but we'll need to find the right place. A place of smoke, a place of ash . . ." Her voice has the same rich quality I heard in it when she whispered the words in the mausoleum, drawing the shade with his book of secrets out into the open. My mind fills with a sound just out of range, a sound like the wind blowing across the opening of a glass bottle. Her eyes drift out of focus, and then snap back to me. The humming in my head disappears. "Do you know such a place?"

I blink. The sudden absence of that crystalline drone is jarring, like the silence that pours from Jay's chest.

"Um, a place of smoke? I guess the Phoenix Project Pyre could be called a place of smoke. It's the only open-air funeral pyre in the western hemisphere." People from all over the country have their bodies brought to it to be cremated under the great blue dome of the New Mexico sky.

"Perfect. It will be full of old charms, easy to twist into something new. You used the mourning brooch and a flame to bind him here," she explains. "So you'll need the mourning brooch and smoke to set him free."

"And that will work?" I ask.

"I think so. But—" She bites her lip, her cheeks flushing. "We'll also need Davis."

"Why?"

"He was there that night you summoned Jay. Not in the room with you, but still, his energy was a part of it. Do you think you can convince him to come with us to the pyre?"

"Maybe," I mutter. "I kind of feel like a jerk asking you for help, especially since it will mean you guys have to spend time together right after breaking up."

Vanessa draws in a deep breath. "We'll be okay. Maybe you can talk to him for me when you ask him to come—see if he's willing to put this behind us?" She looks at me sideways, her eyes glinting. "After all, there's really no point in me even *trying* to free Jay if Davis isn't there."

Annnnnnnd here we go. This is what she's going to hold over my head. If I don't help her get Davis back, she won't help me with Jay.

She may not be using her empath powers, but she's still manipulating me.

But Vanessa is the only one who can help Jay now—the only one who can help *me*. If Jay doesn't move on soon, *now*, the shade will consume him. I need Vanessa. I need her to work her magic, spin her spells, and set Jay's soul free.

So I nod and make promises that I hope I can keep.

CHAPTER 25
THE WAY OF ALL THE EARTH

Davis is sitting on his back steps when I walk up his driveway. With his head bowed and his shoulders slumped, his silhouette looks like the hunchbacked assistant of some mad scientist. He looks up at my footsteps, eyes as deep and dark as a river.

"So," I say. I sit next to him, looping my arm through his and squeezing. It feels so natural; I don't even have to think about how to comfort him.

"So."

"Did you really mean it? You're done with Vanessa?"

"Yes. God, yes. I'm so sick of doing shit just to make other people happy. Everything has to go exactly Vanessa's way, and if she ever does something for you, she never lets you forget it. I learned really quickly that she doesn't do anything unless she gets something in return."

"Yeah, I kind of noticed that," I say dryly. "Everything with Jay . . . I wish I had never gotten her involved. I wish I had never gotten *you* involved."

"Don't worry about it," Davis says. "I want to help."

"You won't." I cover my face with my hands. "Not when you hear what I need from you now."

"It can't be worse than digging for dead bodies."

"It is," I squeak. "I really messed up, Davis. I was messing around with stuff I shouldn't have been. When I was looking for a ghost, I had no idea what I was doing, I was just making shit up, and I kind of . . . bound Jay's spirit here." A lump forms in my throat. How did I let everything get so screwed up? "That's why he couldn't move on even after we found his grave."

Davis puts an arm around my shoulder. "Damn."

"And . . ." I hesitate. "Vanessa thinks she can release him if we go to the Phoenix Project Pyre. But she says you have to be there. Because you were there when I first summoned Jay and the energy all has to match up or something. I don't really get it."

Davis presses his lips into a tight line. "Knowing Vanessa, there's gotta be more to it. So what does she want in exchange for helping?"

"She wants you." I feel slimy just saying it. "She asked me to talk to you about getting back together."

He shakes his head. "Olive—"

"But I'm not asking you to do it," I add quickly. "Get back together with her, I mean. I would never ask you to do that."

"And what if this doesn't work, either?" Davis asks. "What if Jay is still stuck here?"

If Jay is still stuck here, then it will be my fault, and so will everything he does as a shade, including all the attacks on Scary Road. But more than that, I'm afraid of falling back into the pit I was trapped in for the past two years. Drowning in my fear of the Nothing, in complete and utter indifference to everything around me. I managed to pull myself to the top of the pit when I decided to look for a ghost to answer my questions, and now I'm clinging to the crumbling edge with everything I have, but if I have to watch Jay turn into a shade?

Nothing will save me then.

"I just really need to know," I finally say in a small voice. "I need him to move on so that I know there's something else after this life. Something other than the Nothing and the shades. Something that makes everything worth it. Otherwise . . ."

"That's your worst fear, isn't it?" he asks. "That there's

nothing after we die."

I shudder. "Yes."

He tilts his head back, huffing out a breath that lingers like a ghost in the cold air. "I'll come with you to the pyre. And then we'll be done with Vanessa forever."

Relief and gratitude bloom in my chest. I drop my head against his shoulder in silent thanks. I can't believe that after everything I've done—ghosting him and then using him, not coming clean until we were all sucked into this mess too far—he's still there for me. He's still willing to take a risk for me.

Because it is a risk, I admit to myself as Davis stands up and hauls me to my feet. Something tells me Vanessa won't let us shake her off so easily. She'll always find some reason to cling like a thistle to whoever she wants, burrowing into their bloodstream like tetanus spreading from a rusty nail. The thought makes me uneasy, but so does the idea of Jay being trapped in the woods, lost in the darkness, and determined to drag down everyone who crosses his path.

"Come over for dinner," I say to make up for putting Davis in this position. His house is still and silent, and I suddenly feel sick that I let him spend two years alone in that tomb.

"Yeah, okay," he says, shoving his hands in his pockets. But before we can go in, a car pulls into the driveway. Davis stiffens beside me as his father gets out.

"Davis." Mr. Wills's voice is tight with impatience. "I must have called you five times in the last hour."

"Seven," Davis mutters.

"I pay for your phone, so I expect you to answer when I'm trying to get ahold of you." Mr. Wills pulls a cardboard box heaped with papers out of the car and shoves it at Davis, then bends back into the car for a second box. "Come on, we have a lot of work to do. Finding those graves has created a disaster for Wills and Son. We have to call our investors, and—"

"I'm having dinner with the Moranas," Davis says, dropping the box at his father's feet; it lands on the concrete with a hollow slap. "I can't help you right now."

"I'm not asking."

"And I'm not asking for permission."

Mr. Wills puts his box down too, slowly, deliberately, and then takes a step closer to Davis so that they're eye to eye. "I'm sure Olive will bring over a plate if you're hungry, but right now we need to work. You can't let the board think that you got that internship just because you're my son. If you want a place at Wills and Son—"

"That's the thing, Dad. I *don't* want a place at Wills and Son." A vein bulges in the side of Davis's neck as he clenches his jaw. He looks like he's standing on the edge of a mesa waiting to fall, waiting for his father to disown him. "I don't want anything to do with it."

Mr. Wills's eye twitches in indignation.

"You don't know what you want. I built this firm *for you*," he growls, holding up his empty hands like an offering. "So that you could have all the things that I never did."

"No, you built it for yourself." Davis spits the words like they're venom, like he's trying to coat his father in poison so he hurts the way Davis does. I flinch at the contempt in his voice. "I've told you this a hundred fucking times, and you never listen. You just assume I'll be satisfied with you planning my whole life out perfectly for me. Like you're doing me a favor. The internship, then law school, then partner by the time I'm twenty-five, right, Dad? But perfect for you isn't perfect for me, and I'm through letting other people decide what my life is going to look like."

He yanks the atlas out of his pocket and thrusts it into his father's chest. I have to stop myself from snatching it back. It feels like Davis just gave his father a piece of himself, and I'm afraid of what Mr. Wills will do with it.

"What is this?" Mr. Wills asks, frowning and flipping the atlas open.

"My future." Davis grabs me by the hand and yanks me toward his car. "Consider this my resignation."

I didn't think a 2005 Corolla could peel out, but we leave behind a haze of blue smoke that clings to Mr. Wills in the driveway. In the side mirror, I see his eyebrows draw together as he flips through the atlas, and his mouth quirk in an expression I can't quite identify.

I glance at Davis as he rolls through the stop sign at the end of our street. His hands are tight on the steering wheel, shoulders rolled forward and tense. He lets out a shaky breath, half laugh, half groan. "Oh my God."

"Are you okay?" I ask.

"Yes. No." He laughs again. "I don't know."

"Maybe now wasn't the best time to do that."

He shrugs, flicking on the turn signal. "I figured if you're willing to face your biggest fear, I should be, too."

A shiver twists my spine. "So we're really doing this?"

He glances at me, adrenaline dancing over his features. "Now or never. Better text Vanessa and tell her we're coming."

I pull my phone from my purse and send the message, the hairs on my arms prickling. I don't have to be an empath to pick up on the energy surging off Davis. He's riding the high of standing up to his father, and the feeling is contagious, spreading like wildfire until my heart thumps in time with his.

CHAPTER 26
DROP DEAD

The Phoenix Project Pyre isn't the kind of thing you stumble across; you have to seek it out. Like Scary Road, it's on a narrow dirt track that twists through the woods behind Seymour House.

Dad brought me to a service here when I was just a little kid, maybe eight years old. We followed the rest of the guests—you're supposed to call them guests instead of mourners because the pyre is a celebration of life, not a funeral, at least not in the traditional sense—up a path lined with sunflowers, sage, and verbena. Instead of folding chairs on a carpet of Astroturf around a yawning hole in the ground, we sat on old stumps and benches made of rough planks, worn silvery gray from the sun and the wind and the rain. The family carried the shrouded body in a canvas sling and placed it on the pyre, and then we all filed past, dropping bundles of sage and flowers as we went. Then the pyromancer lit the fire, and the sage, the flowers, and the body were engulfed in flames. The pyromancer knows exactly what kind of wood to use and how to arrange it to make the fire burn hot and fast to cremate the body. The ashy white column of smoke rose into the sky, and I tilted my head back, following it up and up and up.

Now I lead Davis and Jay past a hand-lettered sign that reads *pyre →*, following a narrow path that disappears into the hills.

We duck under the low branches of tangled scrub oak that enclose the path. A carpet of dead brown leaves whispers under our feet. I don't know what to expect when we reach the pyre: the confused knot of ribbons from Seymour

House? The candles from the mausoleum? Or something else—veins of molten silver that creep across the pyre like blood, bundles of dried herbs ground into dust . . .

Vanessa said we can use the mourning brooch to free Jay. I made sure he had the locket before we left, tucked under his shirt against his chest, where it hangs like a hollow heart. She brought the rest of her supplies in a small purse slung over her shoulder.

The path opens onto a bald hilltop covered with silver-gold grass that sways as we move through it. Vanessa is standing in a shaft of moonlight next to the pyre, which is just how I remember it: a pyramid of stones with a blackened metal grate on the flat top and rough-hewn benches arranged in a semicircle around it.

The wind blows, blurring Jay's outline so that his bones shine through. I catch a whiff of pungent smoke that dies away as soon as the wind does. Jay's hazy figure leaps back into sharp focus at the same time. *A phantom smell*, I realize. Just like the blood that reveals Seymour House's true nature, I can see the Phoenix Project Pyre for what it really is: a place of smoke, a place of ash.

There's a beautiful kind of symmetry to this. I summoned Jay at Seymour House, where he died—where his body and his life were buried, hidden, and weighed down under secrets. It's only fitting that the pyre is where I will set him free. I still don't know where he'll go, but even the Nothing is a better fate than becoming a shade.

Davis examines the sooty stones that support the pyre. They're blackened from age and smoke, but clean; nothing remains of the last fire that burned here.

"Olive, you stand here, facing west." Vanessa tugs me into position. "And Jay, you stand across from her. Davis and I will complete the circle around the pyre." She smiles at him, her face shining with hope, but he refuses to meet her eyes. Sighing, she fishes a stubby candle and a book of matches out of her bag and sets them on the pyre in front of me. "Light the candle and then hold the mourning brooch over the flame until it catches fire. When it burns away and there's nothing left but ash, blow out the candle so that the smoke passes over Jay and into the setting sun. Then say, 'To free the spirit.'"

"To free the spirit," I repeat in a whisper. My throat is tight. This is my last chance to save Jay from the shade I awakened within him. If this doesn't work, he'll be trapped here as the shadow rolls over him, blotting out his features and leaving him just a shell of what he once was.

And I'll know it was my fault.

Vanessa keeps one hand on her ribbon as everyone shuffles into place. Jay opens the locket and frees the mourning brooch from its clip, then passes it to me, letting the empty locket fall back against his chest. The sun hangs low over the horizon, casting a halo of light behind him. I strike the match against the rough stone of the pyre with a shaking hand and light the candle in the sputtering wind, cupping my hand around it until it burns steady and strong, a memory of other flames that burned here. I hold the mourning brooch over the candle and let the hair spark. There's just an ember at first, a red-orange glow like the eye of a monster, and then the flame singes my fingertips. I drop it onto the stone pyre as the fire devours the hair. When it burns itself out, I lean forward and blow out the candle. A thin column of gray smoke rises into the sky as I whisper, "To free the spirit."

The sun sinks lower behind the hill, staining the sky red. The light is fading, and the trees that ring this bald hilltop stand silhouetted against the night.

My breath comes in shallow gasps as the air around the pyre ripples. Static electricity races across my skin. I feel like I'm standing inside a wind tunnel, trying to swallow air that's billowing and gusting around my face, twisting my hair into a noose around my neck and scraping across my skin with harsh fingers. I struggle to keep my eyes open, blinking out bits of ash and swirling smoke.

At first, I think this sudden wind is the atmosphere parting, a harbinger of the Nothing—but then a gust snags on the tendrils of fog billowing under his skin, lifting his hair to show a network of dark veins creeping across his face.

The shadow spreads and pools under his skin, blotting out the swell of his cheek, the straight bridge of his nose, the cleft of his chin. It rolls over his face, erasing everything it touches and leaving behind a darkness so dense that I feel like I'm drowning.

Horror crashes over me as I realize what's happening: the shade has hold of Jay, and this time it's going to swallow him whole.

The gale dies, leaving behind air so cold that it feels like it's crystalized—sharp and rough in my throat. I gasp, and my breath hangs in the air in front of me, a silver cloud. My feet are rooted to the ground, and the blood in my veins slows, my heart struggling to pump the shards of ice that are left.

Darkness seeps across the pyre, extinguishing the first bright stars on the horizon. It's thick and viscous, and it clings to my skin, draping over the pyre and the four of us like a shroud. Frozen air whistles in my throat every time I take a breath. I close my eyes and open them again, but there's no difference. A muffled yell comes from somewhere to my left, and I twist my head, searching for any speck of light that might break through, but this darkness is all-consuming.

The shade inside Jay has fully awakened. There is no light at the end of the tunnel for him. There is only an eternity in darkness, bound by the misery he felt in life.

Someone shrieks, and then there's a grating noise, like

the metal pyre is being dragged off its stone ziggurat. The darkness hurls me forward, and I bang my shin against the rough stone. The fillings in my teeth give a jolt as a charged howl rushes across the pyre. The air feels like a wool blanket after a thunderstorm. I struggle to swim out of the darkness, struggle to fill my lungs with air so cold it burns. Panic blooms desperate in my chest. I'm drowning, and this time I've dragged Davis down with me.

White-hot sparks ripple across the blanket of darkness, outlining my friends in flashes of light: Vanessa, her mouth open in a silent scream as she claws at a ribbon of darkness across her throat; Davis, flung facedown across the pyre.

This moment is a coin balanced on its side, slowing as it spins closer and closer to its terminus.

Heads or tails. Life or death.

The hairs on my arms stand up as the darkness lifts with a spark like static electricity. There's no sign of Jay; he's disappeared with the viscous darkness. The sky is still black, but it's the natural darkness of night, broken by pinpoints of light and the dull brassy glow of streetlights in White Haven. Vanessa's mouth is still open, but it's not silent anymore. She draws breath, and her scream shatters the night, breaking against the stars that hang over us. Something warm and sticky courses down my hands, and at first I think it's my blood from where my nails are digging into my palm. But then I look at the pyre and see Davis lying in a dark slick of blood, his neck open in a wide grin, his eyes glazed over and dull.

A place of smoke, a place of ash. And now a place of blood.

CHAPTER 27
IN REQUIEM

Vanessa screams again, a ragged sound like a cat being strangled. I stagger to Davis's side, pressing my hands to his throat, to that thin red line traced from ear to ear. The blood that coats my hands flows out thick and fast until I'm wearing a red glove to the elbow. His pulse wanes under my hands. I tighten my grip on his neck: a tiny flutter under my palms. The ghost of his heart.

"He's still alive," I cry. "He's alive! Call 911. Hurry."

Vanessa gasps, fumbling for her phone. Her hands are shaking so much that she drops it on the stone ziggurat and the screen cracks.

"Oh my God," she moans. "There's so much blood. I can't—"

"My phone!" I shout. "In my purse."

Vanessa's just a dark shape on the other side of the pyre, a shadow as deep as the one that poured from Jay's eyes and engulfed us. But then the wispy clouds part over the waning moon, and she's illuminated in a silver glow. There's not a drop of blood on her. I'm dressed in blood, splashed in it, but Vanessa's trailing white dress is spotless.

She tears my purse open, pulling the phone out and dialing while I press my hands so tight against Davis's neck that they go numb. His lifeblood seeps out between my fingers; his skin grows cool. Despair envelops me, bloated and sweet, like meat past its prime or an overripe mango. I try to fight my way out of the whirlwind of emotions sweeping over me, try to slow my dashing heartbeat, but wave after wave crashes over me until I can't breathe.

I curl myself around Davis, whispering in his ear,

"Don't go. I love you. Stay with me."

They're the same words I said to Mrs. H.

But she died anyway.

Vanessa's voice shakes as she tells the 911 dispatcher where we are. "So much blood," she says. "It was the Scary Road Stalker—please hurry."

I let out a harsh cry as her words hit me like a punch in the gut. The horror of the shadow blooming out of Jay's eyes is so big and raw that I can't give voice to it. I can only scream inside my own head.

"Jay." The word is garbled, like I have a mouthful of broken glass. "He—he—"

"We were too late," Vanessa whimpers. "I thought we still had time, but the shadow had spread too much. He's trapped here now. And Davis—" Her hands flutter over Davis's blood-soaked chest, but she doesn't touch him.

"He'll be okay," I insist. "He won't die. He can't die. I can't—" I gulp, choking on the panic that's rising in my chest. I can't get enough air, and my heart feels like it's going to explode. Lights flash in the corners of my vision as I slump forward, hyperventilating over Davis's body.

Vanessa puts her hand to the trailing ends of the ribbon around her neck, twining them around her finger, and then letting them drop in slow loops. Everything falls away in layers as the ribbon untwists: the panic, the fear, the horror, the remorse. I can feel my face drain, my eyes going flat and glassy, my mouth sagging.

I know Vanessa is manipulating me, twisting my feelings, but right now I don't care. Numbness spreads through my body, blanketing the pain in false calm. I can feel the despair just below the surface, but Vanessa's empath powers are enough to suppress it, and I welcome her influence.

"We have to tell the police what happened here tonight so they'll close Scary Road and stop it from happening to anyone else. Stop the Scary Road Stalker from killing anyone else."

"The Scary Road Stalker," I repeat in a trembling voice. He scared Mateo and Evelyn, and he attacked Hugo and Minnie, and he terrorized Ava and Mikey, and now—

Now everything that Jay was has been consumed by the shade.

The rest of the night is a nightmare of flashing lights and wailing sirens, crackling radios and generic police officers. The paramedics take Davis away in a flurry of desperate activity, leaving a cop with eyebrows to rival Dan Levy's to herd me and Vanessa down the hill. He passes around silver emergency blankets and paper cups of lukewarm, bitter coffee, then joins the detectives scurrying up and down the path. Flashes pop in the trees as they take pictures.

They've set up portable emergency lights all around the parking lot, bathing the scene in harsh light and shadows. I only half listen as Vanessa tells the detectives our story, my jaw locked tight against a scream. Instead I'm thinking about Jay. About the way the darkness bled out of his eyes when I blew out the candle. About what he's become. Jay was a ghost of White Haven's past, but he was harmless. What he is now is something dark and sinister, something that lurked in my darkest nightmares, something that I summoned with my candles and stupid rituals. If it weren't for me, Jay would still be the benign, confused hitchhiker trapped in the woods by William Seymour's cruelty.

I cringe, a knife of guilt twisting in my gut.

I sprinkled the salt, bound the spirit, and summoned Jay into his sorrow.

I brought him here, to this place of smoke and ash and blood.

And when Jay drew his finger across Davis's throat, I might as well have held the blade.

Vanessa nudges me in the side. "Hmm?" I blink, trying

to bring everything back into focus.

Eyebrows is asking me a question. "I said, did either of you see what direction the attacker went?"

"Um—no," I stammer. "I didn't see him. Or her. Or them. But I was trying to help Davis." I offer up my hands as proof.

My parents arrive in a vortex of spinning lights. Mom flings her arms around me.

"Oh my God, Olive." She weeps against my neck. "Oh my baby, oh my little girl—"

Dad kisses me on the top of the head.

"When we think of what could have happened—" His voice is thick with emotion. "Oh, God, Davis's parents are going to be devastated."

Vanessa is left alone, her father dead, her mother useless. One of the detectives wraps her in one of those silver blankets they use for shock and bundles her into the back of a police car. The numbing calm she projected over me lifts as it drives away, throwing me back into a crashing sea of panic that I think might drown me.

Eyebrows flips his notepad closed and slips it into his pocket. "We'll need to have you come down to the station to give statements—"

"That can wait until morning," Dad says. "Olive needs to get home. She's been through enough tonight."

Eyebrows hesitates, then nods brusquely.

It must be after midnight, because the only stoplight in town blinks red. When we get home, Mom won't let go of me long enough for me to change out of my clothes, so they dry stiff with Davis's blood. Her hands tremble as she cleans my face with a warm washcloth, searching my eyes for a sign that I'm safe. I can only blink at her through a red fog that lifts when she washes the blood out of my eyelashes.

After a while, Dad convinces her to let me take a

shower. I run the water so hot that my skin screams in protest and my lungs shudder the first time I draw a steamy
breath. The water turns rusty as Davis's blood streams off
my body. My eyes drift out of focus, but every time they
close, I see his body on the pyre. Instead I concentrate on
the way the water swirls in scarlet eddies before disappearing down the drain. I have to, or I'll give in to the panic
trying to claw its way out of my chest and start screaming
and never stop.

Then my shoulders start shaking and my throat closes
up and my vision goes spotty and I think, this is it. The
Nothing is finally going to take me, like it should have two
years ago. But instead of pure terror, I'm kind of relieved.
This is what I deserve. It's my fault that Jay was consumed
by the shade that I was trying to save him from.

I don't want to be alone. The words that I heard at the
Silver Screen leap back into my mind. Those words, that
grating mockery of Mrs. H's voice . . . I thought it was Jay
who got into my head, Jay who showed me what I was most
afraid of, but now I realize it was all me.

It's frankly fucking terrible to think of Mrs. H lying
alone in her casket, but I finally understand that my fear of
the Nothing isn't about what happens after we die.

It's about what happens while we live.

I've spent the past two years since my near-death experience avoiding shellfish like it's the spawn of Satan and
telling myself that it's easier not to let people get too close,
because if it all ends in Nothing, then there's no point anyway.

Now I know this is because I'm afraid. Afraid that if
I let someone in, I'll just end up losing them. To death or
rejection, it doesn't matter. If I offer up my heart, it leaves
me vulnerable to the kind of pain that I can block out so
easily by keeping my distance. It's like every friendship that
grows apart, every parent who throws themselves into

work rather than face their broken family, every hand that slips out of mine, is a little death, all building up to the final one, the one that will send me spinning alone into the Nothing.

Maybe that's why sometimes living feels a little like grief.

CHAPTER 28
SNUFFED OUT

There's a crick in my neck when I wake up, and for a split second, I think last night was just a dream. A waking nightmare. An illusion brought on by stress.

My phone buzzes on my bedside table, the screen lighting up with dozens of text messages from Maren asking if I'm okay. The words on the screen bring everything back: the shadow blotting out the moon, the heavy darkness, Davis lying on the pyre with blood pouring from that sinister smile in his neck.

My stomach clenches like a fist. Last night really happened. Davis's blood is on my hands. The skin on my palms is raw and pink from all the scrubbing in the shower, but I can still see crescents of rust underneath my fingernails. Revulsion twists in my gut at the sight. I can't stand the reminder that everything that went wrong last night is my fault, so I peel my fingernails down to the quick and wince as I brush the dried blood from the tender skin.

"Lolly?" Dad's knuckles brush against my door as he and Mom come in. He pulls me tight against his chest, but his steady heartbeat is a cruel reminder of the way Davis's stuttered and almost stopped last night, so I pull away.

"How's Davis?"

My parents look at me like they're afraid I'm going to break, and I'm suddenly sure that they're here to tell me the worst happened while I was asleep.

"What's wrong? Is he dead?" I struggle to draw in a breath.

"No, honey." Mom strokes my hair. "He isn't dead. He's stable, but the attacker nicked the carotid artery and jugular vein. The doctors say that you saved his life. He would have bled out if you hadn't put pressure on the wound as quickly as you did."

I sag against her, fresh tears flooding my eyes. He's alive, but it's no thanks to me. Whatever Mom and the doctors think, I didn't save his life. I nearly ended it.

"When can I see him?"

Mom and Dad exchange a glance. "Not yet. Right now only family is allowed in the ICU. Davis is still unconscious, and the doctors aren't sure why. And they say . . ." Mom's voice trails off, and Dad finishes for her.

"They say even if he wakes up, he might not be the same." His voice is gruff with tears. "He may not be able to speak. He may have deficits from loss of blood flow to the brain. We just have to wait and see."

If he wakes up. Not when.

The reality of the situation comes over me little by little, like water seeping into a crack.

This might be it. All the years that we've spent together, even the ones we spent apart, and it's come down to this: Davis is hovering somewhere between life and death, and I'm the one who put him there.

Mom brushes the tears from my cheeks, her eyes bright with false hope. "Try not to worry too much yet. Everything is going to be okay."

I cringe. Those words are like a stake in my heart. It was her mantra whenever I tried to talk about what happened two years ago. I know that she was trying to reassure me, but all it did was make me feel completely dismissed. Besides, I knew better than to think everything would be fine. I had been to the Nothing.

"You don't know that. No one does," I mutter. Prickles of hot anger needle at my temples. How can they say Davis will be okay, when I'm the only one who knows where he is right now? He's trapped in the Nothing, just like I was, and he is *not* okay.

Dad frowns, thin lines bracketing his mouth. "It's best to stay positive, Lolly."

I'm on my feet without even thinking about it, my old stuffed rabbit falling to the floor, my jaw clenched so tight that it aches.

"Stop calling me that," I cry. "I hate when you call me that. That's what you called me before, when you promised me everything would be okay and I was stupid enough to believe you. And every time you say it now, it makes me think how stupid *you* are to keep telling me things will be okay when they so clearly aren't. You never even asked me what I saw when I died."

"But you didn't—" Mom protests.

"Yes, I did!" I scream. Startled, a crow rises from the tree outside my bedroom window in a flutter of black wings. "I died! My heart stopped! You can pretend it didn't happen, but it did, and I haven't been okay since. *Nothing* is okay. *Nothing* matters. Because we're all going to die, and do you know what happens when we do? *Nothing.*"

The word bursts out with a giggle, shrill and mean. I think I'm having a nervous breakdown because I can't stop the grating shrieks of laughter from pouring out. Tears stream down my face, an endless river of them, and the more I laugh, the quicker they come, until I'm howling in anger and grief.

Mom wraps her arms around me, guiding me to the bed. I don't want to sit on this bed and think of Davis lying silent and alone in the hospital, but my knees are shaking so hard that I sink down. The wild laughter turns to sobs that shake my body like the earth is coming apart. I clutch my arms, trying to hold my chest together while I cry. It hurts. I can actually feel my heart breaking and my ribs cracking and my lungs deflating and my blood congealing and oh God, if Davis dies, I don't know what I'll do. I would take it all back if I could. I would even crawl back into the pit of despair I was stuck in after I cheated death, if it meant Davis would be whole and well. Even if we never spoke again—if that's what it took to bring him back.

Mom rubs my back while I cry. When the tears finally slow and I can breathe through my nose again, I say the only thing I can think of.

"I'm sorry." I don't know what I'm apologizing for, because I meant what I said. I hate that we never talked about this. I hate that this is what it took.

"What did—" Dad clears his throat. "What did you see, Olive?"

I tell them. I tell them about the endless expanse, the dawning dread, the horror I felt before the paramedics restarted my heart. And to their credit, they listen without interrupting or trying to reassure me. When I'm finally done talking, Mom leans her head against mine and Dad crushes one of my hands between his.

"You've carried that fear for a long time," Mom says. "I'm sorry that it took us this long to listen. I'm sorry that we brushed off what happened to you."

"We should have realized how scary that experience was for you," Dad says. "We were so relieved that you were okay physically that we didn't think about what it meant for you emotionally."

"It screwed me up." I gesture around my room at the coffin-shaped bookshelf stuffed with horror novels, the piles of black clothes, the framed bat skeletons on the wall. "I'm a total mess."

Mom takes my chin in her hands so she can gaze into my face. She looks like a Renaissance painting, cheeks brushed rose gold, lips petal pink. I'm more like a Dali painting with tangled hair, yesterday's black lipstick smeared over my mouth, and everything warped and confused. My heart pinches when I realize that we wouldn't even be in the same wing of an art museum.

"You are what I always hoped for. Smart and strong and completely yourself. And I hope you never change."

CHAPTER 29
AT YOUR FUNERAL

School is like a tomb on Monday. Mom says I can stay home, and believe me, I want to, but staying home from school would be taking the easy way out.

I need to be there. I need to face what I did, face the part I played in this nightmare.

Almost everyone is wearing black. The halls are quiet, and there's a line outside the spare classroom that the district crisis counselor is set up in. Davis's locker is covered by a huge banner that says #Davisstrong, and the floor surrounding it is crowded with flickering candles and objects left in tribute. It looks like a Día de los Muertos ofrenda, but an ofrenda honors the dead, and that feels like a bad omen.

I push away the thought of an ofrenda for Davis, thinking instead about him sitting on the roof of his bus with Monument Valley in the background, outlined by the sun as he traces a path through the worn pages of his atlas. I don't know if he was serious when he told me I should come with him on his trip. But when I think about that hypothetical future where Davis is healthy and whole and I'm a less screwed-up version of myself, I tell myself that I would go with him.

I would follow him anywhere.

The crowd melts away as I approach. I'm not sure how much everyone knows, but I don't have to wonder long.

"She was there when they found him—"

"His friend—"

"Covered in blood—"

I was hoping that detail wouldn't get out. I still see the blood that coats my hands flickering in and out of sight. I know it's still there, just like the Nothing that sometimes breaks through, and maybe I'm not the only one who sees it. In fact, living in White Haven, where almost everyone is involved in the industry of death, it should be a given that there are other people like me, other people who can see the world of bones and blood and darkness that lurks just below the surface.

People who see Davis's blood on my hands.

Because it's my fault that he may never wake up, my fault that Jay now stalks the woods he wandered in for the century since his death. I'm the one who spoke the words that bound him to the life he tried so desperately to escape.

It's a cruel kind of irony that I'm binding myself to the Nothing in the same way. Jay was supposed to answer my questions, give me back some of the light that I had lost, but the cloud of fear and grief that has enveloped me since I watched the Nothing consume Mrs. H is only growing denser.

The whispers die away as Vanessa sweeps down the hall in a black dress trimmed with lace and despair. Her eyes are shadowed, and she dabs at them with a tissue, a picture-perfect devastated girlfriend. Only she wasn't his girlfriend—not anymore. Davis broke up with her, and I'm the only one who knows it. In the eyes of Ocotillo High School, Vanessa is the one who will lose the most if Davis dies.

But I haven't forgotten how she didn't touch him while he lay bleeding on the pyre. She's not the one who bathed in his blood that night. She's not the one who felt his heart-beat slow against her palms.

She takes her place by my side, and we stand silently as more people come to Davis's locker to pay their respects with items that remind them of him. Some of the tributes make sense to me—Davis loves Dr Pepper; he's read *On the Road* a dozen times—but most of them don't. Why do three guys a year younger than us each bring a rubber duck? What's the significance of the Rubik's cube?

They're reminders of the lost years. These are parts of him that I might never have a chance to know.

The crowd around us parts, murmuring in a low electric hum, as Maren approaches the lockers. She's holding a candle with a deep red ribbon tied around it in a drooping bow. I hear someone hiss "Bloody Mary" under their breath.

My belly knots when I realize that every pair of eyes is fixed on us, waiting to take their cue from Vanessa. Maren wasn't even there that night at the pyre, but somehow the news about the unmarked graves in the woods and what happened to Davis have become so snarled together that the kids at school are treating Maren like she's the one who slit Davis's throat.

Her candle flutters, then goes out as she comes face-to-face with us. A thin wisp of smoke rises to the ceiling, just like the candle I blew out as the shade enveloped Jay. Everything changed with that wisp of smoke; what will be different now?

The tension in the crowd sweeps me forward as Vanessa bends toward Maren, balancing on the knife edge of her indecision. Vanessa is a victim, and Maren is a villain, and all it would take for this mob to tear Maren apart is a twist of Vanessa's fingers.

Then Vanessa kisses Maren on the cheek, taking the candle from her hands. "To Davis," she says. "And all the other victims."

She leaves the Seymours out of it, but as the week passes, no one else gives Maren that courtesy. Maren's never been well-liked, but at least she used to be respected. People paid attention to what she had to say. Now her mother is on the verge of a nervous breakdown and their posh Victorian mansion has been graffitied so often that they've stopped painting over the damage.

And I'm not innocent. I avoid looking at her in class and ignore her text messages. The longer Davis lies unconscious in the hospital, the more numb I become to everything. It's like I'm trapped in a nightmare, a slow-moving dream world where everything is tinged corpse gray. At first I think it's Vanessa, anesthetizing my sorrow out of some misguided sense of pity, but the cold numbness lingers even when we're apart and I realize that I'm sinking into the Nothing. Into the pit that swallowed me up two years ago. Mrs. H hauled me out once, but now she's dead, and Davis might be dying, and I'm not going to make the same mistake a third time. Every time I let myself get close to someone, love someone, the pain of losing them is almost too much to bear. Next time it might destroy me.

"Olive."

The gray haze I've been trapped in since the attack lifts slightly at Maren's voice. I blink and close my locker to find her just a breath away. I haven't been this close to her since before the attack, and I'm shaken by how waxy her skin is and how sunken her eyes are.

"I just wanted to ask if you have any news about Davis."

Misery slams back into me. I slump against my locker. It's been almost a week since the attack. The good news is he's been moved out of the ICU. All of his scans have come back clear: no deficits from the lack of blood flow, no brain damage. The bad news is he's still unconscious. The doctors are stumped; they say there's no medical reason for the coma to linger.

I shake my head and grunt a response.

"You haven't texted me back," Maren says in a small voice. "I've been worried about you. And about—"

Someone pushes past, hissing at Maren and lifting

the corner of their jacket to show her the gory plastic Halloween knife stuck in their belt. A whole new wave of shame ripples through me as he whoops and runs down the hall, screaming "Bloody Mary" as he goes. This is all my fault. Maren's entire life has fallen apart because of me. I failed Jay, and I failed Davis, and I failed her. I dragged her down into the Nothing that is my own life.

"Maybe it's best if we don't talk anymore," I say before I can lose my nerve.

Maren sucks in a harsh breath and blinks back tears. "You don't—"

"Everything is such a mess," I try to explain. "I don't want—"

She holds up her hand. "Wow. Okay. I get it." She walks away, then spins back to face me. "You know what, I thought you would be different. I thought that things had changed between us and you understood me. But no. You're just like the rest, blaming me for what happened to Davis. The only difference is you actually know the whole story and you're right." She laughs, the sound masking a sob. "You're right to hate me. I hate myself. Jay died and became a shade because of my family, and that makes everything he's done my fault. I'm responsible for all those deaths listed in the ledger, and if Davis dies, I'll be responsible for that, too." She turns on her heel and slinks away, and I don't go after her.

She thinks I blame her. She couldn't be more wrong. But for Maren, everything comes down to her name, and she has no idea that I don't care about that. She sees everything except how incredible she is, and how I'll never be good enough for her.

One of these days Maren is going to realize that she was wrong and all of this is *my* fault, not hers, and I don't think I can stand to see the look on her face when she does. She'll leave me, and that will be like losing Mrs. H all over again, only worse, because it will be my fault.

So it's best that I don't bother to correct her. It'll be that much easier to ignore my feelings for her if she thinks I don't want to be with her because of her family name and what they did in White Haven. As long as that's the reason we're not together, I can protect my heart from burning itself out.

CHAPTER 30
INTO THE DARK

Davis's parents are sitting at my kitchen table when I get home.

I freeze in the doorway when I see them, letting my backpack thud to the floor. Poppy has shadowed eyes and sagging skin, and Mr. Wills looks just as bad. His normally perfect hair flops over his forehead, and his eyes are bracketed by deep lines that remind me of canyons carved by rivers of tears.

"Olive," he croaks. "We're glad to see you." He twists Davis's atlas between his hands, his thumbs stroking the worn cover. "We wanted to talk to you about what happened that night."

Bile rises in my throat. I clamp my jaw closed and swallow hard. Do they know that I'm the reason Davis is lying in that hospital bed? Do they want to hear me say it, hear me admit to using Davis and putting him in danger? It was bad enough talking to the police. I don't think I can relive that night in front of his parents.

Poppy must be able to read my repulsion, because she says, "Not that, Olive. Not about the pyre. We want to talk to you about what Davis said to his father before all that."

Ah. It's almost worse. Davis only confronted his father that night because of what he was about to do for me. *I figured if you're willing to face your biggest fear, I should be, too.* The last conversation he had with his father before almost being killed was angry, born out of years of resentment. That might be the last thing they ever say to each other. Davis might die without ever waking up.

"We want to know how much you know about this,"

Mr. Wills says, offering me the atlas. "We've been looking through it, and it's clear that Davis has spent a lot of time making plans. But what did he mean when he said this is his future?"

I accept the small book. The inside cover is full of jotted notes in his handwriting. Places he wants to see. Places he might never go.

You could come with me.

His voice in my head hurts so much that I open my mouth to scream. Instead words pour out.

"He was going to go back to the Navajo Nation this summer," I say in a rush. "To stay with his grandparents and fix up an old school bus that his cousin was going to sell him. And then after graduation next year, he wanted to travel. Go all around the country, following the trips he'd planned out in this." I run my fingers over the bent corners of the book. "That was what he wanted to do. Not an internship at Wills and Son. Not law school."

"He never told us." Poppy's eyebrows furrow in confusion.

"You never asked," I shoot back. "Neither of you. *You* only make time for him if he's working at the diner"—Poppy winces at the words, but I turn to Mr. Wills before she can respond—"and he thinks you don't want anything to do with him because he doesn't want to work for Wills and Son."

"Don't want—" Mr. Wills's face drains of color. "Nothing is more important to me than Davis. How could he believe that I care more about my business than about my biye'?"

"Maybe it has to do with the name," I mumble.

Mr. Wills flaps a hand in the air. "Consider the 'Son' dropped. Wills Development Group sounds just as good. I've been ashamed all week about the conversation Davis and I had before he got hurt. I know that I've pushed him too much. I know I haven't listened to what he wants. I was trying to do the right thing for him, prepare him for the future. But these last few days, when I thought we might lose him—" His voice goes all strangled and he has to take a few deep breaths before continuing. "Well. I was wrong. I don't want to push Davis into a life he hates, especially if he thinks that's the only way to earn my love. I'll tell him today."

Tell him? That sounds like—

Poppy shakes her head, reaching for me. "He's not awake. But the doctors think that he can hear us. They say it's good for us to talk to him. In fact—" She glances at Mr. Wills, who nods. "They also said that you can come visit. If you feel ready."

I suck in a deep breath, my chest expanding with hope. I'll get to see him again. I'll get to talk to him again. Even if he dies, I'll be able to tell him how much I love him before he goes. And maybe those words will be a comfort to him in the Nothing.

"I can see him?" I finally squeak out.

Poppy nods. "Just for half an hour. I know it's not long, but they have strict rules about visitation. He's only allowed to have one non-family visitor. We think it's important that it be you."

"We want your voice to be the one he hears," Mr. Wills says firmly.

The hospital lights are harsh and buzzing, an almost inaudible hum that I can feel in my bones. It reminds me of the electric tension in Seymour House the night that Vanessa looked for the ledger. That night ended in someone I love bleeding, too. The thought is enough to set my teeth on edge, twist my stomach into knots. How much blood will my friends lose because of me?

Dad hands me a disposable mask when we get to the door of Davis's room. Mom leans forward and presses a kiss to my forehead, then opens the door for me.

Davis's normally ruddy skin is paper white tinged with gray. Plastic tubes snake across his body, and his neck is swathed in bandages. His hands lie limply on top of the sheets. The room smells like Mrs. H's did on the night that she died.

I freeze in the doorway, balling my hands into tight fists. Sour sweat pools in my armpits, and I shake so hard that my teeth clatter together. I can't go in there. I can't look at Davis lying in that bed and know that behind his closed eyes, there is only darkness.

I can't look into his face and know that he's slipping into the Nothing.

I look at my parents and try to say something, but my throat works soundlessly and all I can do is stare.

Dad takes my hand. "You'll regret it if you don't."

"I know it hurts to see him like this," Mom says. "But if he dies—" Her voice hitches, and she takes my hand. "This might be your only chance to say goodbye. To get closure."

The C-word. Somehow I knew she was going to say it. I still don't know what it means—it's not like I ever questioned if Mrs. H was really dead. I was there when she died. I saw the light go out in her eyes. How much more closure do I need?

"This is how you honor Davis and what he meant to you," Mom says. The steady beeping of the medical equipment almost drowns out her soft voice. "By facing your pain instead of trying to escape it."

The well of sorrow inside me hasn't gone dry yet, and her words bring new tears to my eyes. If only I had listened to her when Mrs. H died—if only I had given in to my grief instead of seeking out a ghost. None of this would have happened, and Davis would be safe and whole.

My skin crawls when I imagine him becoming like Jay: a shade, only a shell of what he once was. I can't bear to think of Davis trapped like that. And now it occurs to me that if he dies and I can't mourn his death and accept that he's gone, I'll be trapping him here as another kind of ghost. The kind that haunts me for the rest of my life.

I don't want that to be how I remember Davis. I don't want to turn him into a ghost. I take a deep breath, and Mom's hand falls out of mine as I step into the room.

What do you say to the only person who ever really knew you? I can't think of any words that make sense. Nothing will be able to capture the storm in my heart. Anguish, grief, sorrow, guilt, love, and gratitude shift and swirl, bleeding together like the aurora in northern skies. One color fades and another takes its place, until the sky is a mottled blend of colors. And like the aurora, I know that everything I'm feeling now will always be there, sometimes hidden, sometimes blocked out, but ready to rise to the surface whenever the circumstances are right. When I pass a stranger who walks with the same loping grace as Davis, or when I catch a whiff of smoke from a candle that's just been blown out. That's when my own personal aurora will resurface and I'll feel this storm just as strongly as I do now.

A month ago, I would have done anything I could to snuff this out, to bury these feelings until they could never rise again. But now I just close my eyes and let them wash over me, and I'm glad to know that I'll feel these things again. There's pain there, but there's also joy and love.

Finally I open my mouth and speak from the heart.

"I loved you when we were kids, and I love you now," I say to Davis. "I think I always will. You're my brother. You're the best thing that ever happened to me. You never gave up on me, and you taught me not to give up, either. No matter what happens, for the rest of my life, I'll carry you right here." I lay my hand over my heart, feeling it beating, feeling it living.

After half an hour, Davis's parents take my place at his side. I squeeze his hand one more time and promise to be back tomorrow, and the next day, and the next, and every day until he's home. Poppy brushes his hair out of his eyes, and Mr. Wills leans down to kiss his forehead. I can see the outline of Davis's atlas tucked in his back pocket.

Now I understand why Jay's mother made a mourning brooch of his hair and wore it close to her heart. The atlas makes Mr. Wills feel closer to Davis. If Davis died without telling his dad about his dreams, it would have been so easy for the atlas to become like the ledger: a symbol of all the pain in Davis's life tethering him to our world as a shade when he was meant to move on. But I don't think that would happen now, even if Davis does slip away. Instead, I think the atlas would become for Davis's parents what Mrs. H's locket was for me. The most tangible, honest thing left of the person they loved.

For the first time in what feels like a lifetime, my eyes are dry and I don't feel one hundred percent miserable. In fact, I feel good. Hopeful. Like things are going to be okay.

I still have the ledger hidden under my mattress. I wonder if Maren wants it back, or if she would be totally opposed to me burning it. It still gives me the creeps to think of William Seymour bent over the book, noting every person who passed through the doors of Seymour House like they were nothing more than a bolt of fabric or a sack of potatoes. Jay's story is just one of the secrets that book holds, and it suddenly seems unfair that the rest of them will stay buried.

Logistically, it makes sense to leave the bodies in place and create a memorial on the Seymour grounds. There are hundreds of bodies in the woods and the only record is a century-old ledger handwritten by a man who had a motive to hide the truth. If they try to exhume the bodies and rebury them somewhere else, someone's bones are sure to slip through the cracks. And that's the premise of at least a dozen horror movies that I can think of off the top of my head.

But knowing those bones will stay in the ground, wrapped in their rotting canvas shrouds, feels wrong. They'll never have their name engraved in stone to mark their final resting place; their loved ones will never have a place to gather and speak memories of them into the wind. Their lives will stay forgotten, and that feels like consigning them to the Nothing altogether.

So as much as my skin crawls every time I have to touch that damn book, I fish it out from its hiding place when I get home from the hospital, and open up my laptop and start typing.

I don't have some grand plan; no visions of a monument that can make up for what happened to them. I'm just typing their names and their dates, one after another, like a string of code that might conjure their memory into reality. If Maren were here, she would probably already have a dozen ideas how to honor the dead. Maybe when I'm done, I'll send her this list and let her decide what to do. I don't know. All I do know is, with every stroke of the keys, each person whose life was recorded in this book feels more real to me.

It doesn't take long before there are red hot pincers jabbing at my temples and a crick in my neck from bending over. Not to mention that I think the scent of leather is ruined for me forever.

One year at the Festival of Death, there was a traveling exhibit about anthropodermic bibliopegy: books bound in human skin. That's a real thing, and the most famous one is a memoir written by a Boston highwayman who died in the 1800s (of consumption, coincidentally) and requested that the book be bound in skin from his own back. The exhibit had the Boston memoir and some other examples, along with displays on their history and the mythology and ethos surrounding them. Curiosity got the better of us, and Davis and I spent the whole afternoon poring over the displays. It was like those shows about popping pimples. I was horrified, but I couldn't get enough.

Anyway, an hour bent over the ledger in my bedroom with the worn cover creaking under my fingers makes me think about those books bound in human skin. And the more names I type out, the more convinced I am that the ledger is bound in human skin, too.

I've typed five single-spaced pages and my fingers are cramping up when there's a knock at my door. I jump, startled out of the world of names spinning through my mind. I slam the ledger closed and shove it under a stack of unfinished homework as Mom and Dad come into the room.

"Lo–Olive?" Dad says. "Let's go grab a bite to eat. Anywhere you want."

I have to stop myself from looking at the corner of the ledger poking out from under my homework. I can't leave this room until I finish. "No thanks," I say, shrugging.

"You have to eat," Mom says. "Poppy's is closed, but there's got to be somewhere else in town with good cheese fries."

"It's not that I don't want to eat," I say. "I'm just not in the mood to go out and be surrounded by people and have to listen to them talk about Davis." My nose wrinkles. "School is bad enough."

Dad nods. "I understand. And seeing Davis today at the hospital must have been exhausting, too."

"Exhausting in a good way," I say. "But it was a lot, and now I just want to stay home. You guys should go. You could bring me something to eat."

Mom and Dad glance at each other. "I don't know,"

Mom says, biting her lip. "I don't want to leave you here by yourself." She reaches out to cup my cheek.

"I'll be fine," I repeat, shifting in my chair to block my computer screen. "Really. It might be nice to have some time alone."

"Come on, Beth," Dad says. "She's right. We've been hovering too much. She'll be fine for an hour."

"I really will," I promise.

Mom looks unsure, but she finally lets Dad lead her out of the room. I wait until I hear the car pull out of the driveway before pulling the ledger out from under the stack of paper and flipping it open.

I'm trying to find the page where I left off when I come across a name that I recognize.

Cold fingers fit themselves between the knobs in my spine. I lean over the book, sure that I misread the entry, sure that when I look again it will say something entirely different.

But the words written in spidery, fading handwriting don't change, no matter how long I stare at them.

Wilhelmina (no surname given) born August 1, 1899, in Frankfurt, Germany; household maid

—and her babe, Vanessa, born July 31, 1915, at Seymour House

Left of her own accord September 10, 1915

This doesn't make any sense. It must be a coincidence, or some sort of cruel, twisted joke that Jay left for Maren to uncover. Everyone listed in this book is dead, and has been for a hundred years.

The rest of the page gives the details of Wilhelmina's employment. It looks like as she was a paid employee, William Seymour did not track the expenses related to her lodging as strictly as he did the other inhabitants of Seymour House. Baby Vanessa, however, was another story. There's a long column after her name: diapers, bottles, powder, and dresses. Each one is marked through with a heavy black line.

I flip through the rest of the book, looking for other columns that have been marked out, other debts that were settled, but find none. As with Jay's entry, the numbers only increase. William Seymour showed no pity, forgave no debts, except for one.

Vanessa, the infant daughter of his household maid.

"Why did he let them go?" I murmur, reading the line at the bottom of the page again: *Left of her own accord.* But there can be only one answer.

Vanessa's voice, rich with secrets, telling Maren and me her mother's story: *My mother, Willa, had the most tragic love affair.*

The shadow show of Edward Seymour as he buried Jay alive: *Help me, Mina, you dirty little gold-digger.*

Other snippets of Vanessa's conversations over the past few weeks race through my mind. *My father was the heir to a wealthy family, and my mother worked in the house as a maid . . . I would take revenge on anyone who ever wronged me . . . He never acknowledged me . . .* and most sinister of all: *Here's to new friends and old grudges.*

Shivers sweep over my body. It's so clear now. Vanessa was not only the daughter of Wilhelmina—she was also the daughter of Edward Seymour, William's son. And when Wilhelmina revealed her child's true paternity, rather than welcome them into the family, William canceled their debt and threw them out with nothing.

I feel like I'm falling, tumbling to my death, as I remember more and more hints of who Vanessa really is: her fascination with Seymour House, the way she always refers to it as the asylum instead of by name, just like Jay. It even answers the question of why she befriended me in the first place: Maren and I were together the first time she met us. She was using me to get to Maren.

Maren.

Her name sends a shock wave of alarm through my chest. I got her involved in all this. I led her right to Vanessa.

I scramble across the room to grab my phone from my bedside table. Swiping at the screen to unlock it, I pull up Maren's number, suddenly desperate to hear her voice and tell her the truth about who—*what*—Vanessa really is.

She deserves more than a warning. She deserves an apology, both for getting her involved in this nightmare and then for leaving her on her own when the wolves descended. Later I'll apologize until I'm blue in the face, but first I have to make sure she knows how dangerous Vanessa is. I have to warn her not to be alone with her.

Sixteen unread texts.

I skim through them, my heart like a crumbling lump of granite when I think about Maren mentioning that I hadn't texted her back, the way her face fell, the way her voice was small in a way that Maren's voice never is.

Maren: I can't sleep. Are you up?

Maren: How are you? If you want to talk, I'm here

Maren: Are you going to school tomorrow? I can give you a ride if you want

Maren: Are you there?

Maren: Can we talk

Maren: I'm worried about you

Maren: Everyone thinks i had something to do with it but i wasn't even there. Did Vanessa say something?

Maren: I know you blame me too. I'm sorry. Please answer me

Maren: I know you don't want to hear from me anymore but I thought of something

Maren: you destroyed the shade that was my great-grandfather when you took the ledger from him. If Jay is a shade now, the only way to destroy him the same way is to take whatever it is that tethers him

Maren: Vanessa thinks its his bones

Maren: his obsession with how he died and his unmarked grave

Maren: that's what tethers him to this world

Maren: If we don't move the bones, no one will and Jay will stay in the woods forever. What happened to Davis will happen again, only next time someone might die

Maren: Vanessa and I are going to destroy him for good. It's the only way I can make up for everything I've done.

Maren: I wish things had gone differently between us

My chest gets tighter and tighter as I read the messages. By the end I feel like I'm trapped in one of the slot canyons we visited in Utah a few years ago. I can feel my ribs closing in, compressing my heart, squeezing it in an iron grip that feels like Vanessa's hand. My mouth sags open and I gasp for breath. Spots of black crowd my vision, the Nothing creeping in and threatening to overwhelm me.

What have I done?

I don't know how long I struggle to breathe, how long it takes for the Nothing to disperse from my vision, but even in the darkness, everything becomes clear.

This has been Vanessa's plan all along.

She's spent years, decades, looking for her chance to take her final revenge on the family that rejected her. As the last blood descendant of Vanessa's father, Maren has been her target all along. Vanessa never intended to help Jay move on. She's been waiting for the shadow to take him, waiting to place Maren in his path so that *Maren* is the next victim of the Scary Road Stalker. Only this time, Vanessa will make sure that Jay cuts deeper and Maren's blood flows faster.

I'm not sure what she is—a ghost like Jay, or something more dangerous—but there's no doubt in my mind that her thirst for revenge trapped her here just as surely as Jay's fixation on his grave trapped him.

Just as surely as I'm trapping myself.

It hits me all at once, a punch to the gut that sucks away my breath. I can see what I'm becoming: a kind of shade. Not one formed from what haunted me in life, but one I've created out of pain and fear and loneliness. Just a shade of myself, of the person I should be. The Nothing isn't coming for me—I've been running directly toward it this whole time.

After I died, I thought the best way to protect myself from ending up alone was to push away my feelings. Tell myself that none of this matters. Lock myself away from the people I cared about.

But that's flawed thinking, because by avoiding relationships to protect myself from being alone, I *am* fucking alone. I'm alone and I'm scared and I think I'm turning into something bitter and corrupt.

I have to slay my demons. I have to face my fears and let someone in, before it's too late. I might have waited too long with Davis. Two years—two wasted years that I could have spent with his friendship. My heart clenches as I remember being grateful that we had found each other again, that we had the rest of our lives to rebuild our friendship. And now the rest of his life may be so short. It stings when I think we could have had more time.

I can't make the same mistake with Maren. It's scary and I'll be vulnerable. Telling Maren how I feel about her—it could all go wrong and leave me with Nothing.

Or it could give me everything.

The vise around my chest loosens at the thought. Maybe I'm not too late. Maybe—

I dial Maren's number from memory, but the call goes straight to voice mail. Her phone is off.

The last text was sent only half an hour ago. I must have been so preoccupied with my fevered typing that I didn't notice the phone buzzing across the room. Half an hour is nothing. Sometimes it takes me half an hour just to find my shoes.

But Maren's not the type to drag her feet when she decides to do something. If she said she and Vanessa were going back to Jay's grave, then she's already there.

I shove my feet into a pair of Doc Martens and half fall down the stairs. The house is still and silent. I jerk open the curtains at the kitchen door. The trees in the yard stand out bare and spindly against the fading light of purple dusk.

The driveway is empty.

Dammit.

I could call Mom and Dad, beg them to bring the car back, but there's not enough time; every minute that slips away is another minute that Vanessa leads Maren deeper into the gloaming.

Groaning, I lean against the window, the glass fogging under my breath.

And stare out at Davis's car.

I suck in a quick breath when I realize that it's really parked there, right next door, just waiting for me. I have no idea how it got back from the Phoenix Project Pyre. Davis drove that night. His parents must have had to go back for it, or maybe one of the other neighbors took pity and brought it back so that his dad didn't have to.

The night is breezy, and a gust of wind whips my hair around my face as I slip across the yard to Davis's driveway. His car is unlocked. I figured it would be; this is White Haven and half the people in town leave their keys in their cars. I rummage through a handful of wadded-up gum wrappers in the center console, wondering if whoever brought back Davis's car is in the same habit, and—there they are. A set of keys dangling from a Navajo Nation flag key chain.

I take a deep breath as I turn the key and the car hums to life. I would do anything to have Davis at my side, but this is a drive I'll have to make on my own.

CHAPTER 31
BRING OUT YOUR DEAD

The Desert Heights billboard is covered in dripping red spray paint and surrounded by broken bottles. The only sign of the police presence that's been here for the last few weeks is the yellow DO NOT ENTER CRIME SCENE tape fluttering from trees on either side of Scary Road.

Even with the moon shining through the bare trees, it's darker than I like. The headlights only reach a few feet ahead of the car, and the darkness presses in on each side. I hit the brights, which throws everything into stark relief: skeletal branches stretching toward me, hints of movement behind the trees.

Maren's car is at Seymour House, tires twisted to the side like she parked in a hurry, the driver's side door still hanging open. I stumble out of Davis's car and lean into the convertible. A high-pitched ringing fills my ears as I take in the spiderweb of cracks on the driver's side window, the blood smeared across the steering wheel, the ragged scratches in the leather seats. Every atom in my body screams to hurry after Maren, but I take a grim pleasure in the disarray. It's clear that, like everything else in her life, Maren refused to sit back and let whatever Vanessa planned just happen to her. She's fighting back, and she's tough.

The thought clears my head like the sharp scent of vinegar, and I realize the ringing isn't just in my mind. The high-pitched beep is the car complaining that the headlights are still on. I flick off the lights and pull the keys out of the ignition. They dangle from an Ocotillo High lanyard that I drop over my head.

Something pricks at the skin over my heart as I duck out of the car. A hammered silver leaf on a key chain, the thin edge honed to a blade sharp enough to shave the hair from my arms. It swings as I move, and I can see the tiny hinge where it closes. This must be one of those defensive key chains that women carry to protect themselves from being assaulted. I slide it closed, then tuck it into my shirt before turning toward the woods.

The scrubby undergrowth is trampled, the path to the gravesites marked by snapped twigs and gouged trees. Sickly gray moonlight, like the ashen color of Jay's skin, filters through the trees. With their bare branches, they look like corpses. I shiver and try not to think of reaching, grasping hands forcing themselves out of the ground and snagging my shoelaces as we pass. But when I reach the first clearing and my flashlight skitters across a grid of twine, each square marked with white flags that ripple like ghosts, it's harder to pretend that I'm not walking through a forest of the dead.

The air buzzes with unseen energy as I approach the seventh clearing: Jay's burial site. I was scared the last time I was here, but that was nothing compared to how I feel now. I keep gulping in shallow, gasping breaths and then forgetting to let them out until my chest almost cracks from the pressure. Maren is on the other side of those trees, at the mercy of the shade that I failed to free and the threat that I failed to see.

A whisper moves through the woods, raising the hairs on my arms and tightening the tension in the air. I grit my teeth against a fresh wave of foreboding. A twig snaps like a bone under my foot. The atmosphere thickens all around me until I feel like I'm moving underwater. Everything is still and heavy and slow. Cold dread swells the air as I slip through the trees to the edge of my nightmares.

Bloated, unnatural shadows darken the clearing. Maren kneels at the center. She holds her arms stiffly at her sides, and her hair, her hair has turned to blood—

"Maren!" I stumble the last few steps to her side. Tendons stand out in her neck as she struggles to speak, but her jaw is locked tight. The fillings in my teeth give a jolt at the energy in the air as I run my hands over her shoulders. There are no bonds holding her in place—at least none that I can see—but she doesn't move. It's like she's been scared stiff.

A pale glow moves across the trees as a luminescent figure drifts into the clearing. Even with his face tilted to the ground, hidden by a shock of corn silk hair, I recognize Jay. He hovers above the ground, the tips of his toes dragging through the dirt and his shadow snagging on the white flags left to mark the burial places of the dead. The way he moves makes me dizzy, almost seasick: wafting on invisible currents of air, like a cork bobbing in the ocean.

The pale curtain of his hair falls back little by little as he begins to lift his face. My lungs empty, all my panicked gulps seeping out in a silvery exhale that hangs in the cold air. I'm frozen in dread, my fear holding me just as still as Maren as I wait to see what I did to him, see how I destroyed him.

But when he looks at me, his face isn't blotted out by the yawning void that I expected. Instead, it looks like it's chiseled out of white marble veined with dark threads that meet and shift at the corners of his eyes. I draw in a gasp of cold air that sends my head spinning. Confusion billows through me like the unfocused outline of his body, fluttering so that I can see his bones shining white in the dark night before settling again.

I don't understand. The last time I saw Jay, the coiled shadow inside of him had broken free and was destroying him, devouring him, and leaving nothing but a shell of who he once was. But this isn't a malevolent shade, devoid of everything that made him human.

This is still Jay, my friend, just another victim of Seymour House.

"Jay?" My voice rasps like a nail being pulled out of rotten wood. "What's going on? How are you still here? What happened at the pyre?"

"It wasn't me," he moans. "Olive, I swear, it wasn't me. It was—"

"But I saw the darkness spread over your face," I interrupt. Jay's eyes, full of a roiling black shadow, widen at something over my shoulder. The hairs on the back of my neck stand up as the air tightens with cold, so sharp that I can taste it. "I saw—"

"You saw what I wanted you to see."

The voice comes from a figure swathed in darkness that ripples like poisonous fog and parts to reveal Vanessa toying with a red ribbon wound around her neck like a bloody smile.

CHAPTER 32
COME TO AN END

I scramble in front of Maren, blocking her with my body, as Vanessa glides to a stop, towering over us. A frenzy of power whips around her, dispersing the black fog that shrouds her enough that I can see her heart-shaped face and her almost violet eyes. There are scratches across her cheek, beads of blood welling up at their ragged ends. One droplet rolls down her cheek, and she swipes her palm across her face, flinging out her hand with a crack like thunder. The unseen bonds holding Maren slacken enough for her to wince.

"Bitch!" Maren spits, her voice full of vitriol. I can feel the angry thrumming of her body against mine as she struggles to free herself from Vanessa's charm. "We trusted you."

Vanessa smiles, her cheeks flushing pink like Maren's curse is a compliment. "You were all just waiting for the shadow to spread and take Jay. You didn't even look around and see what was right in front of your face."

The darkness in Jay's eyes lifts for half a second. Underneath the swirling shadow, they're hollow with resignation. He looks at me like a corpse waiting for burial, his face full of grim acceptance at his fate. He didn't become a shade that night at the pyre, not like I thought he did, but it will happen soon. Vanessa will make it happen. Jay isn't strong enough to resist her dark power. Under her influence, all the horror of his existence will consume him, and she will use him to destroy Maren.

"It was so easy to make you think that Jay tried to kill Davis," Vanessa continues. "When really, it was me. Davis figured out what I was making him do and started resisting. He even tried to pull off my ribbon once. It was time for him to go." She strokes the ends of her ribbon around her finger. It's not the black velvet one that I'm used to. This one is slinky, ruby red. My heart jolts as I recognize it as the ribbon from the candle that Vanessa took out of Maren's hands by Davis's locker. A ribbon that Maren, however unwittingly, gave to her, tying them together.

Vanessa can influence the rest of us, coax us into doing things we wouldn't normally do. Like go to a sleepover and drink with her. But her real power lies in the ribbons that she uses to manipulate those closest to her. The ribbons that she binds with.

Like the black ribbon that came with the bracelets Davis gave her at his mother's diner.

My mind spins, remembering the scratches that crawled out of Davis's shirt collar, the argument I overheard when he told Vanessa he didn't want to do it again, the distress in his voice when he wondered if there would be more attacks.

He knew that if there *were* more, it would be because Vanessa took him out into the woods and whispered poison in his ear.

"Davis was the Scary Road Stalker." I almost choke on the words. "You had him out here stalking Hugo and Minnie and everyone else. You made him *hurt* them."

My hands ball into fists so tight I can feel the sharp bite of my nails against my palm. I imagine digging those nails into Vanessa's flesh, letting her blood flow over my hands like Davis's did. I feel twisted with fury. I worried that she might try to manipulate him, warp his feelings, but it never crossed my mind how far she would go. How could she do that to him? Use him, make him do those unthinkable things, and then discard him like he was a piece of garbage.

"I was just trying to save all those shortsighted, hormonal couples from themselves," Vanessa implores. "Stop them from ruining their lives the way my father ruined my mother's. It's been a hundred years, but you stupid teenagers still can't keep your hands to yourselves. Where do you think my mother got pregnant? In the back of William Seymour's Model T on the dirt road that led to the asylum. And it destroyed her. Olive, you can fill in the details, can't you?"

I grit my teeth, refusing to answer and give her the satisfaction. Tension thrums through the clearing, making my ears ring. Sparks of energy ripple across Maren's skin, then leap to my arms so that the hair stands up. Vanessa tilts her hand, twirling the ends of her ribbon around her finger. Maren moves stiffly against my side, plucking at her hair and wrapping it around her wrist in a macabre parody of Vanessa's ribbon. She gasps as the hair tightens, pulling her head sharply to the side. I claw at her wrist, trying to unwind the hair from her rigid arm, but it's like trying to stretch the spring on a garage door: impossible tension that could kill me if it snaps free. Maren whimpers as her neck bends at an unnatural angle.

Vanessa twirls the ribbon tighter, smiling down at us. She won't stop—not until I reveal the dirty family secret that connects her to Maren.

"Edward Seymour," I shout. "William's son. He was your father, and Mina, the woman he was with when he ran down Jay, was your mother."

Maren takes a sharp breath—the only sign she can make of her shock at this revelation—and Jay's eyes snap to Vanessa. Something shifts on his face. He's looking at her like he's seeing her for the first time.

My skin prickles at that look, at the way the shadows in his eyes tighten and darken. Up to this point, he's been held here under Vanessa's power. But now that he knows the truth about her—that she's like him, another victim of the Seymour family's greed and selfishness—will he give in to the shade struggling to break free and join her in taking revenge?

Vanessa smiles and draws in a deep breath like their shock is the scent of her favorite candle. Her cheeks flush with pleasure. She drops the ribbon looped around her neck, allowing Maren to yank her hand out of the snarled hair, leaving a tangled bracelet around her wrist. Her face is set in lines of anger.

"So why now?" she says through clenched teeth. "Why not take your revenge on Edward Seymour a hundred years ago?"

"Oh, I did," Vanessa says. Her words are bitter but her voice is sweet. "My mother brought me to the asylum to meet him when I was seventeen. She thought if he saw me, he would love me and proclaim me his child. Instead he yanked a ratty shoelace from his boot and threw it at me, declaring that was all I would ever get from him. He thought we were after his money, when what we really wanted was love."

Her delicate eyebrows draw together. "Just love. We just wanted to be welcomed into his family. And he couldn't even give us that. But I took that dirty shoelace like a talisman of my failure, and then I came into my own. I returned to the asylum with the shoelace knotted around my neck and took Edward Seymour to the highest peak I could find—and I told him to jump."

I wince, but it's not Edward Seymour's face I see in my mind. It's Davis, his eyes blank, his mouth slack, Vanessa's hold on him driving him to do horrible things. The velvet ribbon around her neck instead of the shoelace.

"But the shame of my father's suicide didn't ruin the Seymour family the way I had hoped." Vanessa frowns. "I've spent the past hundred years watching the asylum close in disgrace. I thought that would be the end of the Seymours, but they clawed their way back up to the top of the food chain, never mind the pain they caused everyone else. And then last year I saw the land had been sold. They had profited even more off this place soaked in blood. I knew it was time for me to come back and take what I deserve."

"What do you want from me?" Maren says in a brittle voice.

"Why, I thought you were finally catching on," Vanessa says. "I want to destroy the Seymours. And that means destroying you, the last remaining person with Seymour blood."

"You're a Seymour, too, though," Jay whispers, half to himself. "You have the same blood as Maren." He looks like he's trying to make sense of it. Come to terms with what it means for Vanessa to want to spill the blood that she shares. I can feel him teetering, trying to decide if he should join Vanessa in her revenge, or if she's as culpable as Maren.

Vanessa's eyes flash, and the charge in the air surges. "I'm no Seymour," she snaps. "Even if my father had married my mother or acknowledged me, I never would have taken his name. Why pretend that he had any claim on me when I hold all the power? It turns out that revenge is more powerful than love."

She moves in a fury of billowing, dark cold that envelops us like a cloud. I can feel Maren's immobile body ripped away from me. My scream is just another soundless howl in the confusion. The air thrums all around us, and when it settles, Vanessa has Maren by the hair, her head yanked back so that her throat is bared.

"Let her go!" I scream. I try to scramble back to Maren's side but the air is alive with energy that pulses around Vanessa like a force field, holding me back. I don't have to be an empath to feel how my terror fills the clearing. It's mineral-rich, like the scent of blood. "Maren had nothing to do with what your father did."

"Maren," Vanessa says in a voice like broken glass, "has spent her entire life with everything my father never gave me. Respect. Acknowledgment. Money. It's time for her to give back to someone who deserves it."

Vanessa raises her hands and summons the moonlight so that the clearing is bathed in shadows. The light rushes to her, pulsing with her heartbeat, illuminating her face from below so that her cheekbones stand out in stark contrast. It trails from her hands as she sweeps them along her ribbon, the silk running through her fingers like water.

Maren whimpers as a sibilant sound fills the air. The ribbon around Vanessa's neck writhes and twists, sinuous and curling into a snake that settles across her collarbones. It flows across one hand that she lifts for us to see, like she's showing off a new bracelet, then twines itself around her other wrist, a forked tongue tasting the air, feeding on the energy that she has wrapped around her.

Vanessa extends her hand toward Maren. The snake is flowing toward her, its body moving in timeless ripples, when Jay's voice breaks the silence.

"You told me to take revenge on Maren—that finding my grave wasn't enough," he says. "You weren't wrong."

I jerk to the side, eyes wide with horror. All the air rushes out of my lungs. Vanessa must have convinced him with all her talk of power and vengeance.

Vanessa tilts her head, pulling her hand back and smirking. The snake curls in her palm, and she strokes it idly as she waits.

Jay hovers over the crumbling stone that marks his eternal resting place, a storm on his face. "Finding my grave *wasn't* enough, but revenge isn't the answer. Love is."

Vanessa lets out a peal of laughter. "Weak, just like I

said. Next you're going to tell me that love is stronger than power."

"Didn't you do all this for love, though?" Jay points out. "You said it yourself. All you wanted from your father was love. He should have loved you because of who you were, but he didn't. And after you learned to *make* him love you, you decided that you, yourself, weren't worthy of love. You thought that the only way for you to be loved was through manipulation and lies. But that's not real love, Vanessa. I think you know that."

Vanessa scowls at Jay, but he's looking at Maren. Her face softens under his gaze. The hard lines of anger, fear, and defiance smooth into regret and something that looks like hope.

"You shouldn't keep blaming yourself," Jay says. "What happened to me isn't your fault. You did everything you could, and more, to make it right, and I appreciate that. I'm grateful for your friendship, and I hope that you can find peace—the way I have."

The look that passes between them is like a sunrise, swelling from a soft glow into a warmth that fills my chest. I can feel Maren's relief and Jay's peace. My chest loosens for the first time since I entered the woods, and I draw in a breath that feels like pure oxygen.

The snake slackens in Vanessa's hands, its weird glow dimming as the light that she summoned from the moon leaves its body. It's just a limp ribbon now. Movement ripples like white-hot sparks through the clearing, the air around Jay shifting and billowing so that the black cloud under his skin swirls like oil on water. Effervescent light fills his body with a silver-white glow. It's shining in his eyes, no longer inky black, but now pale gray. He looks past us at something I can't see. His eyes drift closed and then blink open. He looks like he's about to fall asleep. But then, under the charged buzzing of the atmosphere, I hear a woman laugh. Jay hears it too, and his eyes crinkle at the corners when he smiles.

"Momma," he says.

The light fades as he drifts apart, losing form until he's just dancing sparks in the dark clearing. And then he's gone.

Gone. Not annihilated like the shade in the mausoleum, not consigned to the darkness that haunts my nightmares. He's passed over to whatever comes next.

I can hardly believe it. I blink, my heart swelling in bone-deep relief. I heard his mother's laugh. I was alone in the Nothing, but Jay's mother was waiting for him, and that means . . .

"You want to see what love really gets you?" Vanessa says spitefully. The tension holding me back abruptly releases as she lets Maren fall to the ground, the charm that immobilized her broken. Maren is shaky and limp from struggling against the unseen bonds. My mind is fuzzy with shock as I scramble to her side on all fours, crushing white plastic flags and ripping out the grid of twine.

"Nothing but pain." Vanessa's face is full of doom as she flicks her wrist toward us. The silence in the clearing is like the roar of speeding death. The air ripples with magic bound up in a dark shadow. When it lifts, Vanessa's ribbon is wound around Maren's neck.

Maren takes a startled breath, fingers flying to her neck, where the ribbon draws tighter, tighter, tighter, until it's like a line of blood across her throat.

"No, no, no," I whimper, trying to work my fingers under the silk as Maren claws at me in panic. Her mouth gapes open. The ribbon is strangling her, making it impossible for her to scream, so I do it for her. I scream as she thrashes in the dirt. I scream as my nails carve furrows in her skin as I desperately try to loosen the ribbon. I scream as her face turns the ugly purple of a bruise.

The whites of her eyes are bloodshot and muddy, but the pupils are still clear. Green dappled with flecks of gold like sunlight shining through tree branches. Something flickers in their depths as she reaches for me. Maren is still fighting, even as her flesh swells over the ribbon, making it impossible to work my fingers under the silk. I lean forward, my tears falling onto her cheeks. Her pinkie twitches against my chest, broken nails rasping against the fabric. She's trying to hook her finger around the object dangling from the lanyard around my neck.

The key chain.

Without thinking, I snap the folding leaf open and slide the cool blade between Maren's skin and the ribbon, slicing through it in one motion.

Maren draws in a sharp gasp at the same time that Vanessa shrieks behind me. I skitter backward through the dirt, pulling Maren with me as a dark ribbon opens across Vanessa's throat.

A sudden wind howls through the clearing, making the trees around us sway and groan. Vanessa's hands clap over her wound, but black vapor spills over them, hissing as it rolls down her shadowy form, stripping the flesh from the bones and leaving behind nothing but choking fumes. It smells faintly of incense and singed velvet, like the ribbons and charms that have held her together for over a hundred years are burning.

Dry leaves spin into a furious, rasping vortex. I clutch Maren tighter, bending across her body to shelter her from the storm.

Vanessa screams again, one hand still trying to stem the flow of fog that pours from her neck, consuming her body as it spreads. Sparks of darkness rush out of the trees, joining the roiling mass and diluting the silver light of the moon so that it's tarnished and dull.

Vanessa stumbles to the ground as the darkness devours her legs. The movement sends the mist billowing around her face, erasing her chin, her jawbones, the lobe of an ear. She gags on another scream as it invades her mouth, robbing her of the barbed compliments and honeyed curses she used to bind people to her will. Her eyes flash once more, burning into mine, before they, too, are choked out by the boundless dark.

The fury of the wind fades as the tattered remains of the fog that consumed Vanessa dissipate, leaving me crouched over Maren. Her eyes swim in terror and she claws at her neck, still struggling against the ghost of Vanessa's charm. Her broken nails rake against her skin and I'm afraid she's going to tear through it like tissue paper, so I clasp her hands between mine and pull her tight against my chest.

"Deep breaths," I wheeze into her hair, before realizing that I'm not taking my own advice. I force myself to slow my breathing. The red haze of desperate fear in my head clears a little more each time I let my lungs fill and deflate. "Take slow, deep breaths. She's gone. You're safe."

I exaggerate the rise and fall of my chest, and little by little, the panicked race of Maren's breathing slows until it matches mine. There's no worrying whistle of damage to her windpipe when she breathes, and the swelling is already going down. She'll be okay—physically. Still, I know better than anyone that emotional trauma can be just as hard to recover from as a physical injury.

But it will help if we do it together.

CHAPTER 33
this is not an exit

"**h**old still." Mom grabs my chin in one hand, angling my head from side to side.

"I can tell you're not used to subjects with a pulse," I manage to sputter out between all the twisting and turning.

"What? Oh," she says absently, and lets go of my face. I massage my jaw. She has an iron grip. "I'm going to go ask if any of the nurses have a makeup light with them. These fluorescents—" She tsks in disapproval and scurries out of the hospital room.

My head still spins when I try to think about everything that's changed in the last few days. What could have happened—what almost *did* happen—is still so raw that I find myself wanting to climb into bed and lock myself away from the world. Pull the covers over my head and push away everyone I love so I don't have to think about how much it hurt to almost lose them.

But every time that fear threatens to engulf me, I see Jay's gray eyes light up at the sound of his mother's laugh. Despite everything—the horror of his existence over the past century, the shadow that nearly consumed him—I know he would say it was all worth it to find her again.

And even though I'm still afraid, I have to agree. Love is worth it.

So who's the lucky guy?

I jerk in my chair as the voice from Davis's text-to-speech app echoes around the stark room. I've barely left the hospital since Maren and I emerged from the woods to half a dozen messages from my mom telling me that Davis was awake. A miracle, Poppy called it, when he suddenly regained consciousness at the exact moment that I cut the ribbon from Maren's neck, destroying the shade that was Vanessa and her hold on him.

"No guy," I mutter. I feel a blush creeping up my cheeks.

Davis takes longer to type out his response this time. He must feel my eyes roving over his face because he glances up once or twice, mouth hitched in a familiar half smile. His skin has lost that greenish tinge, and the bandages on his neck are supposed to come off soon. He's going to have a gnarly scar, but I have a feeling he'll lean into it. Embrace it as part of the brooding, mysterious persona that makes him irresistible to other girls.

"There's got to be a guy. You've never wanted to go to the Sock Hop before. Much less let your mom do your makeup."

I'm not used to the tinny echo that is Davis's new voice, but he did manage to find one with the same obnoxious swagger as his own voice. His vocal cords were cut when Vanessa slit his throat, leaving them damaged and possibly paralyzed. The doctors won't know if he'll be able to regain the ability to speak until he's healed more, and even if he does, the doctors say his voice will be different. Quiet. Difficult to understand. So he's been experimenting with speech-to-text apps and some sign language.

"Well?"

"It's a girl," I blurt out. "It's Maren." My heart flutters in my chest, half panic, half excitement.

He raises his eyebrows, but the expression on his face is one of approval instead of surprise.

"That actually makes total sense. I don't know how I didn't see it before. Your whole 'she's my arch-nemesis, we're total opposites' thing. Kinda predictable."

"Shut up," I mutter, but I can't stop a small smile from creeping across my face.

"I'm happy for you, Lolly. You and Maren will be great together."

I'm still not used to the flutters in my chest that I feel whenever I hear Maren's name linked with mine.

Dad and Davis's parents come back into the room with Mom, who's holding what looks like half the nursing floor's makeup equipment. She finishes my makeup while Poppy and Mr. Wills tell Dad about the plans they made with Davis for a road trip this summer. Poppy promoted one of her cooks to assistant manager, and she's going to leave her in charge of the diner during Davis's recovery. And without the stress of Desert Heights, Mr. Wills is able to take a step back from work, too.

"It will be good to go home," Poppy says as they trace the route Davis mapped out around the four corners states, ending in the Navajo Nation, where she and Mr. Wills grew up.

"Done," Mom says, spinning the chair so I can look in the mirror she has set up on the side table.

"Wow," I say. I lean forward to study my face more closely in the mirror. "That's me?"

I look . . . *hot*. There's no other way to put it. I was expecting pink lips and rose gold cheeks, like the makeup Mom wears, but she stuck with my typical palate—winged eyeliner, dark lipstick—and somehow still managed to transform my awkward goth fifties look into something sophisticated.

"That's you." Mom smiles, brushing one loose strand of hair behind my ear. She glances at her phone. "You better get dressed—Maren will be here soon."

My dress is hanging in the bathroom, wrapped in one of those plastic bags from the dry cleaners. It's all dark florals—burgundy and wine red and purple-black roses. But if you look closer, there's something more than flowers there. That negative space between two blooms becomes an eye socket, that shadow becomes a jawline. And then suddenly the whole dress is covered in skulls, not flowers. It's like one of those optical illusions, constantly shifting between flowers and skulls, life and death.

The hollow of my collarbones looks empty and incomplete without any jewelry. I could ask Mom to borrow something, but it doesn't feel right, wearing some generic necklace. There's only one thing I want to wear tonight. I bite my lip, tilting my head and studying my reflection, tracing my fingers along the empty space where Mrs. H's locket belongs.

Dad wolf-whistles when I come out of the bathroom, and Mr. Wills and Poppy clap. I roll my eyes as Mom bows like they're applauding her makeup job instead of me. Davis grins and moves his hand across his face in the sign for *beautiful*.

"You're giving me a big head." I can't help but glance at my reflection in the mirror on the back of the door. My heart flutters as a staccato tapping in the hall gets closer and closer.

I meet Maren in the doorway. Her dress is exactly what I imagined her wearing: tea-length with a full skirt and an off-the-shoulder sweetheart neckline. The deep red silk matches her hair. She frees a strand from her mass of curls and fiddles with it.

"Hi," I breathe out.

"Hi." Maren bites her lip. She's smiling, but it's a hesitant kind of smile. Like she doesn't want to let herself believe that this is really happening. "Last chance. You really want to go with me?"

I grin. "Of course. You're Maren effing Seymour."

Dad ushers us into the room so he and Mom can take pictures of us posing in front of the window and next to Davis's bed.

"Olive, put your arm around Maren's waist," Mom suggests, lowering her phone until I follow her instructions. My hand slips along the silky fabric of Maren's dress. I'm grinning so big that I feel like a human emoji.

"Straight to city hall," Mom says. "And then straight home. No side trips. No detours." She twists her hands together, pressing her mouth into a frown. She, Dad, and Mrs. Seymour didn't want to let us go to the Sock Hop, but they relented when we pulled the Junior Reaper card and Ms. Hunter promised to keep a close eye on us.

"No detours," I promise.

"Be home by eleven," Dad says, handing me a coffin-shaped clutch.

"Midnight?" I ask, but I backtrack when he raises his eyebrows. "Okay, okay, eleven." I stuff my phone and lipstick into the bag.

"Olive."

I look back at Davis, who holds his hand up with the two middle fingers tucked against the palm and the others extended: "I love you" in sign language.

"I love you, too." I don't even feel awkward saying it in front of Maren and all of our parents. I'll never give up another chance to tell the people I love how I feel about them.

Maren and I glance at each other as we walk down the hall toward the elevator. My heart thuds erratically, and my palms are slick with sweat. Oh God, what if she tries to hold my hand? I rub them against my skirt, trying to dry them without her noticing as the elevator drops to the ground floor, taking my stomach with it.

Outside, the sun is dipping below the horizon, and the sky is shot through with streaks of gold. The ghost of a fingernail moon hangs over the trees. A light breeze blows, just enough to rattle the last few dry leaves across the parking lot. Maren pulls her key lanyard out of a hidden pocket in the seam of her dress and unlocks the car. Should I open her door for her, help her into the driver's seat? I think she's wondering the same thing because we both freeze on the curb and stare at each other awkwardly.

Then Maren laughs—a real laugh, one that reminds me of jukeboxes and milkshakes—and winks at me.

"After you," she says, opening my door and sweeping her hands toward me with a flourish. I let her take my fingers and guide me into the car, then in a jolt of inspiration, I lean over the seat to open the other door for her as she crosses to her side.

On Main Street, lanterns cast a rippling glow over pumpkins and mums arranged in the flower beds. The streetlights are draped in fake cobwebs that flutter in the wind, and the sidewalks are crowded with trick-or-treaters running from shop to shop. Halloween in White Haven draws kids from all over the state; people will haul their children a surprisingly long way to ask strangers for candy in the dark tourism capital of America.

Maren parks in front of city hall. I climb out of the car, pulling the strap of my clutch around my wrist and straightening my skirt. Rockabilly music pours onto the street through doors thrown wide open: "I Was a Teenage Werewolf" by the Cramps, one of those twentieth-century novelty songs. The steps are dotted with poodle skirts and leather jackets, dark wash jeans with turned-up cuffs and bobby socks.

Next to city hall, the cemetery gates are open for ghost tours and graveyard games. Lights bob through the headstones, and actors in ragged turn-of-the-century costumes, hair powdered with dust, pose for pictures. Someone is strumming a guitar and singing a folk song about driving Mary home.

"Wait," I say, hesitating before Maren can tug me up the steps and into the dance. I glance over at the cemetery gates. Mom's anxious warning not to take any detours echoes through my head. I know she'll freak if I don't go straight to the dance, but she's also been telling me for months that I need to go to Mrs. H's grave.

Besides, her exact words before we left the hospital were to go straight to city hall, and the cemetery is technically on the same lot as city hall.

I can feel Mrs. H reaching for me. Or maybe I'm reaching for her. Whatever it is, I'm tired of ignoring it. I want to say goodbye. I want to—and I can't even believe I'm thinking this, using one of Mom's favorite buzzwords—get closure.

"I have to visit someone before we go in. Will you come with me?"

"It can't wait?"

I shake my head. "I should have done this a long time ago."

Maren nods and twines our fingers together. Her pulse beats against my wrist, and nothing has ever felt better.

Pea gravel crunches under our shoes (Converse and peep-toe heels; I'll let you figure out who's wearing what) as we ramble through the headstones. I don't have to check the app on my phone to know where to go. It's the only place I avoided all those months when I was looking for a ghost.

Mrs. H's grave is marked by a white marble obelisk that glows in a pocket of silver moonlight. It's quiet here; the tourists aren't interested in these modern graves. There's something draped around the top of the stone, something that glints in the moonlight—

The locket. My heart warms as I take the chain from the headstone. It's warm, as though it's been tucked against someone's chest or clutched tight in someone's palm. I run my fingers over the secret hinge and squeeze, letting it pop open. Jay's face gazes up at me from the faded picture on one side of the locket. On the other, a scrap of paper is tucked under the clip that once held his mother's mourning brooch.

Maren peers over my shoulder, her breath warm and steadying on the back of my neck. I unfold the paper and we read it together:

Olive—I told you I would find a way to let you know.

I catch my breath as my heart swells. I can feel it expanding in my chest, stretching and aching until it fills my rib cage. Growing pains. The sweet kind of ache that feels so good it hurts.

Maren brushes the hair off the back of my neck and slips the chain over my head. The locket settles just above my breasts like it's meant to be there.

"Perfect," she says.

I take her hand in mine, fitting our fingers together. I can count the faint freckles on her cheeks and smell her clean scent, like sunshine and a spring breeze. Her thumb traces circles on my palm, sending a spray of shivers up my arm, as she looks up at me with eyes half-closed and lips parted.

I lean closer without thinking about it, press my lips to hers, and it's like everything I've been looking for these last two years is wrapped up in this kiss. I close my eyes, but instead of darkness, I see lights dancing across the insides of my eyelids, sparks leaping from Maren to me as our lips move together.

The light at the end of the tunnel.

Maren and I break apart as music spills out of city hall and echoes through the cemetery. I recognize this song, the rhythmic guitar riff and the raw sound of the strings. This is another Saves the Day song. Maren must have slipped it in among the midcentury rock 'n' and swing.

I turn toward the grave with Maren's hand in mine. It still hurts to see the finality of Mrs. H's name etched in stone, but now it feels like a message from beyond the grave. A reminder of her love. At the ragged edge of despair is something soft and soothing, velvety blue like the sky. Wrapped up in all of the sorrow are good memories that I wouldn't have if I didn't let myself feel the pain.

"I should have come earlier," I say to Mrs. H, chagrined that it took me so long. "When you died, it felt like I fell into a pit of despair and I didn't know how to dig myself out. I thought coming here would make it worse. But whatever I saw when I almost died—whatever the Nothing was—I don't think that's where you are."

Maren squeezes my hand, sending a jolt racing through my body to my chest where it jump-starts my heart.

"I think you made it through to the light," I say to Mrs. H. "I think you're with your mother and you're getting to know your brother." Tears prick my eyes as I smile. "And I think someday I'll be there with you, too. I'll see you on the other side."

I turn away from Mrs. H's grave and toward Maren. I'm ready to walk into the dance hand in hand. I'm ready to give her my heart to fill or burst. I'm ready to creep out of the shadow that's consumed me for the past two years.

I'm ready to be alive again.

After my brush with death, everyone asked me if I saw a light at the end of a tunnel. And the fact that I *didn't* scared me so much that I almost convinced myself nothing mattered. But I guess I didn't think about what that expression really means.

To get to the light, you have to go through the darkness.

So I feel the pain, and then I feel the joy.

acknowledgments

Writing a book sometimes feels like a very solitary endeavor because of the amount of time you spend in your own head, creating worlds and characters that no one else will see unless you can find a way to get them down on paper. But the truth is, dozens of people contributed to this book. There are so many people who had a part in creating Olive, and I'm grateful for each one.

Olive would not exist without my sister, critique partner, and friend, Kelsey Down. Literally, because I wrote the first 5000 words while babysitting your daughter. But also because no one has encouraged me, supported me, or listened to me complain as faithfully as you. I can always count on you to be just as excited about a new project as I am, even when it's nothing more than a vague idea and a mood board. Thank you for all the conversations that start out with me asking you to brainstorm and turn into you listening to me ramble for forty minutes before abruptly saying I figured it out and hanging up. Writing with you in coffee shops is my favorite. Love you!

I'm grateful for my friend and mentor, A. J. Sass, who worked with me on a still unpublished MG project in 2019 and has been stuck with me ever since. Thank you for always being a wealth of support and advice!

Thank you to the early readers of *Olive*: Shannon, Jenny, Molly, and Sarah, who told me I should kill someone (in the book). Your advice and patience in reading countless drafts has been invaluable. I love all the work we've shared with each other over the years—I couldn't ask for better critique partners!

My book club, Overbooked, has been a great source of friendship and support over the years. I'm so grateful for the wonderful books we've read together (and the pins we've earned!).

Thank you to my agent, Sharon Belcastro, who jumped into this project full of enthusiasm and has been a wonderful advocate. I'm so glad you're on this journey with me!

My editor, Ashtyn Stann, and Meg Gaertner and the rest of the team at Flux have made this debut experience so wonderful. Thank you for loving *Olive* as much as I do, encouraging me, and pushing me to make this the best book it could be. Ashtyn, thank you for plucking me from the slush pile and making my dreams come true. I still can't quite believe it's happening.

Big thanks to Raluca Burcă for creating a gorgeous cover that captures all of the vibes I imagined before I had even written a word.

I'm grateful to my friend Maddy Smith, who was my Navajo cultural and sensitivity reader. I appreciate your insights so much! Thank you to Black Sheep Cafe in Provo, Utah, which inspired the food at Poppy's, and made my mouth water every time I wrote about it. If you're ever in Utah, Black Sheep is an Indigenous-owned Navajo fusion restaurant that is an absolute must try.

I also want to acknowledge the Navajo people, the original inhabitants of the land in the Four Corners region, where this story is set. White Haven and its history are fictional, but the experiences of the Navajo people and other Indigenous peoples is all too true. Navajostrong.org is a non-profit that was created to aid the Navajo people during the Covid-19 pandemic and has grown to support cultural, business, and farming endeavors. If you're interested in supporting the Navajo community, please give them a look.

Lastly, I am so grateful for my huge, close-knit family. Thank you to my parents, Kevin and Lisa, for your love and support and for giving me the best childhood I could ever imagine. Same goes to my in-laws, Canyon and Jan, on behalf of my husband. Thank you to my siblings and siblings-in-law—all twenty of you—for being my closest friends and loving my children like your own. I'm so grateful I can count on you!

Special thanks to the Allan siblings, who contributed every single pun found in this book, because they are punny and I am not.

And finally, thank you to my husband and four children: Jason, Tempe, Helena, Juno, and Pearl. You are the best thing that ever happened to me. Thank you for believing in me and celebrating with me and filling my life with so much love. You make it all worth it.

about the author

Kate Anderson lives in Utah with her husband and four children. When she's not writing, she's embroidering her favorite book covers, exploring the mountains, or planning road trips to places that are off the beaten path—the weirder, the better. *Here Lies Olive* is her first book. Follow her on Instagram and Twitter @kateanderwrites.